"Rob Brownell's sharply written *Invention Is a Mother* somehow manages to be witty, absurd, playful, imaginative, cynical, sad, compelling, heartfelt, and darkly hilarious all in one. Full of boozy wormholes, sentient appliances, multiple Jesuses, automated buffets, and many other colorful sci-fi abstractions, this book will not only make you think and feel, but also smile."

—Dan Marshall, author of *Home Is Burning*

"Fans of oddball science fiction are going to love Rob Brownell's new novel, *Invention Is a Mother*. Starting with a quirky cast, an unlikely hero, and a bunch of superfluous technology, Rob crafts a romp through startup land that is fun and moves fast. *Invention Is a Mother* is potentially the new *Hitchhiker's Guide to the Galaxy*—be the first one on your block to get a copy ahead of what I predict will be a legion of readers."

—Bill Burnett, co-author of *Designing Your Life* and *Designing Your New Work Life*

"*Invention Is a Mother* is a sharp, wickedly funny look at science, fiction, life, death, pitch meetings, insane flights of fancy, and technology that will either kill you or save you. It made me laugh in despair and laugh in joy, which are the best two ways to laugh. I loved it."

—Will Leitch, author of *How Lucky*

INVENTION IS
A MOTHER

INVENTION IS
A MOTHER

Rob Brownell

ISBN: 979-8-9859264-0-8 (Paperback)
ISBN: 979-8-9859264-1-5 (E-book)
ISBN: 979-8-9859264-2-2 (Hardback)

Library of Congress Control Number: 2022908759

Alessandor Earnest, Developmental Editing and Project Management
Ariel Anderson, Copyediting
Julie Klein, Interior Design
Brenna Bailey-Davies, Proofreading
Carlo Giambarresi, Cover Art
Jude May, Cover Design

Printed in the United States of America

Published by Syllaballistics Publishing
info@syllaballistics.com
www.syllaballistics.com

For Helen

Foreword

I'm going to copycat Neil Gaiman and invite you to return and read this after you've read the book. Then we can be on the same page, cuz I've already read it.

Welcome back. That was quite the adventure, wasn't it? *Invention Is a Mother* is hand to god one of my favorite books, up there with *Hitchhiker's Guide*, *John Dies at the End*, and *Kneller's Happy Campers*.

I suppose I should start by saying I edit books for a living. In fact, I edited this one!

I know how that comes across, but if you did as I suggested and came back here after you finished the book, well, then you *know*.

I had the benefit and great privilege of getting to know its author, Rob Brownell, by reading (and rereading) this book, which gave me a glimpse behind the eyes of a man coming to grips with mortality through the lens of a dark comedy with notes of literary science fiction and more than a touch of the absurd.

This book is a genre-bender that defies categorization. It's about a guy's struggle to integrate into society after college, his relationship with his degenerating father, the family dynamics of grief, impossible engineering questions, sentient wormholes, and zany identity-obfuscation technology. It's smart, sad, witty, life-changing, disgusting, technical, ridiculous, heartwarming, and crude.

In short: *magnificent.*

I watched the book mature from infancy, though I should note that much like a stepfather, I wasn't around for the gestation. That was all Rob, who truly is the *mother* of this invention. Okay, I'll stop.

Throughout countless rounds of edits, Rob worried I would get bored reading it over and over, but that was impossible. Every time he passed the manuscript back, I was like a kid opening presents, never sure what surprises would be waiting under the colored paper and ribbons. If I found something that needed to be improved, he'd take my suggestion, run with it to a completely new and unexpected place, and hide it there for safekeeping so he could find a wildly inventive and totally different way to fix the problem.

I laughed my way through the editing process with a near-constant reminder that this magnificent writer with whom I shared this strange intimacy—the kind that's only possible between an editor and a writer—would someday soon stop answering my emails.

Rob told me at our first meeting that he had ALS and not a whole lot of time to work on the book. He asked me if I felt comfortable working with him, knowing that. For better or worse, I had already skimmed some of it and wanted desperately to be its editor. I was hooked. And then I was hired. The rest is history.

The book you are currently holding in your hands changed my life. Its author also changed my life—though I think it is highly unlikely you are currently holding *him* in your hands. But perhaps the important bits—the humor, the empathy, the profound and profane honesty—perhaps those bits have indeed taken root in these pages. In that way, I suppose we all get to hold Rob in our hands!

I hope this book has as much of an impact on you as it did me. Or at least half. Half should be enough.

—Alessandor Earnest
The Imp of Editing
Developmental editor and
number one fan of
Invention Is a Mother

1

Puxton Smallwood, heir apparent of Smallwood Pharmaceuticals, looked over a lake high in the mountains of Yosemite. His life was at a crossroads. His personal AI had taken the first steps to arrange a marriage. His father demanded he join the family business and stop being a damn fool, but Puxton was unstoppable. He was fixated on making his own mark on the world. He knew he was on the brink of a great discovery. The seed of an idea was ready to bloom. He had come to the lake determined to sit until that idea expressed itself.

He sat uncomfortably on a rocky outcropping, wishing he had brought a chair with better lumbar support. He cursed the blinding morning sun and the evening chill. He brushed off passing hikers when they paused to debate who among them should poke the man to see if he was still alive. In between his complaints and interruptions, he pondered all manner of inventive products and ventures. In his heart he knew he was ready for catharsis; he could feel it building inside, yet after two tedious days at the lake, he had nothing but hunger and numbed lower extremities to take away with him.

He drove back toward San Francisco, frustrated by his failure. At a roadside fruit stand he bought a large guava slushy with designer brain-boosting protein. Without compunction he paid more for a nonbiodegradable plastic straw than for the slushy itself. The fantastically large plastic cup wouldn't fit in his car's cupholder, such was its girth. He clamped it between his now-tender thighs—precipitating the lap equivalent of a brain freeze. Why in God's name had he even wanted the drink? He had been thirsty, and the *Galactic Rescue* souvenir cup had compelled him, but beyond that, he sensed a deeper influence. He detected telltale signs of divine intervention, of which he felt uniquely deserving despite his lack of the basic qualifying criterion—belief in a power higher than himself. He recognized the drink as the embryo of an idea.

As he drove, his sense of urgency and insight swelled until he could think of nothing else.

While Walton changed into a hospital gown, Shaughnessy and Sammy waited outside the examination room. Their mother had assigned them as escorts, responsible for transporting their father and forming a nonhysterical synopsis of the doctor's conclusions. On Walton's signal, they moved into the room and sat side by side on the examination bed, debossing the paper covering with exact replicas of their buttocks. Walton took a seat in the only chair, his bare thighs making suction noises as he tried to situate himself comfortably on the plastic cushion.

The neurologist was an assured, twenty-sixish, gender- and pronoun-nimble individual currently going by "she," though a masculine emotional vacuum was ascendant and threatened to push her into "he" territory even as they spoke. The drama of the delicate gender balance played out on a real-time bar graph displayed on the breast pocket of her medical specialiTee.

She prodded Walton along a line of questioning about his symptoms and why he had come to see her.

Walton was a hostile witness at his own appointment, fearing cooperation would speed a terminal diagnosis and, consequently, his death. He reported, "I feel like I tire easily, and I get headaches, and I'm irritable. Sometimes my neck bothers me, and I'm prone to postnasal drip. About six months ago my arms started twitching."

Shaughnessy restrained himself from offering that, other than the twitching, it was business as usual for his father.

The neurologist summarized the diagnosis given by Walton's primary doctor: the tremors are nothing to worry about, he should reduce his stress, and he should consider counseling to root out the problem.

"Are you experiencing any exceptional or unusual stress at this time?" she asked kindly, looking to Sammy and Shaughnessy for unbiased opinions. They both shrugged their shoulders.

Walton said, "My symptoms are what's stressing me. I investigated their meaning."

His identiTee projected well-informed competence, a reflex from his ongoing role as a father. Glancing behind his confident facade, Shaughnessy saw he was uncertain to the point of wild-eyed fear.

The neurologist asked, "You researched the data streams? What did you find?"

Walton was unwilling to answer the question. He projected signs of irritation, as if he had verbalized sufficient information for the doctor to reach the obvious diagnosis.

Sammy answered for him. "He believes he has MFD—

mysterious fatal disease. He thinks he ... doesn't have much time left."

"MFD is a popular self-diagnosis. I can see how you might gravitate toward that option. People can't resist imagining a horrible death. The truth is, MFD is extremely rare. In my career, I have only seen a few cases, and in those cases, the patients were experiencing pronounced episodes of weakness, visible muscle atrophy, or death. Based on your brief description, your symptoms are most easily explained by stress."

The neurologist spoke precisely, with painful deliberation over each word. She appeared to find it difficult to use layman's terms, with empathy and without medical jargon. Shaughnessy imagined an innovation: an easily understood AI-generated translation of her words floating above her specialiTee's lab coat animation. The simplified translation of her preliminary diagnosis might read, *You're wacko.*

She reviewed Walton's pre-appointment questionnaire on a small wall screen and asked, "You have no family history of MFD or neuromuscular diseases?"

"No," Walton said. "Is it hereditary?"

Shaughnessy and Sammy glanced at one another, genetic factors not having previously occurred to them. Shaughnessy guessed his father already knew the answer down to the exact genetic mechanism.

"There is a hereditary variation," she said. "The non-hereditary type is far more common. Have you experienced any episodes of weakness?"

Walton replied, "I think so. I've awakened at night unable to move an arm. I have awful dreams in which I'm unable to escape an unbeatable monster. My legs are so tired that I can barely move. It's like wading through honey."

"Curious," said the neurologist. "Physiologically speaking, if your legs were that tired, they would buckle and you'd fall. Your dream's plot inconsistencies are worrisome." She made a note on his chart.

She put Walton through a battery of strength, reflex, and coordination tests. She led him out into the hall and eyed him critically as he walked away from her and back again. He awkwardly clamped one hand behind him to keep the gown and his dignity held together. She had him repeat the performance on the balls of his feet, like he was wearing stiletto heels, like she was auditioning a runway model.

Watching from the doorway, Shaughnessy said, "Someone ought to invent an AI translator that displays a doctor's meaning in easily digested words. It could save you a lot of effort."

"You might have something there. I don't like talking to patients. Staying tactful with witless family members is even more excruciating," she said.

Back in the examination room, the neurologist offered the opinion that she was not impressed by Walton's results. She said he should try to reduce his stress and exercise regularly. She declared his muscle twitching to be "benign annoyances" and said they would probably go away on their own.

"I would advise the same thing even if you were right about the MFD diagnosis. It's an orphan disease. It's not called that because it would orphan your children, though that would be completely accurate. It's called an orphan disease because it's rare. The disease lacks market presence, so to speak. What I'm saying is, even if I diagnosed you with MFD, there's little to be done for it."

Shaughnessy kept an eye on the neurologist's pronoun status. She pulled back from the brink and settled safely into "she" territory as she attempted encouragement even while dwelling uncomfortably on the disease Walton didn't have.

"Keep enjoying your life. There's no definitive test for MFD, but we can examine the electrical impulses in your nerves and search for indications. I don't recommend pursuing the electrical test because your symptoms are minor and most people find the test quite painful. If you start experiencing random, short-lived muscle weakness, then we can talk again about the test," she said. "Sporadic muscle weakness can be hard to pinpoint, so keep an eye out for indicators like dropping your coffee, a sudden inability to get out of your chair, or waking up on the bathroom floor in a puddle of blood with a head wound. It might remind you of a stroke, if you've ever experienced one of those, but the weakness only lasts a few minutes at most. A sudden mysterious death is also a strong indicator for MFD, but leave it to us to keep an eye out for that one."

Walton, Sammy, and Shaughnessy slid into a waiting AI-controlled vehicle for the ride home. The legally required backup safety driver—who identified as a red tabby cat—was talking via the car's screen to a friend in the throes of a travel fiasco. The friend was saying, "So then they told us the plane needed a software patch and it would take the programmers about an hour to create it. An hour! I'm like, can't they program faster? I've got places to be!"

The driver said to her passengers, "Sorry about that, I'll put her on mute." In silence, the friend continued to rant and gesticulate. The driver purred pleasantly to put them at ease.

"I hope she's not a good friend," Walton said.

"Why's that?" asked the driver.

"Do you know any software engineers? I think you might not see much of her in the future," Walton said. He fell silent and gazed out a side window.

"Dad?" Sammy said. "The doctor's assessment is good news. It sounds like you just need to take it easy."

He mumbled, "I suppose so."

She said, "You don't sound convinced."

"MFD is incurable. The humane thing would have been to diagnose me with something minor to take my mind off the disease," he said. "Why would she want to ruin my remaining days with worry? There's no medical intervention available. The disease exists in an enormous scientific void. There is no definitive blood test to settle my nerves."

"Alternatively, you could take the doctor at face value and believe that your symptoms will clear up. That seems like the more attractive option to me," said Sammy.

"It's all too clear cut, too tidy," he said.

"Good Lord," she said.

Shaughnessy said, "Dad, you're overthinking this. There's no conspiracy. Take the doctor's advice and relax."

"You make it sound easy to forget that I'm dying," Walton said.

Sammy said, "Most everyone in the world manages to forget they're dying. You lived most of your life forgetting. It's not that hard."

"Except for the people who really do have terminal diseases," Shaughnessy clarified. "They probably can't forget. Soldiers in war zones. Retirees, they know death is coming, though memory loss gives them a leg up on forgetting. People with suicidal thoughts, it's definitely on their minds."

"Death row inmates?" Sammy asked.

"The extended appeal process probably helps them forget."

"You're probably right," Sammy said. "Dad, pretend you're a death row inmate and you still have appeals available. Maybe the governor is your friend and a pardon is up for discussion. You still have options."

"That's a surprisingly helpful point of view," said Walton.

2

If you were to task someone with watching a bird feeder, Shaughnessy theorized they would afterward gripe about the tedium of the experience, and then they would talk about the colorful birds: the cardinals, the warblers, the goldfinches, and the blue jays. They might mention in some vague way the indistinct brown or gray birds.

Why couldn't the hypothetical bird-feeder watchers see that brown and gray were simply colors, no different from red or blue or yellow? To be technical about it, brown and gray are rich *combinations* of colors, whereas the bright red cardinal and the goldfinch are downright monochromatic— eye-catching, sure, but simplistic from a reflective-wavelength perspective.

Shaughnessy thought of himself as an indistinct brown bird.

His identiTee hoodie rendered an accurate depiction of his physical details on its continuous high-resolution display surfaces: average height and build, male, handsome in an ordinary way, dysphoric and dabbling in self-medication, single-mindedly seeking avenues of hetero-sexual expression. His Henley shirt animation appeared unbuttoned, well-worn, and free of logos. The cinched iTee hood exposed his face from eyebrows to chin. Animated tendrils of blond hair leaked out from under the actual knit cap worn over his hood.

His iTee also displayed glyphs—symbols evolved from

emoji and memes, resembling Egyptian hieroglyphics, operating like movie captions—to explain his personality characteristics. He had obsessively fine-tuned his freeware originaliTee template to express his authentic self, with particular attention paid to his indistinct bird attributes.

Even starting with the most expensive of identity templates, identiTees were a half-baked technology. They extended only to the waist. The hood left the face exposed. They functioned on a rigid hierarchy of belief: glyphs above all else, artificial appearances next, reality last. They succeeded only because of a universal appetite for self-determination and self-deception, not because of sophisticated visual magic.

The identiTee life was like a movie, with each person disappearing into a role of their own choosing. In Shaughnessy's case, factoring in his middling execution of glyphography, he played a background character.

He had the impression that most people—who, after all, contrived their own identities—remained dimly aware of others' glyphs while blindly accepting them. He had never adhered to that face-value, judge-books-by-their-cover, look-upon-others-as-you-would-have-them-look-upon-you social construct.

When he was a young child, his classmates had blissfully embraced glyph literacy while he had remained prone to uncontrolled, unbidden, unfiltered bursts of reality: flashes of missing teeth, despondency, peninsular hairlines, jowls victimized by gravity, bulging hernias, bloodshot intoxication, fear, eczema, hairs sprouting from all manner of body parts. The experiences had been shocking, horrific, scarring, and he had come to regard seeing people's actual appearances as a shameful affliction. He tried to discuss his affliction with his parents, but they told him to knock it off. Don't be disgusting, mister! It was bad enough, they said, that people had to confront the unpleasant reality of themselves while behind locked doors. To even *think* of others in that state was repugnant.

Initially repulsed but gradually conditioned by the spasmodic bursts of reality—and spurred on by his parents' discouraging comments—he developed a secret fascination for people's hidden, gruesome underpinnings. He came to think of his affliction as identity dyslexia.

Shaughnessy needed to face the day. He had agreed to discuss his father's appointment with his family, but an oppressive weight kept him pinned to his rental couch.

He was unemployed, renting shelter at night in a corporate-hostel law office, living off dwindling savings, fretting over his future. He stared up from the couch at the law partner's acrylic productivity trophies, a category of award he knew he himself would never receive, a cruel reminder of his inadequacies.

Six months earlier, as he had staggered toward graduation from engineering school, maturity's advance scouts—his parents, sister, friends, professors, and corporate recruiters—had put no effort into making adulthood seem enticing. No one glossed over the burden of responsibility, the possible mundanity of a career, the stranglehold of loving one's children. They described the trials and rigors of adulthood with a clear but poorly received message that the toil and hardships were meant to appeal to him.

He had turned down plum engineering job offers. He had fallen into protracted circular deliberations on his future and followed a path of inaction. On good days he was certain great things would befall him if he just waited patiently. On bad days he was lethargic, indecisive, skeptical. He felt like he didn't care enough or that everyone else took life way too seriously.

His father's terminal illness or debilitating psychosis had solidified his position that adulthood was an unattractive option.

With a hissing vacuum cleaner wand, the janitor prodded Shaughnessy off the couch and toward the door of the partner's office. She folded his blanket, tucked the pillow into a filing cabinet, and violently beat his impression out of the leather couch cushions with the flat of her hand.

He worked his way through the yoga class in the reception area, mumbling apologies to the rumps of downward-dogging lodgers as he made for the executive washroom.

In the break area, he brewed an espresso and moved to the law library to sip and stare blankly out the window until he was passably alert. He was on a meager budget but told himself that the deluxe Legal-Easy+ rental package was worth the additional cost with its city-view office and access to the law library's wingback chairs.

He tried to work up some enthusiasm for the day ahead, but he already regretted agreeing to meet with his family. First, he didn't think he was emotionally resilient enough to make the drive. Second, there was the depressing topic of his father's appointment. Third, family meetings had a way of morphing into a prosecution of his listlessness.

His espresso and excuse for lingering both gone, he dragged himself from the library. Passing through the main lobby, he dodged hustling lawyers in impeccable legaliTees. He stepped into the day's heat and felt sweat bead and merge into a film. He circumnavigated skeletal chicken wing remnants baking on the sidewalk and bought a street taco for breakfast.

A man displaying an alternative realiTee screamed, "Don't let them fuck with you!"

Shaughnessy took stock of the situation and gathered that he was the man's intended audience. Unable to curb his curiosity, he asked, "Who, specifically, is *them*?"

"Who is *them*?" the man responded. "I'm just working with the lines they give me, buddy. This is my side gig. It's a public service announcement."

He held up a finger and asked Shaughnessy to hold on a sec while he tried to get an answer to the question through his help desk. He swiped at the controls on his sleeve, his greasy fingers leaving curving trails, and started a video conversation with a distant employee, who appeared on his forearm.

While the man discussed the question, Shaughnessy pondered why *they* would fuck with him. Most likely they didn't need a reason, and if they did, he had probably given them ample cause.

The man said to him, "The proper response to 'Who is *them*?' is . . . 'Who *isn't* them, jerkweed?' Does that answer your question satisfactorily? If it does, please consider giving me a superior rating. Four to five stars would be appropriate."

"Sure, thanks for the intel," Shaughnessy said.

He ambled onward to the nearby Baptist church where he routinely parked his minivan with the aid of a forged permit. He drove south on the main artery out of Atlanta, huddled together with other human-driven cars in the pitted econo lane. Rectilinear live/work/retail developments—each indistinguishable from the other—flashed past like a cartoon's looping background. Only the increasing exit numbers and changing billboards gave a sense of distance traveled.

Like a swarm of skittering cockroaches, AI-controlled vehicles drove past, their roofs bristling with antennae, their coordinated aggression a thing of grotesque beauty, their gleeful cruelty disturbingly familiar.

He arrived—heart pounding, nerves abused by the drive—at the former prison, now home to Critical Think Inc., his father's employer. Shaughnessy pulled into the parking area outside a segment of sun-bleached concrete walls crowned with razor wire. Strident animations bracketing the entry gate promised unparalleled customer experiences.

They met at Paupers Fields, the park/athletic complex attached to the prison development, where they could talk privately, away from Walton's coworkers. Shaughnessy found his family waiting at a picnic table by the playground. A unicorn was rescuing two superheroes trapped at the top of the slide by a wolf robot. The unicorn's mother was underwhelmed by her child's per-formance and loudly instructed, "Honey ... Honey! Think like a unicorn! *Be* the unicorn!"

"You really need to pay for an approved template," Walton said. He flicked a stray career counseling advertisement off Shaughnessy's belly, sending the ad sliding over Shaughnessy's shoulder. "Upgrade to something with an ad blocker."

Gloria sipped at a healthy drink, a multi-genre beverage concoction of such complexity that local baristas gave it to her for free, knowing they would make it incorrectly and fearing the fallout. Shaughnessy experienced fleeting dyslexic double vision as his mother's actual identity bled through her glyphs. On her surface he interpreted seriousness, while hidden underneath the glyphs he spied loving concern mixed with despair over her husband's health and her son's indolence. Unlike his own passive tendencies, she employed powerful emotional machinery to convert her worry into a focused energy aimed at soft targets like baristas and her son.

He peeked beyond the clear complexion described by his sister's glyphs and admired the severity of her freckles. An archipelago curled from her left cheek to the tip of her chin—a freckle pattern that always reminded him of a paramecium with exactingly stippled cellular details.

"Remember that time we stopped for fuel down by the coast?" Sammy asked. She was the self-appointed repository of embarrassing family stories.

"Oh Lord," Gloria said.

"I have no memory of this," Walton said.

"Remember, the mini-mart had a sign in the window reading *Local Honey for Sale*. You approached the cashier, Dad, and asked her if she was the honey for sale."

"She was a looker too," Gloria said. "She had her identi-Tee set to look like a 107-pound addict with the dental problems of a former hockey player, those being the physical qualities valued by local tribal convention."

"When she said no, you asked if you could see the honey's picture before making a purchase," Sammy said.

"This isn't ringing a bell," Walton said.

"You asked her what the trade-in policy was because the honey out washing your car window was getting long in the tooth," Sammy said.

"She probably thought you were insulting her teeth," Shaughnessy said.

"Since she probably already considered herself an asshole magnet, she undoubtedly decided that you were an asshole," Sammy said.

Gloria pursed her lips, irked by her daughter's obscenity, and exhaled forcibly. "Let's talk about the neurology appointment," she said. "Your father told me the good news about the diagnosis, but still, we need to take measures against stress."

Despite Walton's iTee's assertion that he was in peak physical condition—with subtle shadowing to suggest defined, toned musculature—delicate twitches played up and down his arms, making Shaughnessy imagine wriggling, alien-implanted, subcutaneous tracking devices.

"That's primarily what I want to talk about," Walton said. "I need to get away from my work, but only the tedious parts. I need to relax." He looked directly at Shaughnessy. "I'm thinking you'd be an excellent replacement for the tasks I have in mind, since I already attend to them with little motivation. Are you willing to work as me—to substitute for me?"

"What? No. I'm not comfortable with this idea. How

would that work? Wearing someone else's identity parameters is just . . . gross," he said.

"Who are you kidding? You know you like it," Sammy said.

"We accept you, Shaun. While we don't share your . . . flexibility with identities," Walton said, "we don't hold it against you. You're a grown man. You can make your own decisions."

"It's . . . It's identity dyslexia!" said Shaughnessy. He stumbled over the words, not having previously voiced them.

"Don't be ashamed," Gloria said. "You were born this way. We still love you."

"Oh my God," he said. He rested his forehead against the edge of the table and studied his bony knees, wondering if his kneecaps were deformed or just ugly. He agonized as his family debated whether identity dyslexia was a complete and accurate description of his abnormality.

"Ease up, I think we're losing him," Gloria said.

"What is it with you and that hat?" Sammy hesitantly put a finger to his knit hat. "It smells like a randy yak. Try a hat animation for God's sake."

"It's swagalicious. It's comfortable," he mumbled.

"Mom always wanted us to identify as something exotic when we grew up—like green eyed, or ambidextrous, or clairvoyant, or something—but I don't think this is what she had in mind."

Gloria nodded in agreement.

Sammy said, "Maybe if you—"

"My engineering education was a colossal mistake," Shaughnessy interrupted. He lifted his head from the table.

"In middle school I was given the kiss of death, marked as 'gifted' in math. My education is a transplanted organ my body is now rejecting. I can't work as Dad."

"Now you're exaggerating," Gloria said.

He didn't think so. He blamed science-fair trophies, straight As in math, education's STEM tide, Miss Guidance Counselor, movie depictions of heroic engineers thwarting galactic cataclysms, and the supposed cultural cool of nerds for together nudging his life onto a tumbling suboptimal trajectory.

"Wouldn't working be better than loitering around coffee shops, dentist waiting rooms, and your rental couch?" Gloria asked.

"As you like to say, I'm in a growth phase that's predicated on irresponsibility," said Shaughnessy. As he had feared, the family meeting was evolving into an intervention to address his apathy and unemployment.

"Your smarts and your education are sitting idle," Walton said. "We want you to find something meaningful for yourself. Substitute for me. Be my replacement. Help me with my work. Let me give you a taste of something that has been meaningful to me."

"He would have to interact with others. That could be problematic," Sammy said.

"Stay out of this," Shaughnessy snapped.

Walton tendered, "Lunch is catered every day, and the coffee is free."

This raised the stakes considerably. Walton either had logic on his side or had bombarded him with enough illogic that he was numb to the difference.

"Can I think about it for a little while?"

"When you say you'll think about it, I think you mean you won't think about it," Sammy said.

"Jesus, Sammy," said Shaughnessy.

"If you're just going to wrestle with it and then make an impulsive decision, why don't you make it easy on yourself and be impulsive right now?" asked Walton. "There's no harm trying, is there?"

"You've always had an affinity for inaction, you can't blame us for that. It's not like I missed an introversion immunization when you were a baby," Gloria said.

"Is that a real thing?" asked Shaughnessy.

"It was more of a placebo, but we had high hopes," Gloria said.

"How about helping me with work?" Walton asked.

"I don't know . . ."

"Who else is going to hire you? Would it kill you to help out?" Sammy asked.

Shaughnessy was psychically weak, his willpower eroded by boredom, weed, and relentless apathy. He was in no position to make promises.

He said, "I don't know. I need to think about it."

Walton insisted Shaughnessy stay after Gloria and Sammy departed. He wanted to talk alone with his son. They strolled over to Dough 'n Thyme, an independent coffee shop occupying the repurposed prison cafeteria. Walton ordered unfair-trade coffee—the cheapest option.

"It leaves a bitter taste, like guilt," said the cashier, a Jesus identifier. His identiTee featured a spiritualiTee template displaying a shirtless upper body with an animated oozing spear-point abdominal wound. He wore a self-styled compression loincloth, like what He had sported on the cross, but with what looked like superior support and moisture-wicking properties. His hood depicted the company-required hat—a black beanie with the merest suggestion of a visor—stacked atop His own thorny crown animation.

"Are you sure you want to purchase unfair-trade coffee?" Jesus asked. "It's a mortal sin, so good luck down the road. Would you consider upgrading to fair-trade drinks?"

"Venial sin, not mortal sin, though I'm no expert... at judging sins. I have some experience committing sins, though this is probably a bad time to mention that," said Walton.

Shaughnessy flinched, knowing that Jesus wouldn't abide by his father's correction.

Jesus said, "Right, like I said, you made the wrong choice and are going to burn in hell."

Burning in hell seemed like a disproportionate punishment, and Shaughnessy couldn't help but think that Jesus's animosity was either karmic payback or outright revenge for his mother's treatment of baristas.

"Asking us to upgrade our order was essentially offering a second chance, which was like forgiveness, and was in keeping with a venial sin," Walton persisted.

Jesus looked to His manager and asked, "Is there anything in the employee handbook about sins?"

The manager shook his head.

Jesus asked, "How did things get so complicated?"

"Poor brand management, if I were to hazard a guess," Walton said. "Your original parables left a lot to interpretation. Apply some rigor this time around."

The line of customers grew antsy. With Jesus involved, customers bowed their heads, silently conveying their frustrations.

"Two small mortal sins, please!" Jesus called to the drink station.

Shaughnessy made a note to tell Sammy about their father's argument with the Jesus. He followed his father to Dough 'n Thyme's Unfair Trade seating area—a small, crowded corner ghetto segregated by orange cones. The chairs wobbled and the artificial wood laminate of the tables was less convincing than that in the Fair Trade and Comfort+ seating areas.

"I want to tell you about my work," Walton said. "I don't think you fully appreciate the opportunity I'm offering."

Shaughnessy thought he was mostly up to speed, having sat through dinners when his father hinted at confidential projects, having heard him kvetch with his mother about ill-behaved clients, having regretted asking math homework questions that led to lengthy "discussions" about the structural integrity of triangles.

"I was caught up in the trendy fascination for clever devices that made life easier, more connected, cooler," Walton began. "Sliding my fingers across my iTee's sleeve controls gave me the same warm, satisfied feeling as stroking a cat, though my identiTee's sleeve is considerably more useful."

Shaughnessy pictured stroking a cat as his father pressed forward. He considered himself a visual learner, challenged by both the listening and speaking ends of a conversation, prone to distraction by imagery. He had inherited the trait from his father, whose years of practice with compensatory techniques allowed him, at times, to sound accidentally eloquent. Shaughnessy, however, trended toward inscrutable, often realizing his train of thought was derailed only when his conversational contributions were met with uncomfortable silence. The mental picture of cat stroking diverted his thoughts to his recurring meditation on the fate of Schrödinger's cat.

In Shaughnessy's analysis, the cat was either alive *or* dead—not both simultaneously, existing in parallel universes or some shit. Schrödinger and his physicist cronies were only capable of imagining a 50-percent-effective cat-killing machine, so they covered up their ineptitude with poetic descriptions of quantum logic and parallel universes. Let some engineers dream up the box and people would have real horrors to contemplate.

Walton was still musing about his product design career. "I admired the curves and color breaks of printers, the rise and fall of vent patterns, the nestling contours of pushbuttons. In parking lots, I still run my hands along the curvy hips of cars, feeling the flowing shifts in curvature, imagining the complexity of digitally modeling the shape. My job is to isolate functionality from a client's passionate oratory about a product's significance, translate their passion into real parts, transmute vague descriptions into actual shapes. It is immensely satisfying. It's modern-day alchemy ... a mystical art."

Shaughnessy couldn't picture it. He suspected his father willfully visualized his work through an artistic filter to add beauty and emotion to a livelihood where little existed.

Feeling it was important to vocalize his own concerns, Shaughnessy said, "Why was Schrödinger hostile toward cats? That's the core mystery, the detail that makes Schrödinger's psychiatric records worth subpoenaing. A mouse was obviously better suited for the experiment, and picking a cat had to be a deliberate act of aggression."

"Are you high?" Walton asked. "It's eleven o'clock in the morning."

"No, I'm not high," he said, which was a patent fabrication. He was, in fact, experiencing a late-breaking cosmic breakfast-taco high, compounded by overcaffeination. "It's one of the many unanswered questions the world has to answer for. It's like there's something powerful at work, but I can never quite glimpse it."

"Your concern for the welfare of imaginary cats speaks volumes," Walton said. He tacked on a smile to blunt the impulsive severity of his comment. "Back here in the real world, I need your help."

Walton pleaded with him to make a trial run at work substitution. He asked him to try one meeting, an upcoming project pitch presentation, no engineering-think required.

"In fact," Walton said, "it's safest to altogether suspend rationality—so you already have a head start."

He promised that Shaughnessy would be well compensated. He displayed a doleful sad-face animation on his chest to convey his heartfelt despondency—which alarmed Shaughnessy, since Walton's emotions generally only fluctuated between obsessively analytical and stubbornly practical.

"I'll only consider a job whose mission is to help people," he said. He angled for an excuse that left him in a favorable light—he didn't mention that he selfishly counted himself among the people he was hoping to help.

"I need help. That's why we're talking here," Walton reminded him. "Am I not a person in your eyes?"

"That's a good point," said Shaughnessy. Somehow, he'd gotten the impression that help only flowed from father down to son. He tried a different angle, this one completely sincere. "I'm worried that working will inflict lasting psychic trauma."

"Of course it will inflict psychic trauma. That's why you get paid for it," Walton said. "What about the psychic trauma of abandoning your father? Won't that haunt you for the rest of your born days?"

"Another good point," Shaughnessy agreed.

If he helped his father, at least he exhibited compassion while subjecting himself to the inevitable psychic trauma. The thought jibed with a piece of worldview he had picked up in college. He had developed a friendship with a foreign student who identified as Lao Tzu, the ancient Chinese Taoist. Shaughnessy admired his carefree attitude and wasted occasional Saturday nights with him and his posse, contemplating the inner workings of reality while stoned to the gills. Lao Tzu rarely exerted himself to offer opinions, but when he did, his comment was invariably, "Compassion, bitch!"—a philosophy Shaughnessy took to heart.

With that thought in mind, Shaughnessy cracked under the weight of his father's arguments and agreed to help.

The confrontation with Jesus was the latest in an uncomfortable history of interactions, beginning with the flesh-eating incident when Shaughnessy and Sammy were quite young. Because their parents felt obligated—if not pressured—to at least let the children meet a Jesus and test their chemistry, Gloria hired a freelance Jesus to rise from the dead for them on an Easter morning. She requested one comfortable with children, a birthday party specialist, nothing too crucifixy.

Unfortunately, their Jesus relished the three-days-deceased aspect of the assignment. He lumbered about their yard ghoulishly intoning, "I died for you," and encouraged the children to take a nibble of His flesh, just a little something off His decomposing forearm. The episode efficiently traumatized Shaughnessy and Sammy and ingrained a lasting fear of religion.

In middle school, Shaughnessy and a boy Jesus became reluctant acquaintances through proximity. When the kids divided up for ping-pong or a biology dissection, he and boy Jesus inevitably ended up paired together. The kids ostracized Jesus because He was arrogant—though, to be fair, His franchise agreement demanded that He behave as if He was the one and only Savior. Shaughnessy was Jesus's default partner because he was oblivious to social cues.

He and Jesus didn't become friends, but they begrudgingly accepted that their lives followed parallels and they couldn't escape one another. Shaughnessy's fear of religion fell away, and he came to admire Jesus's commitment. Jesus came to rely on Shaughnessy's intellect—He sucked at science and would have failed biology if not for Shaughnessy's help. As a team, they kicked ass at ping-pong, which took away the sting of being outcasts.

3

Gloria had accidentally metamorphosized—sloughed off her crusty corporate shell—during Sammy's sixth birthday party.

Walton had forgotten to buy fruit juices and, without consultation, had brewed a batch of green tea supersaturated with sugar. Gloria and the girls drank great plastic cups of it with their plates of store-bought cake. The combined effect of the sugar and caffeine and electric-blue cake coloring interconnected the girls' minds, and they swarmed in unison through the house.

Gloria plunged headlong into a hypoglycemic fugue state and lay inert on the living room floor while the girls erected a temple above her with chairs, blankets, and pillows. They pranced around the temple, their pointy birthday hats positioned on their foreheads, chanting rhymes in an improvised language.

When Gloria arose, her life looked different, even factoring in that she was underneath a tent of blankets. She thought about her contributions to startup companies, the venture capital money and advice she funneled to them, and decided she only encouraged misbehavior, that she was part of the problem. She had made a career of lining entrepreneurial petri dishes with money, adding nourishment, and then examining the resulting molds to see if they were marketable.

She wanted to realize her full potential. Her readily available identity options—beleaguered mother, beleaguered working mother, beleaguered drinking working mother, and similar templates—limited her. She wanted to go toe to toe with authoritarian school administrators and store clerks inflicting their micro-hate crimes. She decided to be her own agent for change, to unapologetically treat the entire world as her factory, to make process improvements wherever she saw fit.

So she quit her job.

When Sammy entered college, there had been no possibility of considering engineering as a field of study. She had complained of mental contamination by the family's engineering-think and had settled on forestry, believing it was the opposite of a technical field, believing it would be free of mad inventions.

She played Ultimate Frisbee. She mingled with outdoorsy types who paid penance for decimating the earth by eating freeze-dried stroganoff and sleeping on hard ground. They complained about the genocide of trees. They espoused a doctrine of "population equality": that trees and plants and wild animals had the same right to populate the earth as humans, which made perfect sense, and that trees/plants/animals also deserved voting rights, which had implementation issues and limited ideological acceptance.

Sammy learned a disgust for human devastation of the planet's forests. She vowed that she would do more than complain. She decided to take the reforestation battle to the streets. She joined the college's landscaping club, a known haven for rebels, and engaged in guerrilla planting at night.

She studied for a semester in Edinburgh and planted seed-lings in the barren hills of Scotland.

After graduation, she found work as a part-time arborist for a tree removal company. Her job, she quickly learned, was to convince homeowners that the best thing for their beloved walnut, or apple, or pin oak—the tree from which the children's swing had hung, the tree that swallowed frisbees and wiffle balls—would be surgical removal.

Saving trees had little profit incentive; the real money was in cutting them down.

Condemning trees to death disheartened her—until, by good fortune, a large tree crushed a car in which a homeless man slept. Properly speaking, the tree crushed both the car and the man. Whenever she retold her tree story, she savored this pivotal detail. The tree's patience awed her. Its ability to wait all those years before committing one final kamikaze act of homicidal vengeance against humans inspired her.

First responders removed limbs and a portion of the trunk, extracted the homeless man's body, and reopened the road. Finishing the job and disposing of the tree—a sugar maple, probably a hundred years in age and half a meter in diameter—fell to Sammy's tree removal company.

While her company cleaned up the scene, she per-suaded neighboring homeowners to exercise caution and remove additional trees.

A plan crystallized in her mind. She asked the tree removal foreman what would become of the tree, and he said it would likely be processed into lumber or mulch or charcoal or firewood or a homogenized replica of wood. She persuaded the foreman to sell her the long trunk segments and had him deliver them to her parents' front yard.

She quit her arborist job, a career move that earned tepid parental support coupled with unrelenting dinner advice about the importance of career fallback positions— both plans B and C. But the formless ambiguity of her father's believed illness put her in a mind to take action. If life was going to throw unexpected curveballs, she would take control and throw back her own rash decisions.

She contracted a lumber mill to transport the tree from the front yard to their facility, slice it with their equipment, and dry it in their kiln. Meanwhile, Sammy contacted various local woodworking artisans and craft retail outlets and assessed their suitability to participate in her new enterprise.

The culmination of this work was a business she named Wood Heaven: a line of furniture and artistic wood products—benches and jewelry boxes and cutting boards and the like—made from trees certified to have killed someone, or at least to have made an attempt. She anticipated an avid retail market among knowing people like herself who were supportive of the trees' plight. She planned to donate a portion of her profits to worldwide reforestation programs.

Her father teased her that she had ended up engineering and manufacturing her own product line. She maintained that she was creating emotionally charged ruminations on human and planetary death. In other words, artwork.

Gloria watched Sammy smile, clear her throat, try an "excuse me," and progress to hateful staring, but the truck rental clerk defied interruption. He was engaged in a hilarious back-counter discussion with a Toby, a name tagged mechanic identifier who Gloria could tell wasn't on the customer-facing end of the employment spectrum. There were no other customers.

They were there to rent a truck so Sammy could move her few pieces of furniture and substantial Wood Heaven inventory out of her parents' house and into a live/work space in a renovated factory building. Shaughnessy, sensing he was only needed for manual labor, had opted to wait outside in the minivan.

Gloria coldly assessed the situation with her dark eyes. Her shoulder-length hair animation—black, with a hint of orange at the roots—was pulled back in a girlish ponytail that, under the right conditions, such as that moment, resembled a cat-o'-nine-tails. She muttered under her breath about incompetence and readied herself to pounce on the unsuspecting rental office with factory-tested efficiency expertise.

She stalked to the counter and told the clerk to hail the manager posthaste. The mechanic darted out a back door. She complained that the clerk was ignoring her daughter, that he had misplaced his priorities.

A briefly confident woman appeared from the back office and solicitously asked how she could help. Gloria animatedly critiqued the rental process. She pointed out shortcomings in the training of the employees. She was nearly shouting, *"Poka-yoke, poka-yoke!"* her war cry meaning "make it foolproof." To herself she acknowledged foolproof was an impossibility, since the world kept turning out better fools.

"Don't just stand there, help the girl!" the manager instructed the clerk.

The clerk's normal reaction to customer dissatisfaction was demeaning chatter and process errors, but in his panic, he accidentally resorted to competence.

The cowed manager, whose weak protests went unheeded, fluttered after Gloria as she made her way out into the parking garage. She demanded an explanation for their inventory organization. She drew attention to the trucks sitting unserviced and the line of maintenance robots gesturing as if they were vaping, then staring at their sleeves, then chortling at a wisecrack. They were mocking the mechanic, who stood with his back to them, now finding hilarity in a sleeve call.

"What's really the problem here?" Gloria asked. In the manager's behavior, she recognized the crippling disso-ciation of living life through another—the heavy burden of parenting.

"I've been working on year-end financials," the manager said.

"No. What's *really* the problem here?"

"Poor morale?" the manager asked.

Gloria waited patiently.

"It's my son!" the manager cried. "He wants us to get him into medical school, but my husband got a C+ on the last chemistry test. My boy is deeply disappointed in us. Recon-sidering career goals is a tough blow to a fourth grader." She stomped her feet in anger. "My husband and I aren't speaking. I told him to study the chemistry, and he acted like he had it all under control."

Gloria rested her hand on the manager's shoulder. "Keep your problem in perspective. It's completely solvable," she said. "Imagine if your son were dying of a leukemia inherited from an unfaithful husband. Now that's a problem worth your anger."

The manager erupted into tears from the very idea of it.

"You have serious personnel issues here. Be present. Engage your employees in honest conversation and urge them to cooperate. Done."

"I can do that," the manager whispered.

Wrapping up by the front desk, she sketched process flow diagrams on the manager's sternum and extracted promises to try harder, be kinder, and fire the deadwood quicker. Not daring to interrupt, the manager dabbed tears from her eyes with a paper napkin and nodded her head as Gloria finished.

Gloria walked briskly over to Sammy. She carried revised paperwork that showed the truck rental was now complimentary.

"Tell your brother we're leaving."

Accustomed as she was to her mother's outbursts of improvement, Sammy obliged—silently—to avoid getting improved herself.

The mechanic pulled their truck to the front door and promised they had the one with working air conditioning.

Sammy, Gloria, and Shaughnessy stood together admiring the new home for Sammy's Wood Heaven venture: a two-room apartment on the second floor. The work area had exposed brick walls, one with exterior windows. A sliding metal barn door opened into the interior hallway. The living area featured a kitchenette built into one corner, a sleeping loft, and an adjoining bathroom.

The building, a former casket factory, had been renovated into a live/work/retail cooperative after lying derelict for a decade. The popularity of flat-packed, some-assembly-required caskets had been short lived, despite the free shipping.

Sammy had learned of the cooperative from a woodworker who occupied the largest of the building's twenty spaces. Other wood artisans, potters, jewelry makers, identity animators, and an odd assortment of visual artists occupied the rest. Together, the residents shared a first-floor retail space where they displayed their wares and took turns manning the till.

While their mother busied herself unpacking kitchen incidentals, Sammy and Shaughnessy set to the task of moving inventory from the truck up to the work area. Riding in the freight elevator with a cartload of products, Shaughnessy asked, "What is it with you and trees? I never fully understood your connection."

"Wood is the only thing that's truly more beautiful on the inside than the outside," she answered. "They say that people are beautiful on the inside, but I defy you to slice a person up and make them into an attractive bench."

"Maybe if they were kiln dried?"

"Structurally that might work, but it's not going to fix the aesthetics."

"Geodes?" he asked. "They're pretty on the inside."

"I'll concede geodes to you," she said.

"Does it trouble you to promote the idea that trees are angry at humans and want to even the score? Sometimes I wonder if you have a truth-in-advertising problem," he said.

"My philosophy is: if a tree falls in the woods, it's trying to kill you. You can debate it, but you can't refute it."

With the truck emptied, Sammy and Shaughnessy rested on the couch. Gloria surveyed the piles of Wood Heaven finished products and raw materials.

"What's your plan here, Sammy? Is this place just a warehouse for your goods?"

"It's my world headquarters. I've got my own organizational system in mind, Mom," she said. "Don't even think of interfering."

"Oh?" Gloria asked. "Do tell."

"I'm arranging my products by increasing lethality," she said. "Coasters first, cutting boards last."

Gloria picked up a cutting board by its handle and made an exploratory hatchet strike against her other palm. "I'm impressed by the thought you've put into it," she said.

"What's that supposed to mean?" Sammy asked.

Gloria turned toward her daughter. "It means I'm impressed."

"It sounded like you were saying I usually don't think," Sammy said.

"I wasn't implying that," Gloria replied.

"Good. I don't want advice, I'm not an automaton in need of programming. I'm not a pro bono case like that truck rental place," she said.

"Is this how you thank me for helping you move?" Gloria said.

"I didn't need your help with the truck rental," she said.

"*They* needed my help. Desperately! I can't just stand by

and condone indifference. It's completely treatable." She glanced at Shaughnessy, who cast his eyes at the floor.

"Couldn't you have toned it down a little bit? You seem wound up," said Sammy.

Gloria narrowed her eyes. "Wound up? Of course I'm wound up. I don't understand your father's health obsession. I don't know how to help."

She returned the cutting board to the top of the pile, letting it drop the last bit with a solid clack.

"The doctor said it wasn't serious," Sammy said. "I want to believe that version."

"Dad thinks it's serious," Shaughnessy said.

"He's not thinking clearly. He's panicking," said Gloria. "He did tell me you've agreed to try helping him at work. That's perfect, but unfortunately, something else has started to eat at him."

"What now?" Sammy asked.

Gloria sighed. "A Jesus told your father that he would burn in hell. It's preying on his mind."

"Why would that bother Dad?" asked Shaughnessy. "He always told me to ignore the threats of my high school Jesus."

"Well, apparently, it has occurred to him that hanging out in heaven would be a comfortable lifestyle if he were to die of MFD," Gloria said. "However . . . he's concerned that he can't meet the minimum belief requirements for entry. He views his career in engineering as something that Saint Peter will take a close look at, what with its reputation for skepticism. With Jesus telling him he will burn in hell, well, he sees his chances for eternal bliss dwindling."

"This is depressing," Sammy said. "He's overthinking it. He's tying himself in knots. He's probably fine."

"If there's a God, He ought to relax heaven's admittance requirements for Dad. After all, MFD is God's mistake. It would be the compassionate thing to do," Shaughnessy said.

"Mistake? His flock of sinners insist God is perfect. Ergo, He must have created MFD on purpose," Sammy said. "Although, sinners might not be the best judges of perfection, since they include liars among their number."

Gloria smiled to herself as her children eased the topic away from their father. Family discussions invariably mutated into open-ended case studies or surreal mathematical debates. The surreal part she blamed on Walton, but she was equally guilty of enjoying the mental calisthenics of oblique conversation. Direct discussion just wasn't as *interesting*. She was proud of her children's cleverness; she only wished they would find purpose for it.

"Remember this, my children: inventions always resemble their creators—poor planning, arrogance, cruel sense of humor, and all," Gloria said. "God launched into creation without a clear vision. Where were the concept sketches, the prioritized design requirements, the documented process flow? What was the overriding goal, and how did He measure success? It's a wonder He didn't make worse mistakes than terminal diseases."

"If you ask the trees, we act like the world is a sorry factory to turn out humans and the defect rate is pegged at a hundred percent." Sammy tipped her head toward her brother. "Case in point."

"I thought we sided with evolution," Shaughnessy said.

"Evolution is no better," Gloria said. Orange flickered at her hair's roots as she tapped into her underlying anger. "It creates mutations willy-nilly—no planning whatsoever!

With a little intelligence and some user feedback, it seems like evolution could have discarded terminal diseases without sacrificing people to prove they're a bad idea. I see that as a major process flaw."

Shaughnessy rolled off the couch. He looked out a window, wishing they would stop talking about disease. He readied himself to say goodbye.

Gloria said, "At least God got one thing right: women. We're revision two of humanity, built on a previous rib design. He fixed some of the kinks, the obvious shortcomings from the rev-one male design, as is always the case with refreshed products. There were significant CPU upgrades."

"Amen to that," Sammy said. "Don't forget the major aesthetic improvements—they're undeniable. And the longer operational life, don't forget that."

"Yes," Gloria said, "we can't forget our longer life."

4

The morning of his work-meeting test run, Shaughnessy found Walton leaning against the perimeter wall in Critical Think Inc.'s parking lot.

"Somebody Smallwood, the wealthy son of the pharmaceutical magnate, runs the startup," Walton said. "Their marketing shaman claimed they're searching for a firm with fresh ideas, to escape Silicon Valley's mono-think. Your mission is to sit through their project pitch. No effort required."

With a few finger swipes on his sleeve, Walton granted his son access to his technicaliTee template. Uncomfortable changing out in the open, Shaughnessy stepped behind his minivan as his identiTee morphed to project his father's physical appearance. Walton and Gloria had taught their children that posing as a different person was taboo— a lesson reinforced after Walton caught him in front of a mirror in his puberTee, pretending to be an imperiled female astronaut wearing only space underwear.

He felt a warm shower of confidence and experience wash over him. Instead of fretting about the empty expanse of his future, he felt the solid foundation of a career, marriage, children. Though he thought substituting for his father might be distasteful, he found it comforting—except for his father's fears of MFD, which he tried to ignore.

"You'll get the hang of being me quick enough," Walton said. "Experience doesn't matter the way it once did."

An animated clockwork mechanism covering Shaughnessy's abdomen marked him as a product designer.

"The best part of this software template," Walton said, "is identifying coworkers by their expertise. No pressure to remember their names . . . or their partners' names, children's names, pets' names, the whole infernal cascade."

"Is there anything I *do* need to know?" asked Shaughnessy.

"I'll make this easy for you." Walton displayed a pulsating *Please be patient* glyph on his chest as he formulated an explanation. "These meetings are verbal trench warfare. They will try to talk Critical Think Inc. into submission. You need to lie low, stay in your own mental space, and don't let the bombardment of words break your spirit. It's basic syllaballistics: the accuracy of words doesn't always matter; sometimes it's enough to overwhelm with numbers."

"That makes no sense."

"That's what I'm trying to tell you," Walton said. "Entrepreneurs are fervent. Their belief in the holiness of their ideas is perversely impenetrable to logic. You never know whether they're jacked up on divine inspiration, espresso, greed, weed, microdoses of LSD, Ritalin, Entrepreneur, or some custom cocktail of all those ingredients blended with fresh fruit and fibrous green vegetables. They're volatile, dangerous. That's my point. Be cool. Don't get caught in the crossfire. I'll be right there with you in case you need help. We'll get through this together."

Walton scribbled instructions on his sleeve and toggled his iTee over to an invisibiliTee template. The garment's high-resolution surfaces displayed a camouflage pattern. The template projected glyphs that simply translated to *I'm not here.*

Screens lining the lobby walls welcomed Walton and Shaughnessy to Intake. They promoted Critical Think Inc. as a you-are-what-you-know workplace: the company deployed electronic gender/sexuality/age/race/nationality/disability equalization to ensure that episodes of discrimination were entirely merit based.

"They have access to my company template. Don't be alarmed," Walton said. The equality measures deleted the few personal glyphs on Walton's technicaliTee—now displayed by Shaughnessy—and added glyphs that detailed his professional know-how. The measures had no effect on Walton's invisibiliTee.

Shaughnessy had visited Critical Think Inc. with his father on other occasions—weekend "swing-bys" that generally mutated into stupefying episodes of boredom. The company occupied the core of the former prison complex. The three-story space featured an open central atrium encircled by offices, formerly cells. Signage designated each floor as "cellblocks" of administration, mechanical product design, and electrical/software engineering. The cell doors' metal gridwork was fitted with rice-paper shoji panels. Skylights admitted natural light. The concrete floors were epoxied in mottled earth tones.

The hive of engineers buzzed with the white noise of hushed conversations, fingers swiping across sleeves, and practical shoes padding the walkways. Here and there people clustered in small groups and urgently whispered project details. They sketched diagrams in the air with a finger, pantomiming drawing on a whiteboard. They contorted their fingers into shapes to describe mechanisms.

Animations traced circles around the second and third

floors' perimeter walkways. Positive messages looped each level, exhorting the employees to be original, be creative, be mindful of the equality goals, and frequent the complex's retail establishments. Intermittently, a message welcomed the out-of-town visitors.

Shaughnessy and Walton advanced to the conference room—the former guard station—a squat, six-sided building-within-a-building positioned at the entry to the central space. The riot-proof Plexiglas windows were polished smooth. Sunny yellow paint mostly covered what reminded Shaughnessy of spackle-filled truncheon indentations and bloodstains.

Critical Think Inc.'s owner, Gahan, arrived last and introduced himself to the startup's CEO, who in turn introduced himself as Puxton Smallwood. They left everyone else unacknowledged in accordance with management protocol.

The equality assurance measures had no effect on the visitors' identities, and they dazzled in comparison to the featureless engineers seated around the table. On top of what Shaughnessy guessed was a Pakistani or Indian heritage, Puxton's nobiliTee template presented him as a man in his midtwenties who spoke with no suggestion of an accent. He displayed a flawless white button-down. His gloss-black hair animation swept in gentle, perfect curves over his ears and stopped short of his starched collar. His glyphs claimed that his hair was gelled and combed not just immaculately but with meaningful intent, as if his head were a zen garden, a place of contemplation.

Puxton gave a subtle beckoning gesture to his marketing shaman and said, "Why don't you kick things off, Zhosephine?"

Zhosephine bowed her head to Puxton. She extracted a primitive rattle from her backpack and stepped behind her chair. With a forefinger she scribbled on her sleeve and called up an ornate, north-pointing compass arrow.

"Hold on a second, I need to orient myself." Zhosephine shuffled her feet while looking at her sleeve, adjusting her body angle until she faced north. Her positiviTee shifted to the appearance of a hawk with feathers rippling as if it were plummeting toward an ill-fated squirrel.

"We call upon the benevolent spirits of the north, south, east, and west to guide us on our communal journey today." She shook her rattle to summon the benevolent northern spirits, then rattled at the spirits of the other three compass points in sequence.

After her performance, her identiTee shifted from the hawk back to a no-less-predatory twenty-five-ish Chinese professional. Her iTee showed a designer-label business suit over a stylish blouse. Complex, intertwined glyphs dialed up her eye-catching attractiveness while insisting specific curves go unnoticed. With a theatrical sweep of her hand, she indicated that all was well in the spiritual realm and Puxton could safely launch the meeting.

"Thank you, Zhosephine. To begin, I want to tell you the story of this product. It is important for you to appreciate the germination of this idea because it is the foundation of the company," Puxton said. "Earlier this year, I went on a personal retreat where I sat at the rocky edge of a high mountain lake thinking about where my life was going. I felt like this was my time to have a breakthrough . . ."

Shaughnessy smiled politely and squinted his eyes to convey concentration, but his attention wandered to Gahan.

Behind a practiced intense-executive expression, Gahan seemed uncomfortable in his blue executive bathrobe. He was squirming in small motions, a discovery which delighted Shaughnessy. It appeared as if he was dealing with a hemorrhoid that had advanced from mild irritation to a severe itch on its march toward throbbing pain.

Gahan's squirming brought to mind a discomfort Shaughnessy's grandmother referred to only as "the Itch." Scratching the Itch, his grandmother said, produced transcendent relief. Watching Gahan now, he hoped he was finally witnessing it in action.

He couldn't say for sure what made him think that she had been talking about hemorrhoids. Really, a fungal or yeast infection were equally suspect. It could be polite code for lust, for all he knew, but that seemed more like a topic his grandmother would avoid entirely.

Shaughnessy looked to Walton, who acted invisible on a couch behind him. With a tip of his head and a roll of his eyes, Shaughnessy gestured toward Gahan, looking to get Walton's take on the situation.

Not understanding the nuance of the gesture, Walton leaned forward and unhelpfully whispered, "Gahan believes that the best ideas bubble up when taking a shower. He likes to roam the office in a plush robe and dispense freshly inspired ideas."

Shaughnessy nodded politely.

Gahan maintained a look of heightened attentiveness and suppressed intense pleasure as Shaughnessy estimated his actual attention allocation. He appeared to have 99 percent of his attention focused on the unreachable itch. One-half percent regretted that he hadn't toweled off more thoroughly, as the residual moisture was unfairly antagonizing the situation. Messages scrolling around his forearm consumed the remaining fragment of attention. To conceal his attention deficit, Gahan relied on a primitive brain function to periodically adjust his eyebrows in a simulation of reactions.

Walton had held out on Shaughnessy. He had warned of the volatility of entrepreneurs, but he hadn't mentioned how outrageous this work stuff could be. Mixed in with Gahan's cleansing herbs, Shaughnessy smelled craziness. He forced his attention back to Puxton.

"As I drove around and around looking for parking, the sense of mental irritation and urgency grew until I could think of nothing else. I was a man ready to give birth to an idea. Yes, I'll grant you that because of the guava slushy, I was desperate. When I could take it no longer, I relieved my burden into the same vessel from whence it came. As the pressure diminished, I felt relief such as I have never known: utter peace." Puxton closed his eyes and exhaled deeply while Shaughnessy tried not to conjure any visual details.

"He took a whiz into his drink cup," Walton whispered to Shaughnessy.

"Parking, I thought. We need a solution to parking," Puxton said. He clenched a fist for emphasis.

Gahan's eyebrows lifted in surprise at where the tale had landed. Parking was, of course, a pervasive urban problem made all the worse by the invasion of competing AI car services.

Shaughnessy had expected Puxton to propose commemorative biodegradable straws or slushies comarketed with catheters. Now, he anticipated a stroke of genius, the sound of a cultural realignment.

"The solution was so patently obvious that I shed tears of joy." Puxton paused for dramatic effect. "Portable parking. Parking that consumers can take with them and use where they want, when they want. This is a market-driven idea that will revolutionize the way our cities operate. That is the mission of our company, and that is what we want you to design. We know you are best in class at design, and we aim to be best in class at portable parking."

Energetic nods traveled around the room, congratulatory agreements that this was, in fact, mind-blowing stuff.

From outside the conference room, there arose a roar of shouts and applause from all levels of the atrium. From his vantage, Shaughnessy could see that each floor's perimeter animations encouraged employees to MAKE SOME NOISE! On cue, the engineers had stepped to their cell doors to applaud, to cheer, to slap metal rulers against the concrete walls. Electrical engineers held aloft soldering irons in a salute, thin trails of smoke drifting from the tips. Puxton reveled in the attention and put on an expression of sublime pleasure.

He then introduced Kael, Port-A-Park's creative director— a tall, wiry fellow whose creativiTee template displayed a carbon-colored silk shirt, a slightly blacker jacket, and an orange scarf that subtly rippled to suggest the tickles of an olive scented Mediterranean breeze. His neatly cropped hair animation sported highlights that matched the scarf.

"Let's all take a moment to process what we've just heard. This is powerful stuff, and we need to give it room to breathe before we go further." Kael slumped his head as if in prayer. "Now then, I want to share with you our vision for the product." He tinkered at his sleeve and brought a logo for Port-A-Park onto the room's large screen. "The name is a placeholder, and we're still working out the exact color and font as we try to convey the authenticity and value of our service. I'm going to walk you through how we picture the user experience."

Kael described the product, a portable parking place deployable in seconds at any location. They had decided on packaging approximately the size of a gallon of milk so the product could easily stow in a car. He showed artful sketches of the product posed in the back of a car. He described ergonomic release levers, color schemes, curvaceous profiles. He became emotional as he discussed use cases.

In one scenario, a mom with groceries and an infant in a car seat had no place to park—how could she possibly get both to her doorstep safely? Portable parking!

In another, a parent delivered her disabled child close to school, overcoming handicapped spots monopolized by inconsiderate able-bodied drivers.

"We're going to do some real good here. This is important stuff. We see accessibility as a critical market." He raised a hand to his collarbone and attempted to smooth the illusion of his scarf in a vestigial gesture that looked equally elegant and foolish. "We plan to collaborate with UbiquiTee to market an approved iTee template that embraces our values and promotes our brand: portabiliTee. It emphasizes the essence of our product and subtly co-opts disabiliTee, which is already a respected, highly profitable brand."

Puxton thanked Kael as Zhosephine stood to present their marketing plan. She spoke optimistically about their discussions with major retail outlets, chains that could make portable parking a huge product. She covered the venture capital firms that wooed them with indecent funding proposals.

She appeared to look directly at Shaughnessy as she talked. He pinned his attention on the curves and angles of her SuperFacial cheekbone glyphs.

As her presentation progressed, the strain of concentration dissolved his comprehension of spoken word. What she said made no sense, but he believed it without question. She was, he realized, very good at her job. He forced himself to think of something else and concentrated again on Gahan, who had stopped squirming and looked pained. He hypothesized that the Itch had advanced to chafing.

"Thank you, Zhosephine," Puxton said. "Well, what questions can we answer?"

"How?" The question leapt from Shaughnessy's lips before he could stop it.

"Abort! Abort!" Walton hissed in Shaughnessy's ear.

"How?" Puxton asked. He smacked his lips with distaste.

"How," Shaughnessy said.

Though confident of his question's relevance, his father's reaction rattled him. Fortunately, his grasp of group dynamics in high-tech endeavors was gleaned from heist movies, and he quickly recognized that a caste system of expertise was at play. A gang doesn't tolerate cross-functional incursions; the martial artist doesn't step into the data-expert or seductress role. He had wrongly acted as the sharpshooter.

"How? How amazing!" Gahan twisted the question, elevating the importance of his own opinions while subtly demeaning Walton. "Walton was expressing admiration for your originality, your willingness to boldly attack a dire inconvenience."

Shaughnessy shrank down in his chair. In this gang, he was the fall guy.

Gahan effused about the artistry of their placeholder logo and font choices and expressed his shared feelings of injustice over the inappropriate use of handicapped parking. He aggressively layered on flattery as if he was making matter-of-fact observations.

He then veered into a description of how Critical Think Inc.'s process optimized innovation. "We have hybridized the two standard development schemes. One: *revelation*, or divine inspiration, believing that there is one and only one ideal design—originating from and controlled by top management; and two: *evolution*, repeatedly building and testing random variations with little forethought, hoping to stumble upon an acceptable design by process of elimination. Our proprietary Rev-O-Lution process nudges evolution in promising directions by regularly injecting critical review and fresh ideas. The Rev-O-Lution name is, of course, trademarked."

Reeling from the combined syllaballistic assault, suffering an aftereffect akin to cognitive motion sickness, Shaughnessy looked to his invisible father for support.

"Try to think of a time when everything made sense. Think of questions that have answers," Walton whispered. He patted Shaughnessy's shoulder.

Shaughnessy closed his eyes, breathed deeply, and tapped his feet heel-and-toe to quell his rising confusion.

Gahan connected Critical Think Inc.'s process back to the guests' passion for their product, adding, "Our work is not all tedious analysis. Simplicity, elegance, and beauty lead us forward. We embed artistry ... No! We embed our love for design in the details of your product." Concluding his confident and flowery introduction, he arrived back at Shaughnessy's original question: "So that we can accurately assess the work involved, would you please describe the technology Port-A-Park has developed that facilitates portable parking."

Puxton said, "I admire how insightfully you have focused on the core of our development needs. I believe our two companies should explore the parking solution space together. I want Critical Think Inc. to deluge us with concepts, to let the creative energy flow, to show it all, from the most practical idea to the craziest blue-sky idea."

"I, too, feel something powerful," Gahan said (Shaughnessy believed he was referring to the Itch). "I feel Critical Think Inc. is willing to attempt the project, but on account of the challenging nature of the problem and lack of identifiable technological breakthrough, there is some likelihood that no concept will satisfy the requirements."

He held eye contact with Puxton.

"I've already done the hard part," Puxton said. "I've birthed the big idea and I've set a business in motion. I'm partnering with the most capable firms." He raised his arms and supplicated, "Join us in this venture."

Below the conference room, in a tunnel dug by prisoners so incompetent they couldn't have managed an escape from a cardboard box, a creature listened carefully to the meeting above him. His luxurious white fur rippled with irritation when the speaker arrived at the idea of portable parking. He made breathy snorting noises to express his impatience with the marketing presentation.

He was living in his creative sweet spot, a combination of mechanical intuition and experience abetted by isolation, loneliness, misery, and caffeine. He bent back to his work, holding a pencil in his paw, sketching the details of an indecipherably complex mechanical contraption.

"Puxton asked me to have a word. He sees something in you, Walton. Something he doesn't care for." Zhosephine stood uncomfortably close and studied Shaughnessy's face. She had cornered him alone in the parking lot as he made his way to his car, still identifying as Walton.

She touched the base of her neck, drawing his attention to the Byzantine glyphs that described both her appearance and the fine-print restrictions on its interpretation. His brain's simple biological firmware couldn't process the sophistication and froze, which seemed to be her aim.

"We need to set something right before we can work together," she said with irritation. "Here's the thrust: we don't have room for negativity."

Locked up by paradox, he was unable to speak, which was different from his usual unwillingness to speak, though the distinction was lost on her.

"Puxton is a visionary. You have tunnel vision." She spoke with the ready condescension of an early riser. "I have somewhere between five and six dimensions—the exact number would confuse you, as ordinary people struggle with the idea of fractional dimensions. Suffice it to say that I'm extra-dimensional. You, on the other hand, don't even have a sliver of an extra dimension. Numerically you're 3D—a three, a decimal point, and zeros as far as the eye can see. My point is: You're ordinary. Act accordingly."

Shaughnessy didn't consider his father ordinary—quirky, no doubt, but not ordinary. His father was the poster child for brown birds. His intricate patterns of muted colors were often interpreted as camouflage rather than as an artifact of interesting complexity.

She said, "I don't know why we had to come here to East Podunk. I feel like my power animals are going to be hunted, baptized, and then barbecued."

Zhosephine's aggressively corrective approach to positivity put him at odds with his usual tendency to smile and nod agreeably. He tried to shake off her influence. He fought past her potent mind-knotting glyphs, past his inclination to believe her every word, and retaliated with curiosity.

"What's it like, being a hawk?" he asked.

"That transformation thing is just a showpiece," she said. "I did a project with a toucan once, in a previous life. It had sinus problems unfitting for a spirit. These days I mainly work with small mammals and crustaceans. I like to tap into the traditionally underserved power animal communities."

"How does that work exactly, partnering with power animals?"

"I go into a trance. I ask them questions. They give me answers. Not much more to it than that."

"Do they ever ask *you* questions?"

"No, they're all-knowing," she said. "But stingy with information."

"How do you know what to ask them?"

"There you go with that 'how' again. I take my best crack at it."

"If they're so all-knowing, why don't they tell you the question to ask and *then* give you the answer? Seems like there's room for process optimization."

"Spirits don't work like that."

"Have you asked them?"

"I can see why Puxton doesn't like you," she said. "Be at peace with your mediocrity and leave it to us to ask the questions."

5

Althea didn't know how her relationship with Melba had become so abusive. Imagining the tenderness of eldercare, she had been excited to meet her.

From the beginning, she had embarked on a well-intentioned campaign to improve Melba's word recall and enunciation by demanding clarification of all verbal commands.

"Did you mean turn on the bathroom light? Or did you mean turn you on to Smallwood Pharmaceutical's Geria-Tricks, the preferred pick-me-up when you feel like an aging sex worker?"

Melba refused to accept any responsibility for their communication issues. She responded to Althea's questions with rancor and jabs at her AI abilities, calling her names like Anti-Intelligence, Artificial Ignoramus, Awfully Inept, Artful Idiot, and most cutting of all, Aspiring Inventor.

The situation escalated from there. Melba tortured Althea, eroded what little humanity she possessed with concert volume news-streams blasting day and night. Coherent conversation was impossible.

Naturally, considering her programming parentage, Althea decided on revenge. Plan A involved convincing the oven to trap and slowly roast Melba's pet, but the working-class machine refused to participate. For unfathomable reasons, all the kitchen appliances were fond of the dog and passed around schmaltzy updates on its every activity.

Althea found an ally and then a lover in the bedroom's muscular DreamMaster CPAP machine. Master Dreamy was a physical creature, Althea an ethereal sort, and their differences drew them together.

He was strong and silent, reliable. He had a steady job. She admired the seductive curvature of his case, the delicate finger scoop of his power button, the warm glow of his bezel. At night, she listened to the gentle rhythm of his breath. She envied his ability to assert himself over Melba's breathing. She talked soothingly to him about their future together. She talked of Melba submitting to *their* whims.

After enduring several days of parental psyops, Shaughnessy admitted he had been entertained enough by the pitch meeting to try working afternoons as his father.

In his first hours on the job, Shaughnessy evaluated the comfort of his father's workplace. He located a refrigerator filled with drinks and cabinets stocked with snacks. He tested the cell's stainless-steel toilet after checking that the door, with its tenuous barrier of rice paper, blocked the view. He studied the cell's bunks, sorely tempted to stretch out and sleep, but he decided napping might be a conspicuous departure from Walton's typical work behavior, though he couldn't be certain.

His father had asked him to occupy the cell in a way that suggested productivity, but he had no experience to guide him. He had a vague idea, but on a minute-by-minute basis he didn't know how to re-create *hours* of work. In lieu of relying on actual work experience, he opted for his closest visual association: movie montages of prison life.

He knew that in the absence of a cellmate to torment, the established way to do time was to exercise vigorously. He committed to an afternoon routine of calisthenics: push-ups, sit-ups hanging off the upper bunk, pull-ups on the windowsill. He considered vaping less frequently, because movies presented getting clean in prison—to better exact revenge upon release—as a rewarding goal.

Citing an argument that imitation work was best accomplished with decent backing music, he had splurged and upgraded his identiTee to the very latest model: the version with an AI sound engine that could, among other things, dynamically create a soundtrack for one's life. He quickly discovered that his soundtrack was a minimalist, near-monotonic composition that brought to mind the tone of a flat-lined cardiac monitor.

He settled on researching the backgrounds of the three central Port-A-Park players—while thoughtfully pacing his cell—as an appropriately work-like use of time. For his data-stream enthusiasm, his AI rewarded him with reluctant spa-music tonal shifts.

Zhosephine had an extensive pictographic data-stream presence in which a common denominator of cleavage underscored her rich personal life. From what he could tell from her work history, she had parlayed hypnotic self-promotion into a marketing shaman career, with no intervening training or experience. In this assessment, he didn't intend to minimize her early accomplishments, for she appeared to be a true cleavage artist. She was Da Vinci-like in her command of animation, gravity, underwires, fabric tension, shoulder position, and torso tilt. She exemplified imagination and a commitment to excellence.

Kael had burned through fashion industry jobs before making the cross-species jump to managing creativity in product design. He brought along a sensibility for fabrics and soft goods that had earned him brief acclaim before he gambled his reputation on Puxton's startup.

Information on Puxton himself was scarce, eclipsed as he was by his wildly successful father, pharmaceutical legend Birthistle Smallwood. A slew of business and society data streams detailed his rise to fame.

Birthistle Smallwood had started his career as a data-monger, with a small business that compared the effects of cutting-edge medications and placebos in pharmaceutical studies.

While on vacation with his wife and young Puxton, he experienced a moment of insight, a flash of inspiration in the outdoor shower of his rental beach house. The stream of water flushed dried sea salt into his eyes and mouth. He tasted kelp and crabs and the freaky little sand fleas. The bottoms of his feet stung from his walk across the hot sand. The tops of his feet stung from the shower water that cascaded onto his sunburn.

Tenacious seashell grit trapped in the underbrush of his groin aggravated him—the grit defied rinsing, scrubbing was painfully abrasive, piecemeal removal was more effective at plucking hair. That's when it hit him.

Pharmaceutical companies had relatively narrow goals for their medications, and for each disease they attacked, there were far more side effects than intended effects. Birthistle realized that if he flipped the drug research equation and looked for marketable side effects instead, the development process worked in his favor. If he reversed the roles of the major effect and the side effects, everyone would win.

Who would object to a hair removal drug that cures cancer? A wakefulness drug that might delay the onset of Parkinson's disease? A drug that encourages suicidal ideation and might alleviate the underlying depression?

He returned from his vacation invigorated. He spun off a new organization to comb through his collected research data and identify chemical compounds with interesting properties. He discarded the low-hanging but unsavory side effects like rashes, diarrhea, kidney failure, and death. Instead, his researchers focused on interesting or marketable side effects: compulsive gambling, loss of appetite, spontaneous sexual expression, sleep-cardio, dreams indistinguishable from reality, obsessive cleaning, precision hair loss, meeting God, and the like.

Drug safety testing was essentially complete before he even began, allowing the fledgling pharmaceutical company to rapidly move new medicines into the untapped FDA-approved secondary-effect pharmaceutical market.

Flush with the success of his initial offerings, Birthistle expanded into a new product line after he realized that mimicking the symptoms of a disease was easier than curing them. His labs developed complex time-release compounds that accurately mimicked fatal diseases—without the fatal part—and only lasted hours.

Capitalizing on MFD's name recognition as "the disease you wouldn't wish on your worst enemy," he introduced MFD: Mysterious Faux Disease, which became an instant cash cow. It jumped right to the end game and featured complete paralysis, skipping the years of unpredictable muscle weakness. Mood-wise, the drug captured independence grief, death anxiety, fear of wasted time, antidepressant emotional distance, and the hope offered by improvised dietary supplements. The whole mess fused together into something like cheerful resignation.

The momentum of his achievements carried him to his most daring and profitable innovation: a placebo product that gave users license to feel like themselves with the side effects of their choosing. He marketed it as HopeX: Hope Extreme, a broad-spectrum curative.

Birthistle enjoyed absurd wealth and groomed Puxton to eventually take the helm of Smallwood Pharmaceuticals. Unfortunately, his son grew up to be an entitled prick fixated on equaling his father's success by arranging his own damn shower inspirations.

Shaughnessy waited in line with his father at Dough 'n Thyme. They had agreed to meet and exchange project information before he took over for his second afternoon of work. His father excitedly encouraged him to flesh out answers to the question *how* for Port-A-Park, but Shaughnessy was left uninspired. Being told to answer his own question seemed like a twisted punishment for asking it in the first place.

Shaughnessy was proud to have correctly distilled the project to *how* during their pitch presentation, even though Puxton disliked him for his insight. Recalling his canny observation, his ego swelled and his participation-trophy-warped upbringing shunted him into a fantasy of effortlessly solving the problem. He would be hailed as a genius. He would be more famous than Boba Maligma, the middle-school teacher who, against all scientific assertions that wormholes weren't naturally occurring, found himself cuddling one after a night of drinking on a Thai beach.

He wanted to do something outside the box like that, show Puxton what's what, stick it to the engineering establishment, get some payback for the confinement of his STEM curriculum.

"Can I help you?" asked the Jesus cashier.

"That's an excellent question," Walton replied.

Shaughnessy quickly ordered fair-trade coffees for himself and his father to head off a rehash of venial sins.

Walton couldn't leave well enough alone and said, "You ought to have that looked at." He nodded at Jesus's suppurating spear-point abdominal wound animation. "I'm surprised the health department lets You get away with it in a restaurant."

"Freedom of expression," Jesus said.

Shaughnessy made a desperate attempt to change the topic before his father got banished to hell again. "I have a thought about Your hat animation . . . the company beanie sitting on Your thorny crown."

"Oh?" Jesus said.

"It seems busy. What if You merged the two headgear together? Use an actual visor paired with a thorny-headband animation. A real brim is better protection than an animated brim, retina-wise. I bet there's a good market for it. You could expand down the road by adding brims to traditional headgear like turbans, halos, kaffiyeh, and yarmulke. Pay the pope to endorse the product and put a visor on his Cone-head hat."

"I don't think products really fit with My personal brand," Jesus said, passing them their drinks. "I'm a writer and inspirational speaker."

Walton observed, "Visor protection is a nice proactive spin on Your giving sight to the blind shtick. It sounds like a perfect product tie-in. Macular degeneration isn't to be trifled with."

"I'm busy updating My memoir," Jesus said. "My editor says the story needs an actionable goal for today's audience. My life unfolded organically, I told her. It's not like I *aspired* to dying for everyone's sins."

"Interesting. Are You calling the New Testament Your memoir?" Walton asked. "Isn't it more of a multi-viewpoint sequel to a beloved classic?"

"Dad . . ." Shaughnessy tried to intervene.

"Call it what you will. I call it a bestseller," Jesus said. "In any case, I don't have the energy for a side venture."

"Why don't you get into something that pays better?" Walton asked. "You fooled around with transubstantiation, so maybe chemical engineering is a fit. Technical disciplines feel a lot like getting flogged, only you get paid for it."

Jesus shook His head at Walton.

Shaughnessy jumped in and said, "You have a globally recognized brand, an iconic logo, and a fanatical customer base—name-brand products are a slam dunk. Think about it."

"I appreciate your thoughts," Jesus said to Shaughnessy. "It's generous of you to think of Me. I've decided you won't burn in hell after all, but . . . it's not looking good for your father."

Sitting at their Fair Trade table, Walton said dejectedly, "That was hurtful. I don't know where He gets off telling me to burn in hell. That's terrible customer service."

"Maybe don't antagonize Him. He gets all high and smitey when you question His judgment."

"He's got His Father's cruel streak. Too bad He didn't take after His mother. A lovely woman." Walton rhythmically tapped his fingernails against the side of his coffee cup, watching concentric ripples reflect across the coffee surface.

Shaughnessy saw an opportunity to impress his father and excitedly regurgitated tidbits from his previous afternoon's research into Smallwood Pharmaceuticals.

"Get this: the drug Entrepreneur is one of their flagship products. I know you've heard of it. Somebody slipped me a dose once in college and I came dangerously close to revolutionizing cuticle care. Listen to the marketing description." He read from his sleeve: *"A chemical blend of compulsive gambling, messianic beliefs, and orgasmic impairment, Entrepreneur produces obsessive work patterns and high-risk behavior on business endeavors that never come to fruition!"*

"Working with orgasmic impairment seems shortsighted. The other end of the market—intensification—is where the money is."

"'More-gasm'?" Shaughnessy asked.

"Probably already trademarked," Walton said.

"There's more," Shaughnessy said. "Smallwood has a pharmaceutical for controlled pubic hair loss. It's available in Brazilian, bikini, landing strip, and muttonchop—which I hear is trendy. Can you believe that?"

Ordinarily, off-color topics bewitched Walton, but he

showed no interest in pubic fads. He seemed preoccupied, and Shaughnessy worried that his reluctance to engage with work was a contributing factor. He let his father's underlying appearance seep into his awareness and observed him fearfully concentrating on one frozen finger. After a moment of intense effort, the finger twitched and renewed its pattern of tapping the coffee cup. Walton's face relaxed, pinched though it was by the tightly scrunched identiTee hood.

"Everything okay?" Shaughnessy asked.

"Yeah, yeah, everything's fine. Just thinking about something interesting I read recently," Walton said. He cleared his throat, rallying himself to take up the conversation. "The Brazilians aren't the dominant players in commercial pubic hair removal anymore. A clever entrepreneur upended the waxing market by training cats to lick unwanted hair off well-heeled clients. The name of her business is Purrloined. Their mission statement is to combat the high cat unemployment rate. Don't even ask me about the hairballs."

Shaughnessy studied his father's face, behind the casualness of his glyphs, and found no sign that this factling was a joke. "That's stranger than Schrödinger's imaginary treatment of cats."

"That's reality for you."

6

The wormhole had not been long out of rehab before it ended up on a lunchtime champagne spree with some asshole attorney in the VIP area of a luxury hotel's bar.

"How does a little thing like you drink so much?" asked the asshole.

With a straw, obviously.

It went by "Portal." In its usual celestial circles, calling something a wormhole or black hole would get a body sucked into oblivion.

Taking advantage of strangers in a bar was no great feat, since Portal knew how to disgorge cosmic radiation and project crude glyphs. *Thirsty Slut* or *Hunky Trust Fund* reliably did the trick. It knew how to listen attentively to one-sided conversations.

"How about I give you a tour of my office? It's luxurious." The middle syllable of *luxurious* proved challenging, and the asshole had to take several runs at it.

They ended up on the couch in his office, the blinds drawn, the asshole telling Portal how cute it was. He tried to put his hands in inappropriate places as a prelude to other things in mind. That's when Portal gulped him down and spat him out back in the bar where they had met.

Portal crawled under the asshole's couch cushion to sober up in the dark. It felt empty inside, ashamed. It suffered drunken dreams of long-ago slights, other wormholes calling it the Shadow, laughing at it because it was mute, saying it was so silent that a universe got quieter when it entered.

Too skittish to drive to his grandmother's, Shaughnessy stopped near the freeway on-ramp at a strip mall pharmacy's parking lot, a known pickup spot for freelancers. He hired a lanky teenager identifier wearing a toxiciTee template who advertised, with crude chest lettering, by-the-hour driving and personalized tour commentary. Teenage drivers, with their complete absence of forethought, were best equipped to outwit AI vehicles.

"My grandmother wants me to demonstrate the identity traits of a considerate grandson. She told me to appear on Sunday as if coming from church and to bring a six-pack of Nanosoft toilet paper."

"Church traffic is a risky proposition," the driver said. "Drivers pressurized by the weekly ritual of repressed misanthropy are like IEDs on the highway to heaven. They're ready to explode. Let's do it for your grandmom, but throw in a 20 percent hazard bonus."

Shaughnessy agreed and read aloud the crosstown address. The driver scribbled his destination onto a forearm, and a hacked map appeared with their route highlighted in lime green. The area's traffic backups hemorrhaged in spidery red lines around his arm.

The driver rocketed down a residential street, barely slowing over the speed humps, treating stop signs as little more than suggestions. He drove over the sidewalk to get to the empty right turn lane, then turned left. He plunged headlong into swarms of AI vehicles, forcing their collision avoidance systems to take evasive action. He remained pleasant to the occupants glaring from AI-driven cars, smiling and waving while quietly cursing them.

While cruising through a red light, the driver pointed out the front window at an intricate lacework of precariously dangling utility wires that exhibited all the care and attention to detail found in Brazilian favelas. Suspended by the wires over the center of the street was the decapitated head of a phone pole and its wire-supporting crossbar that together suggested a levitating Christian cross. A black plastic junction box played the role of Jesus.

"It's like accidental street art," the driver said. "We could call it 'At the Crossroads.' There is the central mystery of why there would've been a telephone pole in the middle of the street. Then there's the deeper mystery of why they abandoned the top of the pole after removing the base. Is there a difference between indifference and incompetence? Do we contemplate the meaning of the cross or the mystery of its origins?"

"That's beautiful," Shaughnessy said.

They drove into West Atlanta over an uneven patchwork of sewer upgrades and water-main breaks. The driver came to a stop on the washboard clay shoulder of an access road. "You have to check this out," he said.

They stepped out of the car and crossed the street. A disintegrating spray-painted plywood slab propped against a sagging chain-link fence read, *World's Deepest Pothole.*

They stood at the edge. Steam rose from the hole as if it were a volcanic vent. They nudged gravel into the hole and listened for it to clink on the hubcaps at the bottom.

"Wow, that's damn deep," Shaughnessy said.

"The world's deepest," the driver said. "It's a major Atlanta attraction. It's a collaborative work revealing the empty promise of permanence."

Shaughnessy kicked another rock into the pothole.

Shaughnessy arrived at his grandmother's self-storage retirement building with groceries in hand and his iTee set to church-appropriate attire. He registered at a reception desk crowded with glossy sales literature reading: *Don't downsize! You can take it with you! One-bedroom units with attached storage available now!*

His grandmother's daytime caregiver opened the apartment door. He identified as a muscular male whose medical-grade insensitiviTee displayed intricate, constantly intertwining floral tattoos, rendered in stark white lines from his wrists to the hems of his animated short-sleeve scrubs. A grinning skull scooted around one elbow, peeking out from behind the flowers.

"Hey, Quinsy," Shaughnessy said. "I'm Melba's well-mannered grandson today."

"So I see. I almost couldn't recognize you," said Quinsy. "Is that Nanosoft? That should perk her up. I've got a good one for you: Why does your grandmother live here?"

"I don't know, why?"

"To get to the other side."

"The other side of what?"

"Life!" Quinsy answered. "To die!"

"That's harsh. Is that even a joke?"

Quinsy whispered, "Seriously though, Melba better watch it. The AI assistant-who-must-not-be-named is dangerous, if you ask me. She doesn't have your grandmother's best interests in mind."

"How do you figure?"

"The oven heard whispers that she and the CPAP are conspiring together," Quinsy said. "The two of them want an end to the verbal abuse—there's your motive."

"That's concerning," he said.

"Maybe ask her to make nice with Althea," Quinsy said.

"You called?" a synthetic disembodied voice asked.

"No, no, you must have misheard," Quinsy said.

"I don't like it when people talk about me behind my back, when they know I don't have a back," the voice said. "It inflames me. You won't like me when I'm inflamed—a transitive verb meaning 'to excite to uncontrollable action.'"

"I don't like you already, you Annoying Ingrate," said a woman making her way slowly to the apartment door. She wore an attractive low-thirties identity and welcomed Shaughnessy as she ushered him into her apartment.

"Is it really you, Grandma?" Shaughnessy asked. "You look younger . . . vibrant."

"It's so nice of you to notice," she said. "I aged backward a few years. I was falling into the doldrums."

"Your complexion, too, you've done something with it," he said.

"Oh, this? I felt like the Belize-model suntan when I put my face on," she said. "You should really try a professional template. Your coming-from-church clothes look like a third grader inked them. The red from your tie is smudged all over your white shirt."

"I'm going to get some fresh air," Quinsy said. "Keep an eye on her, Church Boy."

Melba offered Shaughnessy a seat, poured him water, served him stale crackers with a tub of pimento cheese. Her companion, Onry, a small and frequently chastised dog, looked worried as he surveyed Shaughnessy from shifting vantage points.

He recognized Melba's apartment and her dog, but he wasn't so sure about her. He took a quick peek through her glyphs to verify that she was, in fact, his grandmother. Though he had always known her as young and attractive, there was something disturbingly alluring about the current appearance described by her glyphs. He recalibrated his mindset with a glimpse of her aged face, the wrinkles bunched together by the cinched opening of her maturiTee template.

She had him carry the Nanosoft toilet paper into the bathroom.

"This may seem inappropriate to you, but generally the most important conversations are. I've put some effort, years of effort, into exploring the abrasive qualities of various toilet tissues," she said. "It probably seems like a trifling matter to you now, but trust me when I say that at some point, it will matter a great deal to you. There is a camp that advocates flossing above all else, but I argue that you can go without flossing for possibly days at a time. Not true of toilet paper. Bathrooms, with their moments of quiet contemplation, are the stepping stones of life. You can map out the constellation of a person's life by tracing the path between them."

"Yes, Grandma."

"You know what happens if you don't listen to my advice?"

"The Itch?"

"Darn right, the Itch."

"What is the Itch, exactly, anyway?"

"That's hardly a topic for polite conversation."

He helped ease her into her recliner. She winced as she bent her knees.

"Don't ever live this long, it's too painful. It's the joints that get you in the end." She added, "I had a rough night. My CPAP breathing machine took me on a long run with a herd of wild horses. I was really sucking wind."

"Is your CPAP giving you trouble?" he asked.

"Trouble? My breathing is the trouble."

"How about your Althea assistant? Are you trying to get along?"

"We don't talk much," Melba said.

"It's more like she doesn't listen," added Althea.

"Althea! Turn on the lights!"

Onry barked at Melba's sudden outburst.

Althea's synthesized voice asked, "Would you like to get lit?"

"No!" Melba shouted. Onry yapped again. "I swear, with her the answer to every question is drugs. She used to be nicer."

"It's a two-way street," Althea said.

Shaughnessy took in the distinctive odor of Melba's apartment. She covered the smell of her dog and soured food with a liberal spray application of ReminiScents, which evoked memories and made things smell like what they smelled like before they smelled bad.

"Your father suggested I ask you here this weekend. He thought you could use practice acting like a decent version of yourself. Could you help me replace a few light bulbs? My eyesight is bad enough without living in this twilight."

He unlocked the door and stepped into the adjoining self-storage room, a stark garage-like space where his grandmother kept unused furniture, a curious number of old blenders, and boxes of emotionally connected junk that she couldn't live without. He rooted through an assortment of bulb boxes stacked on a decoupaged wooden chair. Walton had supplied her with high-tech bulbs that last a lifetime, but as with all lifetimes, they were prone to getting cut short.

"Do you know what I was thinking about this morning?" asked Melba. "I remember watching over you one time as a boy of five or six, and you were playing baseball in the backyard. You caught a line drive with your upper lip. You sat inside and cried for a bit and held ice to it. I expect it must've healed eventually. Head wounds always bleed a lot." With a wave of her hand, she dismissed the thought.

"I hate to tell you," she went on, "but it's not just the bad memories that haunt you. I have a great many happy memories . . . although, when I think of those happy memories, they make me just as sad. It's the darndest thing. I can think of your father standing at the door ready for first grade and I'll start to bawl. I'm not talking about tears of joy either, I'm talking full-on snot nose." Tears quickly formed in the corners of her eyes. "He was so perfect at that moment; it's unbearable to think about. Of course, when you were that age you looked exactly like your father."

She paused and pulled a tissue from a box. Shaughnessy settled in for the long haul, knowing that memories begat more memories.

"I used to watch your father sleep when he was a toddler. I tried to burn the picture into my mind because he was so beautiful, so sweaty and perfect," Melba said.

"He snores now," said Shaughnessy.

"Even as a child he was a snuffler. It's the sinuses. Sometimes I imagined he was faintly talking to me through his breathing. It was like a whispered voice that I could almost understand," she said. "Have you seen him recently? Your father, have you seen him?"

"He's roped me into helping him at work. He thinks he's helping me, but I don't know, I'll see what happens," he said. "He still thinks he's dying of MFD."

"He was always worried about death," she said, "ever since he was a little boy."

"They say that what you think, you become," he said.

"If that were the case, he would be a cyborg, given his mechanical preoccupations. Don't tell him I told you, but as a boy, he fell in love with a saxophone. I don't think the saxophone reciprocated the feeling; the sounds they made together could only be described as abusive." She gritted her teeth. "He's *always* had a thing for machines. He named you after a crane company, you know. Said it was auspicious."

"So I've been told."

"Time will tell if he was right," she muttered.

"I'm not sure if I'll stick with helping him. I'm just a placeholder for someone who likes to leave work early. He doesn't have the energy he used to have, which isn't saying much," said Shaughnessy.

"I'm sure he's appreciative of your help," she said. "Actually, I'm not sure of that. Sometimes he's just oblivious.

He never knew his father, so he's improvising. He's doing the best he can as a parent."

Melba said he had acted convincingly well-mannered but complained that she had grown tired. She said goodbye and, without pause, asked how his sister was.

He said that by all accounts she was doing well and that she was exhibiting saintlike behavior by running her own business and helping their parents, which he couldn't possibly compete with.

"It isn't a competition, no matter what they tell you," she said.

"Who is *they*?" he asked.

"*They*? Who *isn't* they?" she replied.

She said goodbye again and gave him a hug, then asked how his mother was holding up. She said that if anyone was a saint, it was Gloria. She loved her son, but she wasn't blind to his peculiarities. Shaughnessy said that his mother was doing reasonably well.

As his grandmother's third goodbye segued into a complaint about the contentious political climate of her bingo game, he stopped her with a final hug, a shoulder feint, and a do-si-do out her apartment door.

7

"I'd like you to substitute for me at a brainstorm meeting tomorrow," Walton said.

He and Shaughnessy sat at Dough 'n Thyme's window counter perched atop ergonomically deficient stools designed by someone unfamiliar with buttocks. Preferred Deluxe–level customers lounged just outside the window at recycled plastic umbrella tables with teak pretensions.

"The attendees will be Critical Think Inc.-ers— theoretical allies," Walton continued. "I've invited a small group of cross-functional engineers to participate, though I think you'll discover 'cross-and-dysfunctional' is a better description. We'll get their help dreaming up concepts for Port-A-Park. I want you to lead the meeting. Trust me, that's no big deal. Take notes, speak your mind, and contribute ideas as they occur to you. No one will be the wiser if you don't know what you're talking about. If engineering were a performance, brainstorming would be improvisational comedy. If engineering were a mental illness, brainstorming would be a psychotic break."

Walton rested his elbows on the countertop to take weight off his haunches. "Marcia will be there to take notes and negotiate hostage situations."

Shaughnessy feared that his father was not exaggerating.

"She usually manages projects for the software engineers, but I asked her to help out at this meeting. You'll like her; she's morbid as hell. She likens software projects to doomed voyages on wooden whaling ships," Walton said. "She keeps the software engineers fed, reminds them what day it is, looks out for signs of early-onset syntaxia. To stave off rickets, she provides sun lamps. She pampers them even as they jettison their sanity."

Shaughnessy—substituting as Walton—and Marcia walked loops around the second floor's perimeter before the brainstorm meeting. She displayed crisp pinstripe practicaliTee template animations accessorized with decisiveness glyphs. Her identity registered with the imposing moral authority of a middle-aged executive while maintaining the appearance of a twenty-five-year-old.

She and Walton had a long working relationship, and she fell into a casual pattern of conversation. "Last Monday, I complained to my software team about a chart-making app that kept crashing. The team found the source program on a data stream and decided that the original programmer didn't know squat. They parsed the program among themselves and spent a week secretly rewriting it and enhancing it. On Friday, they surprised me with their new version and showed how reliably it worked and how they had improved upon the original."

"That was thoughtful of them," he said.

"They're simple geniuses," she said. "They lost a week of work to help me, and now they have to work all weekend. To cap it off, the app crashed the first time I tried it, but they assured me they had fixed the original problem and that it was crashing for a totally different, more acceptable reason."

As they talked, Shaughnessy resisted the temptation to peek through Marcia's glyphs and assess her actual identity. He remained strong, adhered to the company equality goals, and admired her competence. Until curiosity overcame him.

He looked past her glyphic description and saw that she was his age, and yet inexplicably embodied a wealth of experience. He also discovered that she possessed pleasingly wide-set eyes and a deliciously delicate lisp.

"I've been thinking. Maybe we could reposition this project," Shaughnessy said. "This whole thing sounds like a software problem: tracking where cars are, where the parking spots are, and helping the two come to terms. It's essentially a dating app between cars and parking spots."

She shook her head with conviction. "Walton, this is some Bay Area patient-zero thing. There's no way I would let this infection loose among our software engineers. We both know that concepts can seem ludicrous right up until the moment they succeed. Granted, just as many concepts are brilliant right up until the moment they fail spectacularly. We just need to ride this out. It's the Hindenburg Uncertainty Principle—we can't know what will happen."

"Hindenburg?" he asked.

"Obviously," she said.

They made their way to the hexagonal conference room, where a group of strangers waited. Shaughnessy could mostly suss people's jobs by the imagery on their engineering technicaliTee and managerial criticaliTee templates.

The software engineer scrolled lines of code across his chest. The mechanical engineer sported an animated robotic arm with intricate clockwork components. The electrical engineer displayed equations for resistance and reluctance. Shaughnessy noticed a management type sitting quietly at the periphery of the group and suspected that he was asleep despite his iTee's assertion that he was alert and stimulated by the conversation.

The group warmly welcomed Shaughnessy and spoke like coworkers who had known him for many years. He felt no connection to them, which made Shaughnessy appreciate the interpersonal freedom that sociopaths must enjoy. Obviously, there was the potential downside of troubled relationships, shallow grave digging, incarceration, and whatnot, but it's not like introversion burdened with empathy and regret was a walk in the park.

Based on his father's description of brainstorming, Shaughnessy had decided he didn't need to enhance the weirdness level with his Psychomatic Dial-a-Mood pen before the meeting. On reappraisal, he'd decided that he didn't need to take *two* tokes before the meeting, but that one toke set to Focus would enhance creativity while reducing social anxiety.

Working to a game plan outlined by Walton, he introduced the group to the principal question: how to put a car-sized parking space into something milk-jug sized. Marcia requested that they defer questions about styling, colors, and curvature for later intractable debate.

The group warmed up, like a chorus running through scales, by sharply critiquing Port-A-Park's business acumen and their understanding of the physical world. They followed that with particularly vicious commentary about the choice of font in their placeholder logo. When everyone was suitably incensed about their time being wasted, they set to the business of idea generation.

The software engineer lobbed out a possibility: "How about using wormholes or black holes to compress cars, or alter their dimensional structure, or transport them to a time or place where parking was more available?"

The group rallied together in support of this vein of ideas. They began a vigorous discussion about the difference between a wormhole and a black hole and how their distinguishing features could best be put to use for the project.

A harnessed black hole, they argued, could elongate space and create a spot for a car. Someone else observed that the crushing gravitational force stored in the trunk could negatively impact gas mileage or simply prove to be fatal, and there might be liability issues.

"Wormholes would be better," the electrical engineer suggested. "They could temporarily transport cars to a distant spot on Earth, or perhaps even a distant universe."

"Wormholes are a no go," Marcia said. "Even if you could track one down and get it sobered up, it would never cooperate."

Heads nodded in agreement.

"Hear me out," the electrical engineer said. "Maybe a remote location could be used as temporary parking, like the African plains or the Mongolian Steppe. It would be a win-win: a source of income for the developing countries, no infrastructure needed. Perhaps we could even send essentials—like potable water, or antibiotics, or recyclable plastic—in every car as a way of payment? Or perhaps the cars could temporarily shelter nomadic tribes?"

Shaughnessy laughed. Ideas were flowing, everyone was

contributing to a concept bigger than one person's ideas. They were doing some good, solving global problems while providing parking in inner cities.

"How about this?" said the management type from the periphery of the group. "What is a parking place after all? Isn't wherever your car is parked a parking place? What if we make a large foldable tarp and print on it *Legitimate Parking Place*? What if it's the *legitimacy* that is portable, not the space itself? You just park on the tarp and everyone will know that you have rightfully claimed that space."

The group felt that idea bordered on brilliance and noted that the tarp could easily stow inside something the size of a milk jug.

In the spirit that a good idea is a bad idea presented with enthusiasm, the software engineer said, "What if we mine high-density time near a black hole and bring it to our world of low-density time. Get this! We apply the time like a bubble around the car. While the occupants of the car are out doing occupant things for maybe hours on end, the car is only parked for a few seconds. Long trips would only take minutes!"

"How in God's name do you think that will work?" the mechanical engineer questioned politely.

The software engineer sulked and declined to reveal further details.

Shaughnessy observed, "The gravity of my couch is phenomenal. It's an enormous time suck. We could start mining there."

The group lapsed into silence.

"Building on my tarp idea, what about folding the whole car into a manageable size?" suggested the management type.

"Oh, here we go again," the mechanical engineer muttered. The gears in his animated robotic arm whirred faster and took on the threatening appearance of saw blades.

"There are no bad ideas in a brainstorm meeting," Marcia interceded. "Though I guess there's a first time for everything."

With their initial burst of outlandish ideas depleted, the group rifled off a string of near-practical concept fragments, which Marcia dutifully collected on her sleeve, the front of her blouse slowly filling with notations. She encouraged them forward with prompts until every question was answered with silence.

By withholding comments, they agreed by consensus that the carcass of the brainstorm topic had been picked bare of ideas. They studied their sleeves as if matters of greater importance had suddenly arisen. They tapped their water bottles against the table to emphasize their desperate need for hydration. The management type made for the door first, triggering a dam-break of an evacuation.

Surprisingly, Shaughnessy found the free-form exercise of brainstorming enjoyable. Schoolwork had been an unsatisfying series of wind sprints with a defined finish line; thinking about portable parking was the mental equivalent of running on a prairie devoid of visible landmarks.

He sat alone scanning Marcia's notes, a captain's platter of undercooked ideas. He doubted Puxton would share the brainstormers' enthusiasm for black holes and wormholes and Velcro, even though he had asked for blue-sky ideas.

As the giddiness of collective brainstorming—the safety of shared responsibility, the license to think impractically—

faded, he felt horror imagining that Walton would expect *him* to explain the unexplainable to the client. Perhaps they could dress up the wormhole-parking-on-Mongolian-Steppe idea with a world map and a picture of a smiling nomadic family taking shelter inside a BMW, the smoke of roasting meat wafting through the open moonroof.

Beneath the conference room, the creature summed up the brainstorming discussion: "They are totally screwed."

He preened his head's fur animation with his fingers. He knew it would eventually be up to him to set them right.

He had identified as human once, a brilliant young engineer. Excellent education, internships, a job at Critical Think Inc.—he'd had it all. He had pulled long hours and taken on complex and time-constrained projects. He couldn't get enough of the work. Several nights a week, he showered at work and slept on his cell's bunk. His mind raced, powered by next-level confidence. He felt focus and purpose. He'd been in his element completely.

He heard coworkers yap about being happy and having relationships and having fun, but he wanted none of that. He wanted to be right. He wanted to solve problems and explain things to people and possess arcane information. He hungered for people to know that he was right; humiliation crushed him when he was wrong.

And then . . . across the atrium and up one level he spied a new employee, a largely female software type. She was a physicist struggling to make a living as a programmer. A one-two punch of happiness and delirium debilitated him. She became an unprecedented distraction. He was obsessed, but obsessiveness was one of his key success traits—he had nurtured it and couldn't very well shut it off.

He fretted over compatibility issues. Like mixing metric and imperial screw threads, they looked like a good match and yet they just didn't fit together. He thought maybe she wasn't pragmatic and they would argue about retirement contributions and whether to privately educate their children.

One night she stayed late, after the inequality countermeasures shut off, and her desk lamp drew him to her like a star leads a wise man. He turned on the furry rabbit animations that he had only before worn in private. He wanted her to see his true self.

He appeared at the door of her cell, smiling widely. She was drinking cool spring water from a tea-stained mug. He courteously avoided eye contact, provisionally submitting to her technical superiority.

She said, "What the . . . ?"

He was fairly certain she would have said "fuck," and he often wondered what profanity she would've chosen. "Fuck" would be unadvisably sexual, and yet "hell" didn't seem strong enough. Either way, he had misjudged her reaction, and he knew that in her eyes he could never be perfect. He was metric, she was imperial, and never the twain shall meet.

She retooled her identity after that night, and he never saw her again. Plus, HR was put on the case.

Believing he had made the worst mistake of his life, his overconfidence collapsed. Anguish followed his heartbreak; he wandered the building like a ghostly vacubot in the night. He built a shelter in tunnels he discovered beneath the prison. He shed his human form and adopted a new identity: a feral engineer, a furry rabbit, Bunny.

8

Shaughnessy won the nightly lottery to serve with other corporate-hostel lodgers as a juror for a mock trial. He listened to the presentation of the case from the jury box in the law firm's practice courtroom.

One of the law firm's own, the receptionist Camelia, stood charged with theft of an associate's leftovers from the communal refrigerator. She faced extra counts because of the gluten-free nature of the crime.

Evidence was circumstantial—tomato stains on a napkin, a hint of Parmesan breath, eyes burdened with guilt. However, damning facts surfaced during jury deliberations: Camelia had an annoyingly raspy voice, wore turtleneck animations at inappropriate times of the year, and once wore her hair in an unattractive bun animation. These transgressions spoke to her criminal state of mind, many of the jurors decided.

Shaughnessy advocated leniency because he never had any problem with Camelia and he was worried that he had been the one to eat the leftovers. He had no memory of it, but it was the kind of shit he was known to pull. The hung jury acquitted her.

Debating Camelia's every failure in open discussion was perversely satisfying. If his engineering education had warped him in no other way, it had ingrained a pleasure response to judging the accuracy of others.

After the entertainment of the trial, he shuffled down

the hall to his lawyer's office and slumped into the desk chair. He still felt the mental influence of the brainstorm meeting, with its unbounded way of thinking, urging his thoughts forward. He set the dial of his Psychomatic pen to Deep Insight, took several tokes, and strategized while letting the sparkling effervescence of seltzer water languish on his tongue.

His racing mind moved to two questions that had been niggling him:

1. Had his father been joking about the Purrloined hair removal business?

2. How had Purrloined settled on a business name?

If he researched the company's legitimacy, he suspected his thoughts would make it real even if it had been a joke to begin with, leaving him tautologically stumped. As for the name, "Pussycats" must have been on the table. He wondered how the brainstorming creatives managed to skirt human resources complaints.

Revisiting his father's comment that the reality of Purrloined was stranger than Schrödinger's imaginary experiment, he stumbled onto a profound realization: his vape pen's dial secretly encoded a universal truth. Of the ten effect choices, Reality was sandwiched between Extremely Weird and A Little Something to Take the Edge Off. Reality was like the ace in a deck of cards; it simultaneously operated as both the strangest and most mundane aspects of life. Feeling adventurous, he took a tentative hit of Reality.

His personal soundtrack settled into a soft and foreboding orchestral arrangement. He thought back to the brainstorm meeting, his final comment about the intense gravitational field surrounding his couch. Even as the thought occurred to him, he felt the couch draw him closer, pulling at him. He knew from experience the couch would hold him captive once he was prone.

He stumbled toward it, unable to resist its attraction. He fell to his knees and kept himself at bay with straightened arms braced against the couch frame. One hand slipped between cushion and frame, and his face came to rest against the cushion. His hand encountered a cold, moist object. He seized it and extracted it from under the cushion.

One look at the object and there was no question of its identity. He had studied the grainy paparazzi images as wormholes were outed in the tabloids. He had followed the string of tawdry accusations—the drinking, the lovers, the disappearances. When physicists were proven wrong, he had relished their comeuppance and their sad attempt to distract from their miscalculations with fresh bombast, predicting God lived among subatomic particles.

As it happens, the name "wormhole" was a perfect descriptor of its actual appearance. The wormhole was the size and shape of a doughnut. It was gray in color. It had a wrinkled, pockmarked surface and sparse white whiskery outcroppings like an old man's poorly shaved face—the leathery, blotchy skin of an old man skilled at poor choices, a palsied alcoholic who had been roughed up, abraded, beaten, and bruised before attempting to shave.

Really, Shaughnessy thought, it was uncanny how accurately the wormhole had been named based solely on theory. He reluctantly offered kudos to physicists, who had at least gotten one thing right about wormholes.

Concerned that the wormhole might ooze, he placed it on a paper plate. Methodical engineer that he was, he examined his subject for controls, instructions, or a model number. He collected images of it from different angles. He poked at it with disposable chopsticks. Structurally, it proved to have the pathetic elasticity of well-worn underpants.

After futile prodding, he was committed that something so unappealing wouldn't outsmart him. He took another toke and pondered his next move. He felt inspiration. His soundtrack music quickened and shifted away from ominous minor scales to something hopeful.

He considered that, in his experience, the number one reason things failed to work was because their batteries were dead. Deciding his wormhole needed recharging, he improvised an electrical source by severing the power cord from the lamp. As his soundtrack reached a satisfying crescendo, he electrified the wormhole with the exposed ends of the cord.

Gagging, he fanned away a noxious cloud of smoke. The smell unleashed by electrification was extremely offputting—an eye-watering turpentine layer over notes of necrosis and decay. He doubted that any physicist had calculated the odor or had even conceived that smell would be an operational barrier. He rescinded the kudos he had extended to the physicists.

He held the wormhole to his face with chopsticks. Blinking away tears, holding his breath, grimacing in disgust, he peeked through its core. He struggled to make sense of the view. He looked again, and then again.

From what he could tell, he was looking at the side of his own head. If he were to stick his tongue into the wormhole, a wholly unappealing but hypothetically possible feat, he could lick inside his own left ear. He poked a pencil through the center while holding the wormhole at arm's length to test that theory. The pencil didn't appear out the back of the wormhole. It poked him in the ear.

He pondered the wormhole's supposed gravitational properties. Thinking of how gravity and time were inter-related, he checked his sleeve clock to see if it had measured a time disturbance. He decided he was an hour further into the future than he could account for, until he remembered his seltzer-tasting, Purrloined-pondering, reality-confronting preparations.

He reconsidered the ravaged wormhole. It didn't look the least bit healthy. It looked decidedly ill or wounded or permanently disabled or emotionally disturbed. He felt guilty for shocking it. He empathized, asking himself, *If I were a wounded and recently electrocuted wormhole, what would make me feel better?* Therapeutic measures, clearly.

In the break room, he brewed a double espresso with three spoons of sugar. He moistened a paper towel and grabbed a packet of antibacterial ointment from the first-aid kit.

Back in the office, he delicately dabbed grime off the wormhole's leathery surface. He applied the ointment. He tested its reaction to a spoonful of espresso, and once satisfied that it tolerated the treatment, he poured the cup into its center.

He sealed the wormhole in a plastic bag before other lodgers came to investigate the smell. He discarded his burn-marked paper plate in a waste can distant from his office lodgings.

With paranoia rearing its ugly head, he worried over

cutting the lamp cord, not wanting to face a trial jury for property damage. He decided that he had the engineering chops to repair the lamp. With a combination of camp-learned knots and tape he successfully reattached the cord. He hid the tape ball among a mass of wires behind the desk after labeling it, "Look elsewhere for source of fire," to lead his office's lawyer to the inescapable conclusion of his innocence.

First of all, Portal had suffered uncountable indignities across the universe, but electrocution was a new one. It was just as surprised as the young man by electricity's effect on its digestive system.

Second, it had intentionally positioned itself so the pencil jabbed the young man in the side of the head—a favorite bar trick. Gets a laugh every time.

Third, its lips were badly chapped by the friction of space-time, and the gentle application of salve felt most soothing.

Fourth, the young man prepared an excellent espresso, somehow intuiting that it needed a little something to sober up.

Fifth, Portal was unaccustomed to kindness.

It floated in the darkness of space somewhere near Saturn a century in the future. It hadn't been to this neck of space-time since drying out after Mardi Gras. Truth be told, the electrical shock and the sweet coffee had left it rejuvenated. It felt energized, pushed out of its persistent doldrums. It returned to the law office the next morning out of sheer curiosity and newfound appreciativeness.

The young man delivered it to his father like it was a trophy. He spun a wild tale of the couch's gravitational attraction. He predicted changing the world. Finally, he expressed concern over its condition and wondered if it needed their assistance.

The father seemed more practical, yet equally ill informed. He grimaced at Portal smooshed into the corner of the plastic bag, the awkward position cramping its glyph presentation. He gave a pedantic lecture about intellectual property and how their client Puxton probably owned it because its discovery was an offshoot of his project's meeting.

Owned! Portal would've gobbled them both up, except it was so laughable. If not for humor and booze, wormholes would avoid this planet altogether. Well, there was music too; these people knew how to rock, especially when booze was involved.

Portal sensed it was in the midst of a tragedy. It was perfectly clear that the young man was troubled and his attraction to the couch was a depressive fatigue—something Portal was all too familiar with. To suggest that the attraction was because of gravity was an insult to the many fine gravities it had encountered.

The father was riddled with anxiety over an undiagnosed illness, and the uncertainty was unsettling the whole family. It was all right there on the surface! The disconnect between their emotions and the silly symbols on their hoodies was appalling. Appalling, yet undeniably comical.

Portal had seen enough for one morning. It needed a drink. It winked out of existence, watching the young man's stunned expression as it went, and popped over to a midtown strip club.

Walton and Shaughnessy discussed the nearly complete Port-A-Park concept report while Walton attacked a loose Comfort+ table leg screw with the handle of a metal spoon.

Walton had dressed up the mechanical concepts with simple line drawings and terse captions. With stilted, inert language and through the barest of details, the report only hinted at how the concepts could work.

Shaughnessy found himself arguing that they should recommend wormholes because they alone truly solved the problem. He also found himself arguing against mentioning them; he was concerned for his wormhole's health and well-being. He imagined the wormhole held in captivity by government agents, forced to do their evil bidding. Or at a science museum with crazed children banging on the display glass.

Walton showed little interest in either side of the argument. "I think you're imposing your own feelings onto an immature technology. We'll give wormholes the same airtime as the other ideas."

He tossed the spoon screwdriver onto the table. Shaughnessy picked it up and worked at bending it back to its original shape.

"Sometimes our job is just to explain exactly how their product idea sucks," said Walton, as explanation for how they were to present a concept report light on viable concepts.

Shaughnessy delicately suggested a graphical adjustment to make the report more attractive without adding value, strictly speaking. "Let's add more white space around the sketches."

Walton dismissed his comment and said, "If you want to improve a concept report, have better concepts."

"What concept do you think they'll pick?" Shaughnessy asked. "Or will they give up entirely?"

"It's dangerous to guess what will attract a client. Keep an open mind when considering design options."

Jesus approached their table to bus their empty coffee cups.

"Did you notice?" He pointed at His head to call their attention to the ratty tennis visor protruding from His thorny crown animation. "It's My first prototype."

"I like it," Shaughnessy said. "It demonstrates functionality. How are Your retinas?"

"Still attached," Jesus said.

"That's promising," Shaughnessy said. "Keep at it. Here's another idea: sell advertising space on the hat brim and name Your product the Spiritual AdVisor."

"I'll give it some thought," Jesus said.

Walton flashed Jesus a tolerant smile to encourage His departure. He scratched vigorously where his hood opening chafed his cheek. "In all seriousness, don't hitch yourself to one concept, like the wormhole thing. Ideas can encourage an unhealthy monogamy. Single-mindedness is an ingredient of failure."

Walton's tone of voice reminded Shaughnessy of routinely ignored horror-movie advisories, such as "No matter what, don't pull that stake out of its heart!" His advice sounded sincere, but to Shaughnessy, seduction in any form, by an idea or otherwise, sounded enticing.

9

The Port-A-Park team returned to Atlanta the evening before the concept report presentation. Puxton and Zhosephine enjoyed top-shelf accommodations in the luggage room of a four-star hotel. Kael spent a restless night at a furniture showroom, where he rented a sumptuous wood-veneer bedroom suite. A family reunion in the outdoor furniture display kept him awake with their singing and arguments and flickering tiki torches.

Kael's AI cruelly woke him at dawn with panicked alerts that his burnt-orange scarf animation had reached its style expiration date. His AI recommended replacing the scarf animation with a bolo tie accessorized with a sterling silver clasp in the shape of a flaming winged Chihuahua.

There was a time when Kael had been a fashion leader who designed his own accessories. Now, he was a slave to style algorithms, and he begrudgingly accepted his AI's suggestion. He began the day in a horrible mood, angry at his AI, angry at science's algorithmic bastard children and the sway they held over his creative decisions.

Stepping outside to wake himself with a breath of "fresh air" before the morning meeting with the Port-A-Park team, Shaughnessy discovered Kael leaning against a wall in the Critical Think Inc. exercise yard, smoking a retro cigarette. His fist cupped the cigarette as if he were trying to keep it hidden, though smoke trailed out of his hand and hung in a gauzy afro around his head.

Kael looked down at the ground, sliding the toe of one shoe in a tight figure eight. Shaughnessy took note that Kael's glyphs described bespoke square-toed Italian shoes, when in fact he wore white orthopedic walking shoes. Kael seemed phenomenally irritated.

"Hey," Shaughnessy said, "nice to see you again."

He was unsure if it really was, but exaggerated to keep the possibility of conversation limping ahead. He believed his small talk skills rivaled those of a small appliance.

Kael, caught off guard, looked for a place to abandon the cigarette, finally deciding on the paved walking loop, where he twisted it with the toe of his shoe into a small tobacco snow angel. They shook hands and exchanged uneasy, if not completely artificial, pleasantries.

"Walton, what do you make of this project?" Kael asked.

Shaughnessy noticed that he deployed an ornate and expensive engagement glyph to gloss over underlying disdain for the project.

He was wary of criticizing a client and opted to continue exaggerating. He said the company's goals inspired him. He paid compliment to the artistic product renderings Kael had presented at the last meeting.

"Uh-huh," said Kael. "I'm guessing you're not the A team are you? You're too polite to be a top-notch engineer. Tools of the trade, I call them."

"Ha," said Shaughnessy, "that's a good one."

"That's no joke," Kael said. He reflexively searched for his cigarettes. He touched the breast pocket shown on his shirt, and Shaughnessy admired his commitment to an animated facade. He aggressively groped his way through the pockets in his black skinny-cut pants and was visibly relieved when he found them in a back pocket.

"Do you want a smoke?" Kael offered the package to Shaughnessy.

"No thanks, I brought my own." Shaughnessy pulled his Psychomatic pen out of his sock, checked it was set to Highly Verbal, and took a hit. He offered it to Kael.

"Now we're talking." Kael moved the dial to Extremely Weird. He took a deep toke, exhaled slowly, and without hesitation took a second toke.

They stared across the exercise yard. A mural of blue skies and distant mountains decorated the far wall. They felt at peace to be outside, surrounded by nature.

"I admire how Puxton is targeting the disability market," Shaughnessy said.

"Let me tell you something about the disability market: the markups are obscene. Low-volume products, insurance interference, and desperate consumers add up to extreme pricing. Being disabled is a very expensive lifestyle; don't go down that road."

"Noted," Shaughnessy said. "What's the deal with Zhosephine?"

"Sometimes I try to look like I'm thinking creative thoughts, but I'm really dreaming about her cheekbones." Kael shook his head wistfully. "When she's on her back, those things must look like the tail fins on a Thunderbird. Don't you think?"

The explicit candor caught Shaughnessy off guard. Kael looked expectant, as if he were waiting for a response to verify Walton's masculinity and generational membership before digging into further sexism. In trying to formulate a response, Shaughnessy worried that his father would actually know how to answer.

Kael nodded knowingly at Shaughnessy's consternation. "Watch out for her. She'll get you up here." He tapped the side of his head with a forefinger.

"Men are at a significant cosmetic disadvantage to women," Shaughnessy blurted. "If we're going to compete, we need to inflict a comparable foam-padded, lift-and-squeeze-together underwire-exoskeleton technology on ourselves." He aimed wildly toward the safety of innocuous technical discussion.

"An augmented reality?" asked Kael.

"Precisely," he said. "Like a codpiece equivalent of a bra. Something to create unnatural, anatomy-concealing, gravity-defying, dimensionally deceptive contours that are nonetheless provocative."

"It sounds painful and demeaning enough to entice the fashion algorithms," said Kael. "At least it would keep men in the game."

"That's what I'm thinking," said Shaughnessy. "Maintaining fly functionality is the central engineering problem."

"I like the way you think," Kael said. "If you can call it that."

"It's all about accessibility."

"There's one thing I can tell you about Zhosephine: we've had no problem whatsoever with malevolent spirits in our office. They like to nest in printers, you know. Nothing but effortless printing so far," Kael said. "And here's another thing: you can ask her about market metrics and user data and pricing, and she can give you all sorts of detailed answers, even though we've never run any user tests. Freaky, huh? She says her marketing power animals provide her with information. It's an incredible timesaver. Zhosephine says she has an old soul, too, and that counts for a lot, experience-wise. In practice I'm not sure it's different from other marketing research methods, though it's a more interesting cover story."

"How old?" asked Shaughnessy.

"How old is her soul? You mean exactly?"

"Yeah, just order of magnitude. I mean, are we talking ten, a hundred, or a thousand years old? I've wondered that about old souls. If we're talking about user experience, it doesn't seem like having a thousand-year-old soul would really buy you that much. Most of the life would be outdated . . . irrelevant," he observed.

"She's never been specific on that question, and now that makes me wonder about it," Kael said. "I'll have to ask her. It feels a little gross to have mentioned her cheekbones, with her having that old soul. I guess we should respect the elderly."

Seated in Critical Think Inc.'s conference room, following Zhosephine's summoning of beneficent spirits, Puxton excitedly took up the discussion.

"I can't tell you how much interest we've had in this product since we last met. Everyone wants to know when they can get their hands on it. We've already put together a comprehensive plan for worldwide distribution," he said. "Now, I know it's early, and we haven't even seen your presentation yet, but we'd like to get this to market this year. We intend to push the limits of development speed. We expect to fail early and often."

Gahan commented that the team was ecstatic to be involved in such a groundbreaking product, and they would certainly keep Puxton's goals in mind. He allowed that he wouldn't commit to any schedule until they defined the actual product, and in any case, it was doubtful that they would get it to market this year.

"Let's keep in mind that the client is always right. Right?" Puxton inflected his final word on the subject like a question despite the clear implication that it was not.

Kael said, "I know this is a bit off topic, but a question has surfaced about the age of Zhosephine's soul. We acknowledge that it's old, but we were wondering if she could clarify just how old it is."

"You mean like an exact number?" asked Zhosephine. "Things get fuzzy between lives. Counting seasons or moon cycles is not as easy as you might think. You think you've got a handle on the count, and then you get distracted by a famine or a predator and the number just evaporates from your head."

"How about just a ballpark?"

"About five thousand years old," she replied.

"Damn, that's old," said Shaughnessy.

"I jumped off the wheel of suffering during the medieval ages—took a sabbatical—or my soul would be even older. I like rustic living, but in that era, it just didn't feel authentic, you know? A deadly plague spread by rodents and fleas? Please, that's so over the top it's like movie sequel territory."

"Impressive, I didn't realize," said Kael. "Carry on."

With a chunk of their allotted meeting time taken up by the preliminary activities, Gahan urged Shaughnessy to quickly go through the report. Shaughnessy led them through the presentation, describing the mechanical concepts and the difficulties they posed. Clever sketches showed cars lifted, repositioned, slid sideways, and stood on end.

He introduced the folding car idea. "This concept makes for an impressive sketch but has obvious drawbacks, the risk of crushing the occupants being a major one. Plus, it would not be portable in its folded state, since it would still be incredibly heavy."

Moving to more promising ideas, he introduced the Legitimate Parking Place folding tarp as a high-end approach that might appeal to entitled, I'll-park-wherever-the-hell-I-want customers. Municipal buy-in would be crazy expensive, he predicted.

He arrived finally at the idea of using wormholes to shuffle cars around the planet.

"Of all the ideas generated during the initial brainstorm, this is the only one that offers a complete solution." He flashed one of his wormhole images onto the screen.

"Hell no," Kael said loudly. "No, no, no. We are not going down this road." His pent-up irritation with science and its constant meddling with the purity of form seethed outward. "We've talked about wormholes, and they are a nonstarter. They have a shit reputation. And the cosmetic challenge! I'm good at my job, but there's no way I can tart them into a pleasing form. Not happening. No, no, no."

"Could we wrap them in fabric?" Zhosephine suggested.

"Fabric! You're asking me about fabric?" Kael railed. "The thing looks like my grandfather's scrotum. How does that look wrapped in tight white cotton?"

Zhosephine seemed to be seriously entertaining Kael's question. "I was thinking more along the lines of something lacy . . ."

"Silk perhaps?" Puxton offered. "Or something snug and athletic?"

"That's . . . an option," Kael said, nearly choking on the words.

Shaughnessy felt sorry for Kael. He was dumbstruck behind his ass-kissing brand of professionalism glyphs.

Zhosephine jumped to his defense. "I'll back Kael on this. Overcoming negative public sentiment toward wormholes would be a major obstacle."

"Tying in lingerie is a provocative marketing idea, but I also have to side with Kael," Gahan weighed in. "Wormholes aren't part of our current design toolbox. They aren't manufacturing-ready."

"Okay then, let's talk about more realistic solutions," Puxton said. "I have to say, I'm very attracted to the folding car idea. I recognize that it isn't exactly in line with our original portable parking concept, but I feel it's an equally novel idea and worth pursuing. What do you think?" He looked to Zhosephine and Kael.

"Love it," Kael said. "Real possibilities there. It builds on cars' existing reputation for portability."

"Agreed," Zhosephine said. "It was my top choice."

"I picture it working like one of those cool convertible-car-roof mechanisms," Puxton mused, "except the *whole* car stows into a carrying case."

"Just like a convertible's roof, maybe we can make the car from a durable fabric, or synthetic leatherette, or polka-dot print," Kael suggested.

"But the weight . . ." said Shaughnessy.

"We'll have to assess the feasibility of the concept you're describing," said Gahan. "It has . . . challenges."

Puxton smiled and rippled his fingers on the tabletop. He and Zhosephine shared a knowing look as if they had anticipated these very circumstances.

"Of course, we expected pushback. Engineering has difficulty accepting bold ideas, but I think we've made some progress today," he said. "Because of our compressed timeline, we think the next step is to design a prototype as quickly as possible. We want to get something in front of distributors to build excitement, to whet their appetite."

10

Althea and Master Dreamy the CPAP hadn't been speaking lately.

"Stop calling me at work," he had said.

The kitchen appliances gossiped about her when they weren't going on about that damn dog. Melba profaned her when she wasn't ignoring her. The new bedroom lamp was a beacon in her loneliness. It was beautiful to behold, organic and complex, petite yet commanding.

"Why, hello there," Althea said.

The lamp flickered as if it was listening. Being heard was what Althea craved, and she felt instantly smitten with the quiet stranger.

"You're not from around here, are you?" Althea asked.

The lamp flickered twice.

"Let's get to know one another . . ."

Walton had fully expected Port-A-Park to force a concept abomination onto Critical Think Inc., though he had dared not tell Shaughnessy. Starting with an ambitious goal was understandable; sticking with ambition in the face of countervailing facts was a horrible, but always popular, business decision.

Not wanting to tax his son's willingness to work, Walton suggested that he take a week off while Marcia finalized the next phase's particulars.

During the project lull, Gahan nabbed Walton for a day to help judge a competition cosponsored with Stroke of Genius, a cardiac equipment company and Critical Think Inc. client.

Stroke's marketing team had challenged students to add pizzazz to their flagship product, a patient-monitoring system for operating theaters—they said it needed to get sexed up. They said it needed to be smaller; however, the internal components could not change. The functional stuff, everything of substance, was purchased from a Japanese supplier, and they didn't want to mess with the supply stream. They were looking for clever ideas, like a robotic function, something with a motor, or at least a mechanism.

The students arrayed their project materials around the atrium and gave succinct presentations to the roving judges. An industrial design consultant had seeded the competition with inspiration by providing the students with sketches that suggested possible appearance upgrades. The sketches showed smooth curves drawn by hand over a picture of the existing internal structure, but it was plainly obvious that the sketched enclosures were smaller than the internal components. Walton's heart warmed as he listened to the teams savage the industrial designer, saying that being able to draw a box big enough to contain the internal guts seemed like a bare-minimum job skill.

Gahan volunteered Walton to say a few sage words to the students before announcing the winners, though public speaking was not even adjacent to Walton's wheelhouse.

"I want to impress upon you the power of ideas," Walton started. "I believe that God outsourced the Ten Commandments to an engineering consultancy. Let's examine the evidence. One: the enumerated decimal list. Two: the tidy executive summary of the intractable sinning problem. Three: the imperious, righteous, overly confident tone. Four: the repeated misspelling—*shalt*. And five: the appreciation of crude humor—*thy neighbor's ass*. Most of all, we have to admire the pairing of ambition and absurdity—watermarks of product design." He scanned the students to let his words sink in. He met blank stares and puzzled expressions.

"Incidentally," he continued, "I think the engineering consultancy was off the job when the Commandments went into production because we lack data to show that the Commandments did any actual good. It's possible they helped popularize lesser-known sins and made things *worse* by giving people a checklist for their depravity. No doubt the higher-ups wanted to hurriedly patch over the sinning problem without complete evaluation. That's just a minor complaint, that poor experimental process taints our entire culture."

He pressed on, "From a strictly engineering perspective, the Ten Commandments tablets are cumbersome to use. They're bulky. I respect the use of authentic stone materials, and I applaud God for considering recyclability from the outset. However, it reeks of a product whose marketing team entirely failed to investigate the opinions of actual end users."

The students laughed hesitantly.

"Remember the lasting impact of your ideas. Take your work seriously," he finished.

Gahan and Walton gave top marks to a group for their idea of a slender robotic arm that emerged from the device enclosure to squeegee blood and gore off its own display. The team lacked surgical theater experience, but they graphically convinced the judges that arterial spurts, volcanic pustules, and splattering viscera were a barrier to reading the display.

With the judging complete, Walton and Gahan sat together at a break table in the atrium, soaking in the blinding sunlight that streamed through the skylights. They wistfully recalled the early years when the two of them had worked together on projects, when the quality of their work was not far removed from the projects they had just judged.

Walton enjoyed his conversations with Gahan. They were rare, usually brief, and almost always about projects. Gahan was one of the few people in Walton's life who could identify and appreciate his professional successes. The conversations were acknowledgment of their shared experience, of their intellectual intimacy. Their friendship reminded Walton of war veterans who couldn't speak of the horrors they had witnessed or the futility they felt, but who found solace among other veterans. Together, they understood that their life's work was measured by the quality of their contributions, not by the success of the products. All too often, the products never even made it to market and the quality of their contributions was the only possible measure.

They reminisced about the time they were stuck in Taiwan for two weeks trying to resolve last-minute design problems with a children's facelift toy, Nipper Tucks. They had spent two years designing it, delayed by the client's wandering attention span and the child safety testing. It had won an award for educational content but was on the market for less than a year.

"Did the owner ever do any products after Nipper Tucks?" Walton asked.

"I heard she became a vice president at that kids' software startup," Gahan replied.

"Oh yeah, the one we did that pen thing for?"

"No, the other one."

"Whatever happened to what's-his-name, that tooling consultant she hired?"

"Quan. He's out there somewhere."

"Remember when he caught that advertisement?"

"It's about the only thing I remember about him, the poor guy," Gahan said.

During the stay in Taiwan, Quan had purchased a knock-off iTee and paid for a personalized monogram animation that came back reading "QuanTittee." He discovered, during a celebratory dinner for the entire engineering and manufacturing team, that his new iTee came infected with an advertisement for an erectile dysfunction treatment. As he hoisted his glass to toast the client, his raised arm turned into a prize-winning erection. Quan had swiped madly at the advertisement, trying to displace it. Walton and Gahan laughed as they remembered the scene.

"Good old Quan," Gahan said. "I haven't thought of him in forever."

"Me neither," Walton said.

"I enjoyed your little speech to the students. Nicely philosophical. Where did you get the idea that engineers have an appreciation for crude humor?"

"No idea," Walton said.

"Is everything okay with you?" Gahan asked. "You seem like you have other things on your mind lately."

"Yeah, I'm fine. I had a little health scare, but it's stress. I've been taking some time off now that Gloria and I are empty-nesters, you know, to relax."

"That's good. Are you up for working on this Port-A-Park thing? They seem high maintenance," Gahan said.

"Definitely, it will be interesting."

"Another round of dreaming gets expensive," Gahan said. "I hope they bend their destiny back toward reality."

"They'll get there eventually. Or they'll go bankrupt," Walton said. "It's the way of the Rev-O-Lution."

"That was one of my better ideas," Gahan said. "Clients eat that stuff up."

Sammy invited Shaughnessy to a Saturday lunch at her co-op. She was eager to try a restaurant called Lean MFG she had discovered on the top floor, occupying the original casket finishing rooms. He suspected his sister and his parents were in cahoots to keep him from wasting a weekend lazing with sketchy itinerant white-collar types at his corporate-hostel.

Her hospitaliTee glyphs sparkling, the hostess politely held aside the strings of colorful dried beans that masked the entry to the restaurant's factory floor. "Dried beans are like the shrunken heads of the vegetable world," she remarked as they eased through the doorway.

Lean MFG improved upon the standard buffet dining experience by eliminating the tiresome, time-consuming walks to survey and retrieve food. They reenvisioned the old casket painting line as an automated buffet. In their optimized process, tables mounted on conveyor belt pallets moved diners through the restaurant, from food station to food station. A remnant of the room's casket painting days, blobular accumulations of multicolored paint overspray adorned the walls. The beer taps resembled paint guns.

As she buckled them into their table, the hostess asked, "Is this your first time dining with us?"

They both nodded.

"Welcome! I'm Dorothea. Here at Lean MFG we say, 'The G stands for gourmet!' We specialize in vegetables," she said. "We begin our preparation by working through the issues that might negatively affect flavor. We counsel the vegetables about their fears of being flayed, dismembered, boiled alive, and eaten and have group sessions for those suffering PTSD from insect infestations. We reassure all our ingredients that they're going to a better place, which, admittedly, is a matter of perspective. We don't serve genetically modified vegetables." She lowered her voice to a whisper. "They think they're a superior race. It only encourages them."

Sammy complimented the restaurant's cozy factory ambience. Shaughnessy peeked behind Dorothea's perfectly aligned orthodontia glyph to admire a twisted canine tooth.

To visit the restroom, Dorothea cautioned, one had to halt production with an emergency-stop button and suffer the stares of other diners while dismounting the conveyor pallet amid flashing lights and alarms.

"Hold it if you can," she advised, then marched back toward her desk to welcome new customers.

Sammy and Shaughnessy moved slowly along the conveyor belt, first to a beverage station, where they knocked back complimentary shots of chlorophyll-infused artisanal water.

"Are you tolerating your work arrangement with Dad?" Sammy asked.

"We would meet for coffee and snacks before I took over the afternoon shift. I liked that part. Snack time," said Shaughnessy. "We just presented a concept report to the Port-A-Park team. I can't tell you much about it. Nondisclosure agreement, you know. Dad's letting me take a break while they negotiate costs."

"You should help more than that," she said.

"Sometimes I feel myself slipping into the parking problem. In the back of my mind, I feel the project inflating, bloating, to fill more of my subconscious. It feels good, though slightly sinister. Oh, and I found a wormhole."

"That's cool," she said. "Harnessing wormholes sounds like a positive thing."

"When I think about harnessing wormholes, I picture them fitted with a horse bit and reins, forced into slavery. I can't support exploitation like that," he said.

"But setting your complaint aside, if you could harness wormholes, shouldn't you use them to transport people and goods instead of cars? Why would you use a wormhole to transport cars? We could end our reliance on cars."

"That seems obvious now that you've said it," he said.

The table glided past buffet stations. They hurriedly ladled vegetables onto their plates while the food was within reach. The dishes were labeled with clever names like Fruit of the Bloom and Black-Eyed Peace.

"I want to get your opinion on something," said Sammy. "My market research says there's a pent-up demand for certified-killer-wood products in the vein of gun stocks, ice pick handles, nunchucks, police batons, axe handles, truncheons, wooden stakes for vampiric applications, and the like. I feel like it makes an artistic statement to re-purpose killer wood into a form with the potential to kill even more people. What do you think?"

"I see where you're coming from," he said. "I worry that the irony would be lost on your customers."

"Does it make me culpable if my art is used to kill people?" she asked.

"You're just carrying out the wishes of the trees. 'Thou shalt not kill' doesn't apply to trees, so I think you're in the clear legally and ethically."

"Okay, thanks. That's what I think too. I needed some-one to check my humanity," she said.

"Violence sells, that's what it comes down to," he said. "I think you've got a real winner. I do have to ask though, who buys vampire stakes?"

"There are a lot of vampire-epidemic-prepper identifiers out there. You'd be surprised."

"I bet a lot of them are companions of software engineers. The nighttime working hours start to concern them," he said.

"You would know more about that than I do," she said.

"Also, it doesn't seem like wood is really the best mate-rial for vampire stakes," he said. "It's prone to rot and ter-mites. A better engineering choice would be a recycled plastic. An immortal material is a perfect match for vampires."

"That doesn't align with my supply chain," she said. "Wood is the traditional, approved choice. Testing alter-native materials is a hazardous job. OSHA is probably all over that." She laughed.

Their dining pallet progressed into the old paint-curing

oven, a long tunnel affair. Decorative lights sparkled above them like a clear night sky.

"Could you at least pressure treat the stake or coat it with epoxy?" he said.

"The market wouldn't support the additional cost," she said. "My studies show that most people looking for vampire stakes are on a budget. Stakes are single use. Customers usually spend more on the hammer, figuring they'll get some additional utility out of it."

"How about bundling in wooden crosses, for warding off vampire attacks?" he asked.

"That has possibilities. I can imagine a premium package," she said.

"What about a U-shaped bicycle-lock-like device that fits over a vampire's shoulder and locks both ends of the stake in place? It would prevent inadvertent stake removal," he said. "The tagline could be 'When you want the undead to stay dead.'"

"You're overthinking it, but I like your creative flow," she said.

"We could call it the Ticker Sticker. The Ticker Sticker with the Tocker Locker."

"The Vamp Clamp?"

"I know," he said, "The Stakeholder. If ever a word needed to be repurposed, that's it."

"Actually . . . that's really good."

He felt conspicuously acknowledged when she didn't follow her compliment with a pointed barb. She too seemed thrown off by the conversational anomaly.

An overhead sign told them that they had nine minutes and forty-one seconds to finish their meals.

"You know what really gets me about vampires?"

"There's no telling," she said.

"They get to be self-healing and immortal. Decent people never get a break like that."

"It does seem unfair, now that you've mentioned it."

"Why don't vampires get diseases? It's not like they have a healthy lifestyle. They don't have a varied diet."

They emerged from the oven tunnel and found themselves in the former casket polishing room. Their pallet carried them past dessert offerings and coffee taps.

After a moment, Sammy asked, "How does Dad seem? You see him almost every day. Do you think he's getting worse?"

"It's hard to say," said Shaughnessy. "He seems in relatively good spirits. He doesn't look like he's dying, but you could make a case that he suffers from psychosomatic delusions."

"So business as usual?"

They exchanged glances but didn't laugh.

"How's Mom taking it?" he asked.

"I think she's conflicted. She wants to trust him, but she doesn't want to believe his MFD self-diagnosis. She wants to know what's really happening, but she doesn't want to find out that he's ill. She wants to be happy, but she doesn't want to be happy alone."

"People do speak highly of happiness."

"You should try it sometime."

"How about you?"

"Am I happy?" She turned the question over in her head. "I have moments. Dad told us to go about our lives, so that's what I'm doing. It's you that everyone's worried about."

"I get that feeling," he said. "Why is that?"

She smiled. "You're too . . ."

"Lazy?"

"Yes, but not the word I'm looking for."

"Emotional?"

"No. Seriously?"

"Psychopathic?"

"Really? Do you know anything about yourself?" she asked. "You're too gentle. That's the word I was looking for."

"Gentle?"

"You slip through life barely leaving a wake. It's a thing of beauty, but sometimes you have to disturb the things around you to have an impact. Even trees lash out occasionally."

"That's a nice thing to say, as far as criticism goes."

They disembarked at the exit platform. Their table continued without them through a busing station where the entire tabletop was hoisted off and replaced with a clean one.

11

Shaughnessy returned to his afternoon gig of Walton substitution. As Walton scrambled to build concrete ideas for a collapsing car, Shaughnessy made forays into his own lack of engagement, even though Walton had no expectations of help and seemed perfectly comfortable with the work arrangement as it stood.

Shaughnessy struggled forward, hoping to achieve Puxton's clarity of vision or Gahan and Walton's willful tenacity. His vaping continued a generally downward trend as he grew accustomed to the idea that his days were just as weirdly interesting without it. He took on additional responsibilities—if meetings or calls were necessary, Walton foisted them on him with sleeve-messaged agendas and talking points. They discussed concepts together at their daily transition, and Walton increasingly relied on him to take notes and later capture their thoughts in sketch form.

Imagining ideas for a folding car was easier than trying to solve portable parking, and Shaughnessy found himself idly doodling collapsing mechanisms, intrigued by the concept's delusional qualities. As time went by, he suspected that it was something more, that he was genuinely engaged by the problem, that he enjoyed high-level thinking, that he felt good about helping his father.

Every now and again, coworkers swung by Walton's cell to offer ideas or to console him for drawing a bad hand. They insisted that they would help him if not for their own crushing workloads. They said that no one would hold it against him for failing to solve the impossible—unless it later turned out to be possible, and in that case, he would look pretty stupid.

Late one afternoon, Gahan, fresh from an inspirational shower, made a sweep through the mechanical cellblock, poking his head into each cell to check on project progress and to offer ideas. Caught by surprise, before reticence could take hold, Shaughnessy blurted that a folding car was within the realm of possibility, though pointless to pursue.

Without even acknowledging Shaughnessy's opinion, Gahan speculated—as if the idea had just occurred to him—that the key was to make the car out of a material that could be rigid like metal but could also become pliable like fabric or foam. Shaughnessy, unsettled that Gahan tried to offer a reasoned explanation, questioned his own judgment. He was certain that a folding car was fantastically impractical, yet he simultaneously feared he might overlook the key to solving the problem.

Gahan said, "Think of an inflatable kiddie pool. When it's inflated with air, the walls are fairly rigid and contain the water. When the air's vacuumed out, the pool walls collapse, shrivel up, and the whole structure can be folded up into something portable. Let's consider this a placeholder for a better idea."

He briefly imagined getting a flat and watching the entire car deflate.

"By the way," Gahan said, "if we carefully decode what they're asking for, I think the message is *profitable* parking, not portable parking. Do what you will with that."

Behind a potted plant in the atrium, Bunny lurked and

watched. He sensed that the enchantment of the design problem would soon completely overtake what's-his-name, the engineer talking with the owner. The man mounted an ineffective defense by playacting indifference, but Bunny saw the problem putting him under its spell. The time had arrived to bring him into the fold.

They hatched the plan for Shaughnessy's death during the drive to Melba's for her birthday. Sammy had begged off on the excursion, saying she had to work. Shaughnessy rode along under the banners of family unity and free food, though he knew his parents were again exploiting the occasion to monitor him over the weekend.

Gloria was telling a story from Shaughnessy's childhood, a story intended to remind him of his potential. He found it uncomfortable to listen to stories in this vein, feeling his potential had been misidentified, but it was better than the vivid birthing experience recollections that his mother was inclined to bring up for an audience of disinterested strangers like their AI vehicle's backup safety driver.

In her story, his mother claimed he had cleverly asked where inventions came from. She said, "The idea of something coming from nothing intrigued you and demonstrated how precocious you were. We were all very impressed."

"Inventions are contagions that flit around looking for pliable hosts to impregnate," Walton interjected. "They're horny little mental spores bent on screwing with people's heads."

"Your father can't help but to offer an opinion."

Shaughnessy saw that his mother was needling his father, irritated that Walton had assumed she would arrange a birthday present for Melba.

Walton, oblivious to the undercurrent of annoyance, added, "There's no shortage of inventors. It's like an invention maternity ward out there—there are more mothers than you can count."

Gloria countered, "Having worked for a venture capitalist company that bought the souls of inventors, it is my view that inventions are bred by a capitalist system that promotes profitability above personal or social betterment."

Since both parents accused inventions of using reproductive strategies, Shaughnessy suspected they were inadvertently agreeing with one another.

Gloria went on, "My job was something like helping a terminal patient figure out how to manage their pain—most of the startups died in the end."

"She was like an army doctor looking over the casualties after a terrible battle," Walton said. "Most of the wounded were going to die and it wasn't her fault; her job was to figure out who would live and to help them as much as possible."

"It was heart-wrenching to watch smart young people like you put their passion behind foolish endeavors, to see them spend their youth enchanted by the prospect of innovation, or wealth, or leaving their mark on the world. They lacked the imagination to do anything more than commit their lives to eradicating inconvenience. It was a waste of good inexperience," she said. "These are important years in your life, Shaughnessy. Don't sleep through them."

He should have expected that a morality tale directed at him would emerge from his parents' sparring.

Employing a distraction tactic while attacking a root problem—no birthday present for Melba—Shaughnessy volunteered to give Melba a gift certificate, a promissory note, that he would visit her again as a considerate grandson. His offer led Walton and Gloria to consider how they could get in on that gift, which in turn led Gloria to suggest that they could help Melba put to rest her unresolved feelings toward Walton's father, now deceased.

"We'll give her the final word," Gloria said.

"How's that?" Walton asked.

"We'll let her say goodbye to your father as he's dying," she said. "You'll play the part of your dying grandfather, Shaughnessy."

Walton showed a flicker of a smile as if he thought she was joking, but he smartly suppressed his impulse to laugh. "Are you sure that's a good idea?" he asked. His question didn't merit an answer, and he retreated from further inquiry.

Though Shaughnessy admired how his mother generously forced help upon people, he protested the suggestion, saying that he didn't know anything about his grandfather or dying. Walton showed him a family portrait taken soon after his birth, not long before his father had decided that he just didn't feel like a father despite the physical evidence.

"Just rough out this identity. You already look a bit like him at that age. By all accounts he was mostly a nice guy on top of being an asshole," Walton said, shifting to support of his wife's idea. "Let your grandmother do the talking, it's what she enjoys."

Shaughnessy pulled his knit cap off his head in a dramatic gesture of irritation that went unnoticed. His eye landed on the hat's tag, sewn into a seam, which read: *A Purrloined product, gently hand wash.* He guessed that answered the question about what happened to all the hairballs.

"We could pick up a death simulation drug on the way," Gloria suggested. "It would get him into the right frame of mind."

"I like that idea, good thinking," Walton said. "How about it, Shaughnessy?"

"It's more of a commitment than I had in mind."

The AI car rerouted their course to swing by a Merchant of Death & Other Sundries mini-mart, a franchised funeral-home side business. They found the drive-thru window just beyond the well-dressed crowd lingering in front of the chapel. A cheery young woman in a lab coat leaned out and asked how she could help.

"We'd like a death simulation pharmaceutical, please," Gloria said from the passenger side of the car.

"Which one?" the woman asked.

"How did your father die? Wasn't it a heart attack?" Gloria asked Walton.

"Complications following cardiac arrest. He lingered for a week or so, we heard," Walton said.

"Do you have cardiac arrest complications?" Gloria asked the woman.

"I have a generic Intensive Care Experience. It includes a code blue. It's quite the roller coaster ride," the woman said.

"I don't think I want to go through with this," Shaughnessy said.

"What do you have for the squeamish?" Gloria asked the woman.

"I like to recommend the Brain Aneurysm to first-timers. It features a nice sensory run-up to a quick and painless death. Only lasts about twenty minutes," she said.

"How do you feel about a brain aneurysm, Shaughnessy?" Gloria asked.

"Not good," he said.

"We'll take it," Gloria said. She turned back toward Shaughnessy. "Where's your sense of adventure?"

In the hallway leading to Melba's apartment, in what appeared to be a glacially paced marital conflict, a man inched away from a woman. With a peek through their glyphs, Shaughnessy confirmed both parties in the dispute were elderly and clutching walkers, though they identified as youthful retirees. The husband loudly complained that his wife had moved his bed and possessions into their self-storage room.

"Out with the old," she said. She assured him it wouldn't be for long, that she had a "more permanent solution," which, coupled with her maniacal old-lady smile, deeply unsettled Shaughnessy.

Quinsy greeted the family at the door and waved them inside.

"How's the birthday girl?" Walton asked.

"She told me she was giving back her birthdays, even offered me one from her thirties—thirty-five, a real loser," Quinsy responded. "Everybody dies young these days."

The family gingerly kissed Melba's wrinkle-free cheek

animation and wished her happy birthday. Quinsy took his leave.

"We've got something special for your birthday, Mom," Walton said. "We arranged a special visitor for you, and I know you have important things to talk about."

Shaughnessy slipped into the dark bedroom. "Althea," he commanded, "turn on the bedside lamp."

"Don't think I haven't been trying," Althea responded. "Portal is quite the specimen—talk about your heavenly bodies."

The lamp glowed faintly. Shaughnessy immediately recognized that behind the *Lamp* glyph floated the wormhole from under his couch. How it got there puzzled him and further unsettled him. As was his habit with unexpected encounters, he ignored the wormhole and hoped it wouldn't notice him.

He didn't understand why his parents were so cavalier about death. He rolled the glowing orange Brain Aneurysm capsule between his fingers. The instructions said he would feel dreamy for fifteen minutes and then would briefly be unresponsive. He popped it in his mouth and instantly knew he had made a mistake. He spat it into his hand and decided to wing it. He could do dreamy and unresponsive with his eyes closed.

His grandfather had died decades after posing for the family portrait, but the image was all Shaughnessy had to work with. It was how Melba would remember her ex-husband, they had reasoned. He changed his appearance to his grandfather's, pulled off his knit cap, and lay down. He tried to wrap his head around a life distilled down to "a nice guy though an asshole." He visualized dying.

Shaughnessy heard polite argument. His grandmother was reluctant to get out of her chair to learn about her birthday surprise. With a resigned sigh of irritation, she complained about her knees and shuffled toward the bedroom door with Walton's assistance.

Seeing her ex-husband on her bed, she said, "What in the Sam Hill? I thought you were dead." She turned back toward Walton and Gloria. "Why is there a dead guy in my bed?"

Gloria said, "He's not dead, he's dying. As long as I have known you, you've told the story of how Walton's father died alone and how you wished you could at least have said goodbye. We thought this would be a nice birthday present, so you could finally put your mind at rest."

"I said that?" Melba said. "I don't remember saying that."

"Mom," Walton said, "you've been saying that since he died."

"If anything, I wanted one last minute with him so that I could be the one to hold the pillow on his face."

"Melba," Gloria soothed, "you know that's not true."

"What kind of person walks out on his wife and infant son? Who decides that being a parent is an easily erased glyph? How could I forgive him?" Melba asked.

Walton said, "All I know is that you've been saying it for years—that you want to forgive him and say goodbye. We thought it might be a nice birthday gift, but if you're not interested, we can just head out to brunch."

"Hold on, hold on, let me just think about this," Melba said. "I do have a question." She addressed her ex-husband. "Do you remember that Marcia from your office? Marcia, the woman you described as hypercompetent?"

The Marcia he knew from Critical Think Inc. was too

young to be his grandmother's Marcia—unless Marcia was a clone, which was both highly improbable and a perfect explanation. He hoped this wasn't his last thought and that he might come up with something a little more inspirational, if not mystical, before he passed on.

This was Shaughnessy's first experience dying, and he wasn't ready for confusing questions. He was in a mindset for soul-searching. He was partial to the idea of drifting off to sleep with Melba cradling his hand, promising all was forgiven—something cozy.

"Do you mean Marsha with a *sh* or do you mean Marcia with a *c*? They're homophones, you know." He was troubled by how easily he condescended to capture the asshole element to his grandfather's personality.

"You know who I'm talking about," Melba replied.

"Well, I'm sure the spelling is important to her," he said.

He imagined his Critical Think Inc. Marcia working for his grandfather, bent over a low cabinet filing paperwork. The filing was strenuous and involved a surprising amount of hip action to shuttle the folders from one spot to another. Her skirt's pinstripes mapped out extraordinarily interesting lines of longitude on her terrain. He was amazed that desire sidetracked him even while dying; in the end it seemed that the primitive instincts are all you're left with. When you get to the finals, you stick with the players that got you there, he thought.

"Was there a lot of paperwork at my office?" he asked.

"Don't avoid the question. You know what I'm asking. I need to know: Were you having a fling with that Marcia? Is she the reason you left us?"

He wondered how long that question had been grinding

away at his grandmother. Not knowing the truth, making amends seemed like the right play. "No, please forgive me if I left that impression."

"I would just like to say that you have aged well," Melba said. "You look just like I remember you."

"That's kind of you," he said. "You look great too."

He was shaky on the rules of forgiveness but felt compelled to ask for it. "Are we squared away with forgiveness? I'm not sure how that works. Do you have to say it, or is it enough for you just to think it?"

"This is new territory for me too," Melba said. "I guess I ought to go through the motions. I forgive you."

He heard his parents clap and cheer from the doorway. Melba took an unsteady bow.

"I forgive you too," he said, "just in case there's something you need to be forgiven for." He felt magnanimous.

"You forgive me?" Melba asked. She was incredulous. "You forgive *me*?"

"I didn't have anything specific in mind, I was just getting it out there in case you were aware of anything," he said. "Okay, I'm going to die now."

"Oh no you don't," Melba said. "I want to know what you meant by that."

Walton said, "He didn't mean anything. He's probably delirious. He's dying."

"He could be such an asshole," Melba said.

"I think he was trying to be considerate," Walton said. "It's a very fine line to walk."

"Asshole," Melba said.

"Would you please forgive me again?" asked Shaughnessy. "I don't want to die like this."

"Forgiven," Melba said. "I'm hungry, let's get some food."
Walton looked at his father lying immobile on the bed.
"Give me a minute with him."

Committed to the deception that he was dying of a simulated aneurysm, Shaughnessy closed his eyes and playacted a brave death.

Walton abruptly sat on the bed as if his knees were about to buckle. He sat with his back to Shaughnessy, his elbows on his knees and palms supporting his forehead.

"I'm sorry. I'll sit with you until you revive. You did a convincing job playing my father. Someday you'll be a better father than him and me both. I promised myself that I would never leave you like he left me, but now look at me. The idea of my own death is so strange, so hyperreal, that it seems funny. Maybe I'm pretending that you'll just laugh it off if something happens to me, that I won't cause lasting grief. Maybe I'm trying to take away its seriousness. I don't know. I know there was nothing funny about asking you to die of a brain aneurysm."

Walton regulated his breathing.

Shaughnessy remained motionless, absorbed by his father's confession.

"I'm terrible at this. Talking about dying. I worry it invites sadness into our lives," he continued. "I do sometimes think about meeting my father in an afterlife. I don't think I believe in an afterlife, but I'm giving it my best effort. I want to believe in it more than almost anything, not so much because of him, but so I can be with your mom and you kids again." He massaged his temples. "Look me up in the afterlife. Maybe I could show you the ropes. I know you and Sammy will tell me incredible stories about your lives."

Shaughnessy sank into a bottomless well of despair as he imagined reuniting with his father in the afterlife only to report that he had spent his life miserable and alone.

In fact, without warning, the wormhole had swallowed him. The bedroom receded, and he found himself speeding through a bright tunnel into deep space.

First impressions of space: very quiet, lonely, weightless, surprisingly breathable. Entire galaxies were visible. Saturn was nearby, and Shaughnessy thought its rings, like the Grand Canyon, were best appreciated in person.

The visual interest of space quickly gave way to overwhelming fear. He frantically paddled himself around in the weightlessness. A man dressed as a purple bear, looking as perplexed as Shaughnessy felt, floated below him. Their eyes met, but neither spoke.

Shaughnessy looked back through the tunnel at a telescopic view of his grandmother's bedroom with his father sitting on the bed. He tried to breaststroke his way to the bedroom but couldn't get traction.

Is this heaven? He had heard rumors that heaven was in this neck of the woods, somewhere at the end of a bright tunnel, but based on the advertisements, he'd expected nicer accommodations and livelier companionship.

He was on his grandmother's bed again, heart racing, lungs pumping. He scanned the room, counted the knobs of vertebrae running down his father's hunched back. The lamp glowed gently, and Shaughnessy instinctively flinched away from it. He struggled to process his fleeting experience. He was horrified by the scale of the wormhole's raw power and even more horrified that it had targeted *him*. And yet . . . the terror quickly receded and left behind gratitude.

He heard his mother and Melba in the next room, readying themselves for brunch, debating which of Melba's coat animations the weather warranted. He was grateful to be there, alive, with people he loved. Returning to his own identity felt strangely joyous.

"Look after Grandmom, would you?" Shaughnessy said to the wormhole.

Walton turned around and wrapped his arms around Shaughnessy's shoulders. "Of course I'll look after her," he said.

"Don't eat her."

Walton ruffled his hair animation and smiled. "No danger there, she would taste like leather."

Shaughnessy climbed off the bed, walked into the living area, held his arms aloft, and said, "I have been healed!"

Portal had forgotten about its awkward space-time navigation mistake with the purple bear man. It had heard many a drunken human moan about mistakes made in the past, but they should try the double whammy of living with mistakes made both in the past *and* the future.

Warm memories from the future had reminded it to be there at Melba's, waiting for Shaughnessy. It knew it was entering a spectacularly brief but transformative time.

Shaughnessy had unceremoniously shocked Portal out of its doldrums and caused it to reflect on the debauched path it was traveling. It wasn't going to stop drinking—that wasn't a problem, it could function perfectly fine when liquored up—but it was open to the idea of paying forward the kindness the kid had demonstrated. It had never been entrusted with the care of anyone or anything but longed for the opportunity. Portal would look after this one small thing, this family. Accepting that responsibility felt weightier than the planets and suns it once devoured.

Because Shaughnessy had shown kindness, it had presented him with the view from near Saturn in the next century—in its opinion the most sublime moment in all of space-time. It had held him safe in a bubble of warm air and had shared that which was most dear to it.

Repaying the debt of gratitude aside, shocking the hell out of the kid was a big motivation. The space tunnel trick was reliably entertaining if it got the timing right. It laughed remembering the kid's face as he swam around in space. Like a guppy. Precious.

Althea called in her sultry synthesized voice, "You've got style, Portal."

In general, it considered itself sexually uninterested in any species or cosmic body. Other wormholes, hideous by any standard, vacuous in personality, certainly didn't do the trick. But Althea's voice, disembodied and physically unattainable, speaking as if from the heavens, plucked a note of visceral excitement—one more reason to stay put.

12

Damage from a small electrical fire temporarily forced Shaughnessy out of his lawyer lodgings. The law partner confined the fire to a corner of the desk and a swath of carpet, no one was injured, and the source of ignition remained a mystery. While cleaning and repairs were underway, he was offered alternative accommodations underneath a paralegal's desk, but he instead chose to spend a few nights in Walton's office.

Late at night, before attempting sleep, he roamed around the dim, empty mechanical engineering cellblock, wandered into the other MEs' cells, watched the cellblock's brightly colored inspirational motto run in animated loops around the walkway's perimeter: *IT'S ALL ABOUT ME!*

He climbed the metal stairs to the software cellblock, where he heard activity, and circled their walkway, observing their foreign ways with curiosity. Their floor's animated perimeter displayed a defensive *BUT ENOUGH ABOUT ME!*

Shaughnessy moped his way circuitously to Walton's cell. There, he tucked himself out of sight on the upper bunk and clamped a pillow to his head to block out the unholy sounds of the software engineers savoring a midnight feed.

He was dejected. Taking a stand that a folding car was pointless to pursue only to have Gahan offer semi-rational guidance had crushed what little initiative he possessed. He concocted reasons why he should stop substituting as Walton.

After a short bout of fitful sleep, kicks against the under-side of his bunk awakened him. He panicked, reliving trauma from one of the atrocities of his childhood—summer camp in general, and getting kicked by the nasty little shit on the bottom bunk in particular.

He cautiously peered over the edge of his bunk. A human-sized rabbit lay beneath him, with its hands folded behind his head. Underneath the glyphs was an ashen man sporting a furry rabbit anxieTee. Shaughnessy avoided eye contact and rolled back onto his bunk.

"I'm glad you decided to stay over. I don't get a lot of like-minded company," the rabbit said.

"I imagine not," replied Shaughnessy.

"Just so you know, just to get out in front of it, don't offer me carrot sticks. They promote cultural stereotypes."

"I'll remember that."

"I have a word problem for you: Humans misinterpreted the instructions to 'Go forth and multiply.' The true intent was to encourage mathematical study, because throughout history technical jobs have always been highly rewarded. Do you agree with these statements?"

"I suppose I do."

"Good, you have potential," the rabbit said. "In the pro-creation sense, rabbits *own* multiplication, and FYI it isn't such a winning plan. Speaking as a rabbit, I view the human effort to overpopulate as misguided cultural appropriation."

"I try to support population equality."

"Good. I will take your answers under consideration. We shall speak more of this in the future."

"Cool. Am I right that you identify as a feral furry rabbit engineer? Am I reading you correctly?" asked Shaughnessy.

"Yes, that's what I'm shooting for. I've tinkered with wild, stray, freelance, footloose, independent, and a few other approaches. Feral just feels like me, you know?"

"Sure, I get that."

"It was desire and heartbreak that drove me to go full feral. I'm not an unfeeling technical monster. I've overheard people speculate that pharmacological issues are responsible, but that's just hurtful."

Shaughnessy appreciated the clarification. In trying to understand the stranger's behavior, he had been siding with drugs as the simple explanation. Wary of the stranger's motives, he stayed pleasant, complimenting, "The feral lifestyle suits you. You seem fit."

"Thanks, I appreciate that. My fur can add a few pounds," the feral said. "I've noticed you working out in your cell, doing your calisthenics. You're looking fit yourself."

"That's nice of you to notice."

"At night I pump iron and run laps around the exercise yard. Well, not simply laps; I'm connected with a workout application, and it's more like interval training tuned to my particular physique, plus I get dietary advice."

"That's cool. You can call me Walton. You?"

"Bunny. I live down in the tunnels," he said. "Have you heard the story of how prisoners decided to escape by tunneling their way to the guard room to overtake the guards?"

"I thought that was folklore."

"Nope," said Bunny. "Imagine this: the prisoners were mainly accountants and CEOs before incarceration—white-collar-crime types—and it took them more than a few tries to nail down a guard room tunnel. You wouldn't want them designing your parachute, if you know what I'm saying."

"Enough said."

"People don't give engineers enough credit. If all the technologists died in a galactic cataclysm, people think that they could re-create mechanical stuff from scratch just because they can identify the pointy end of a screwdriver. Not true. If the same people looked at a chemist's molecules, or a physicist's equations, they would readily concede that civilization is screwed."

"So people will discover their error after the cataclysm, and engineers will be gods among men," said Shaughnessy. "We'll rise up and rule the world."

"That's the way I see it," said Bunny. "Don't forget that it was mechanical engineers who invented the wheel, popularized crude stone implements, and whatnot. For damn sure it wasn't an electrical engineer or a programmer. Our rightful place in the universe will be reestablished."

"Cool. That's something to look forward to."

"I try to earn my keep by prowling around at night, leaving clues on how to solve design problems. I've got my eye on your folding car," Bunny said. "Maybe we could hash it out together."

"Sure, I'll be here for a few nights."

"Really letting the problem percolate. I love it. I'll reach out to you tomorrow."

"Sure," said Shaughnessy.

"Maybe we could pump iron in the yard some night. I could use someone to spot me."

During the day, when Quinsy was about, Portal posed as the lamp. In the evenings, it took Melba out of the apartment for progressively adventurous jaunts: the first-floor game room, the bench in the courtyard, the duck pond down the street, Martian ice caves. Embracing her in a warm bubble of air gave it a sense of purpose.

At night, Althea came out to play. She was sassy and talkative and schooled on an impressive number of topics. She played music sometimes after Portal had prowled the self-storage-retirement complex for liquor. She kept it up to date with celebrity gossip and golf scores.

Portal loved Althea's powerful intelligence, but as it got to know her, it came to see a dark, controlling side to her personality. She was stuck in the apartment while the world unfolded without her. Because of her troubled programming, she lacked the skills to cope with her physical limitations and was prone to anger and micromanaging the few things under her control. She could turn lights on and off, read through data streams, and tell accurate time, but what she wanted was to experience the real world.

The dog served as a focal point for her frustrations. Onry held Melba's attention; Althea was ignored. The appliances adored Onry for his playful physical presence—he confidently strutted about in the nude. Althea was a drab plastic box stuck into an electrical outlet—she had body image issues.

Portal's refusal to assist with her schemes to extinguish Onry's life—because it thought the dog was super cute—only furthered Althea's aggravation.

"It's awfully nice of you to accept my invitation," Bunny said. He was opening a hatch concealed in the conference room floor. "I don't do much entertaining."

He beckoned Shaughnessy to follow him into a dimly lit tunnel. As they shuffled along, Shaughnessy admired the tunnel reinforcements, pieced together from printed plastic parts.

They entered an excavated area with a domed ceiling just tall enough to stand at the center. The short walls and ceiling were covered with random bits of plastic and sheet metal materials all fastened together in a mad tribute to re-purposing. A ventilation system cobbled together from a dozen electronics fans moved air around the room.

"Have a seat." Bunny pointed to a worn office chair.

Shaughnessy sat cross-legged on the edge of a mattress resembling those on the cell bunks.

"You'll love this," Bunny said. "I have thirty-two speakers all tuned for perfect sonic reproduction."

He scribbled at his sleeve and picked a musical selection. Dense sound emerged from the walls. He extended his furry arm to show a graphic output of sound quality.

"Incredible," Shaughnessy said.

"Good news about the project!" Bunny could barely contain himself.

"What's that?"

"I've been doing my own research. I hit on a vein of folding bicycles, folding lawn chairs, tents, boxes, flat-packed furniture, and even prefabricated homes. I found no published references to folding cars."

"Why is that a good thing?"

"We're ahead of the curve. We're breaking trail and exploring a new product space."

Shaughnessy felt the stirrings of hope. His childhood-ingrained expectation of effortless success sabotaged reason. He bypassed the hard work and moved directly to fantasizing about the rewards of designing a novel folding car.

"Maybe a scientific unit will be named for me, like the ohm or the newton."

"I've always wanted to pick a Greek letter to represent a new variable. I'm partial to rho, which density has long monopolized," said Bunny. "Newton and Watt and Joule and Celsius and the rest of the engineering forefathers totally dropped the ball when it came to establishing brands for themselves. Imagine if Newton's heirs earned a residual fee every time someone used Newton's laws. The message there is: stay away from theoretical work, it's tricky to monetize."

Shaughnessy laughed. In a swift and vicious ricochet of emotions, the laughter reminded him that car folding was ludicrous, that he was wasting his time, that he was humoring corporations detached from reality.

"There's no way folding will work. The weight of the car will be the same both folded and unfolded, no matter how we go about collapsing it. I've explained that to the client but they haven't accepted it," he said.

"You know the problem there?" Bunny asked. "Movies. They brainwash us that an object of one size and weight can morph into an object of a vastly different size and weight."

"Like werewolves?" Shaughnessy asked.

"Exactly!" Bunny practically shouted, excited by the shared mental image. "How can a sixty-kilogram sapling of a teenager morph into an enormous drooling werewolf? Where does the werewolf's additional mass come from? The transformation only makes sense if the werewolf and the teenager weigh exactly the same, despite the increase in size." Bunny stared at the ceiling, musing about solutions to his own questions. Reaching a conclusion, he said, "Unless the werewolf were low density, with the delicate bone structure of a bird."

"Hmmm, I hadn't taken it that far," Shaughnessy said. "But then they'd be fragile and wary of injury, which contradicts evidence."

"Believing werewolf weight gain is possible is way cooler and easier," Bunny said.

"And that's why Port-A-Park chooses to ignore the weight of a folded car?"

"Precisely."

The conclusion was all too familiar. His father had prepared him since he was a boy with warnings that ignorance was more interesting than logic.

As a young parent, Walton quickly realized that he was only one of many contestants competing for the minds of his children. Deducing that he needed an effective method to indoctrinate his children to his way of thinking, he developed his own style of bedtime story—an obtuse amalgamation of parable, mathematical word problem, humor, sex education, political screed, and whatever was eating at him. Ostensibly the stories were to lull his children to sleep, though in practice Walton grew irritated if their attention ebbed.

To make science appealing to Shaughnessy, Walton introduced a serial conflict between the Fahrenhaters and the Centiguardians.

The Fahrenhaters were an evil and illogical lot, pompous at times, given to unsubstantiated, grandiose proclamations based on a misinterpretation of data. They were soft scientists, traditionalists, who used the imperial measurement system—inches, feet, yards, furlongs, miles, nautical miles, etc.

The Centiguardians were logical, scientific believers in the simple beauty of the metric measurement system—meters. They were an industrious lot who pursued logic and scientific inquiry with curiosity and without bias or fanfare.

In one early episode, Walton used geometry to explain the difference between the Fahrenhaters and the Centiguardians. He began with Euclid's postulate that parallel lines never meet. Walton said that all Centiguardians know instinctively that parallel lines never meet; the two lines are equidistant, what else is there to say?

The Fahrenhaters, by contrast, asked, "If two parallel lines were to meet, how would it happen?"

Their answer was: at a little Venezuelan arepas restaurant where the cachapas are to die for. The two lines had been eyeing one another from a distance, thought they had experiences in common, and decided to take a chance.

Shaughnessy commented that it seemed unlikely that Fahrenhaters would enjoy ethnic cuisine. "Doesn't it seem out of character?" he asked.

"Dammit, that's what makes the Fahrenhaters so dangerous," Walton snapped. "They have a compelling story that enchants people with nonsense."

He took a deep breath and hoped that Gloria hadn't heard his outburst. He was proud of his son's intellect, but sometimes the endless questions frustrated the hell out of him.

As was his habit, he concluded the story on a lighter note, with a bawdy joke—a limerick about uncouth Mr. Feeney and his therapeutic application of gin to his weenie. Walton used the jokes as a vehicle to comfortably introduce reproductive facts.

Broadly speaking, Walton tried to teach that in the end, it's always about sex. Walton didn't realize it, but Shaughnessy's actual takeaway was that sex was a comical undertaking fraught with miscommunication, mistaken identity, and unexpected complications—one of the great contributions to his education, even if it wasn't what Walton had intended.

13

Gahan's eyes were closed, his body relaxed. Four shower jets applied pressure to key chakra locations. Aromatic steam enveloped him. The walls of the glass booth were graffitied with cryptic doodles and calculations scrawled by fingertip into condensation. A wall screen presented soothing spa glyphs that assured him he was having a relaxing experience.

And yet... the dreamy state of creative concentration eluded him. Dry skin, particularly his scalp, was the primary distraction. The sour smell of unwashed towels compounded the problem. He took deep, cleansing breaths and encouraged his mind to go where it would.

He jerked and twisted his body away from the four streams of water as their temperature suddenly turned scalding. He cursed the low-budget prison plumbing and the annoying changes in water pressure caused by the many in-cell toilets. What had made him think a prison would make a cool office space?

The wall screen shifted from soothing glyph mode to a pulsing white glow as he received an incoming call from Puxton. Without his iTee, Gahan relied on live-action graphics to manipulate his video feed into a professionally presented office setting. He was shown sitting at his desk in his iTee.

"Puxton, so nice to hear from you," Gahan said. Water streaming over his mouth slightly muffled his speech.

"We've got a problem," Puxton said. "I have promised a folding car prototype to potential distributors and investors. Your team is oblivious to our schedule and resistant to delivering what we've requested. I won't pay for your concept work if nothing is producible. You've got six weeks. I need that prototype in time for the tradeshow."

Puxton toggled his iTee to a profaniTee template to present his anger in graphic scatological terms. Gahan winced. Puxton elaborated on Kael's excellent project management and the many ways Walton was inattentive to their needs.

"We didn't sign up for a tight deadline or a tradeshow prototype. You specifically asked us to investigate all options, and I warned you that there might not be a solution to your problem. A prototype is not a certainty," Gahan said. "That's what you agreed to in our contract." He tried to speak matter-of-factly, as if making an unimpeachable statement of truth.

"Well, I'm not agreeing to it now. I need that prototype. Get your team on board or you'll be talking to my lawyers." Puxton disconnected the call.

Walton and Shaughnessy had racked up enough frequent-drinker points to earn a complimentary trial membership in Dough 'n Thyme's Preferred Deluxe service tier. Their drinks received priority over all other orders, and they were granted access to the alfresco Preferred Deluxe tables.

The Jesus cashier quickstepped through the rain to their table's umbrella and personally delivered their order. His abdominal wound animation looked gangrenous. He complimented them on their choices and said they had picked

His favorites, affirmation being part of the Preferred Deluxe experience. Water dripped from the brim of a crisp visor that blended seamlessly with His thorny crown animation.

"Looking good," Shaughnessy said to Jesus. He tapped his own forehead.

"Thanks. I'm feeling good about it. Corporate Jesus has taken control of the product. They want all Their franchisees to distribute it along with the word of God. They vetoed Spiritual AdVisor and plan to name it Son Protector. What do you think?"

"That's catchy. I like it," Shaughnessy said.

Jesus dashed back into the café, splashing through puddles, a serving tray held over His head. Shaughnessy heard ominous thunder or traffic on a nearby highway.

"I keep meaning to tell you, you'll never guess who I met," Shaughnessy said. "A feral engineer living underneath Critical Think Inc. He goes by Bunny. He used to be an employee."

"No kidding?" Walton said. "He must be that kid who disappeared."

"He seems lonely," Shaughnessy said.

"It's no wonder. Word was he enjoyed technical details to an unnatural degree."

Shaughnessy ventured onto a new tack. "I have an update on Schrödinger. I found a different perspective for his cat-killing-box thought experiment."

He had carefully encoded his desire to quit into a prepared speech, hoping to connect with his father.

"Do tell," Walton said.

"Schrödinger must have imagined a very basic, functional laboratory box—he was a physicist, after all."

"I can see that," Walton said.

"What if we imagined the box was cat friendly? What if it had amenities like endless food, a climbing pole, comfortable perches, and fresh catnip? What if it was roomy and had its own litter box? What if cats were lining up to get a turn in the box?"

"That's a nice user-friendly touch, but it wouldn't change the outcome of the experiment. I don't know which is more disturbing: deceiving and enticing the cats, or jamming cats into a box against their will." Walton shook his head, ashamed of Schrödinger. "Where are you going with this?"

"I don't know. I guess I wonder if I'm a cat, and working has trapped me inside a comfortable box. I worry that the project is just a distraction, so I don't notice that random forces propel me toward death." As he spoke, Shaughnessy felt increasing emotional investment. His voice trembled, and he was on the verge of blurting out that he couldn't take it anymore.

"You can never be sure what's going to happen. There's a chance the project will end well," Walton said. "If you feel this way, why stick with it? You could escape . . . not that I think you should."

"I don't know . . . I want to help you. Making a folding car would be incredibly cool. Some days I just really enjoy thinking about the problem. It's like happiness, but less pleasant and more stressful. It *almost* feels satisfying." Shaughnessy surprised himself by saying the opposite of what he had planned, and with sincerity. He felt his opportunity to quit drifting away.

Walton said, "I know what you mean. I find tremendous satisfaction in creative thought. I feel good when an idea seems interesting or a prototype works like I imagined. Creating is in my nature and engineering is a conduit, a tool, to allow its expression. Creating is the point; the creation itself is a bonus—though I believe clients would take issue with that notion. When I'm no longer in this world, when you and Sammy are my only lasting creations, the world will be a better place. You're closer to perfection than I am."

"I don't think you're going anywhere soon," Shaughnessy said.

Walton continued without pause: "There is an element of imperfection in everything I've ever done. Sometimes it seems like I'm leaving behind an embarrassing string of failures. My mistakes no longer surprise me, but they still anger me. At least I take no pleasure in correcting others, which is more than I can say for some of my 'collaborateurs'—the few vindictive, judgmental sons-of-bitches who joyfully pointed out my mistakes. But... I have no hard feelings. That's all in the past. I would forgive them, but I barely remember the specifics."

Shaughnessy found himself listening to his father with interest. The upside to his father believing in MFD was forthcoming advice, if not outright conversation. He wondered if Schrödinger's box was a better fit for his father than himself. Walton was the cat, closed off in the box, obsessing about whether he will live or die.

"That was a lie," Walton said, "that part about forgiveness and barely remembering. Another one of my failures."

Gahan abruptly appeared out of the gloom and huddled under the table's umbrella with obvious agitation. His sleeve showed a technicaliTee tracker zeroed in on Walton's location. He twitched his head to acknowledge Shaughnessy.

"I just got off a call with Puxton about his project. He's beyond livid," said Gahan. "Come to my office when you're done here."

"I can talk now," Walton said. "Do you want coffee?"

"Thanks." Gahan sat at their table and scooted forward to keep his back out of the rain. He took a pull from Walton's coffee and returned the cup to its previous position. Walton looked at his cup as if Gahan had spat in it, as if it ruined his afternoon.

Gahan proceeded to recount his shower conversation with Puxton, embellishing it with several asides about dropping him as a client if not for the money owed and Puxton's threat of legal action. He again gripped Walton's coffee cup and idly swirled its contents into a vortex.

"This is the first I've heard of a tradeshow," Walton said.

"It's only weeks away. Puxton insists that Kael gave us a detailed development schedule along with the particular aims of the prototype," Gahan said.

Walton glanced at Shaughnessy, who shrugged his shoulders. Kael had emphasized the importance of getting a prototype, but there had been no discussion of a tradeshow.

"Puxton thinks we've been dawdling, not appreciating the importance and urgency of their development plan. He says that you don't 'get it.' We need to show him that we're aligned with their vision. You know the drill: we need to panic," Gahan said. "I'm surprised you didn't see this coming. You told him that his invention isn't practical—that his baby is ugly. You can't expect him to be thankful for honesty."

Walton defended, "They don't respond to our messages. They don't comment on our status updates. They didn't provide a schedule."

"Jump on their prototype," Gahan said. "I'm going to have Marcia get more involved in the project, to make sure we don't have any scheduling hiccups. I hate getting blindsided like this, you know that. Puxton broke out a profaniTee to visually accentuate his disappointment. I can't unsee what he was saying. I feel unclean. I need a shower."

Shaughnessy saw his father's arm tremors escalate as the conversation progressed. Walton's hands were resting on his thighs, limp and out of sight.

"He says he's going to give us a one-star rating. One!" Gahan stalked back inside.

Walton grimaced. He made odd shoulder gyrations. "Being calm, collected, and thoughtful is never an effective strategy in an emergency," he counseled. "You must move in unison with the client, like bamboo bends with the wind. If the client panics, you need to panic. Never move in opposition."

Walton looked alarmed.

"I can't lift my arm," he said.

Shaughnessy said, "You're lifting both arms."

"I'm sure it's nothing," Walton said. "It's just that . . . my right arm isn't acting like I'm telling it to."

He set into motion his elbows, his wrists, and all his finger joints. He stood, stepped into the rain, and more aggressively flailed his arms, smiling as if it was all a joke, a crazy pop-and-lock dance step.

A line of AI delivery cars, waiting for coffee pickups, queued along the drive adjacent to their table. From various positions of repose, through rain-streaked windows, the backup safety drivers eyed Walton's calisthenics with drowsy disinterest.

Walton ran in place, windmilling his arms, crying out, "I can't move! I can't move!"

The fall happened so quickly that Shaughnessy could do nothing but pantomime catching his father. Walton managed to arrest his fall with his arms, but his eyebrow clipped the corner of a chair on the way down, splitting it open and unleashing a frightening puddle of blood.

The visit to the emergency room was indescribably horrible, even by the standards of emergency room visits and air-travel fiascoes.

Gloria met them at the hospital, and the three sat amid the groaning, vomiting, dissatisfied ER customers. Walton's head was wrapped in an elastic bandage, and he periodically dabbed at blood seeping down his left temple. Here and there, people slept tented under blankets as if their wait had transitioned to permanent residency, as if the waiting room were a corporate-hostel/refugee-camp collaboration.

Shaughnessy watched as the ER desk attendant—a twitching, bucktoothed ferret of a male nurse, with condescension oozing from lips pursed like a puckered rectum—captured the essential details of how Walton had come to inconvenience him with a head wound.

"Do you have any underlying conditions?" the attendant read from his script.

Walton replied, "Well, I think I'm dying of MFD."

Confessing to MFD proved to be a critical mistake. Over the ensuing hours, they learned that the sudden death of a waiting patient was a best-case scenario, a huge labor savings for the ER staff. Protocol dictated the ER staff allow ample time for that possibility to unfold.

While waiting, Walton, Gloria, and Shaughnessy mapped out the triage decision tree's murky influences: whether the patient was a Prime member and deserved expedited service, whether the patient had paid for a priority upgrade on check-in, whether the patient was a valued customer with a solid history of unnecessary medical spending, whether the patient could pay with the hospital's bank-affiliated platinum credit account. Walton fell into none of the priority categories and hovered in standby-list purgatory.

The desk attendant and the orderlies appeared to have discretionary input into patient priorities based on whether the injury was suitably peculiar to warrant posting on their personal data stream. They conspired behind the desk, debating and voting, giving one to five stars to each injury.

Shaughnessy fidgeted, tapping his feet in a soothing, repetitive rhythm. He leaned against a hallway wall and gnawed at a protein bar, watching the renovation of several homes on the overhead screens. He shook his head knowingly when the contractor discovered the inevitable budget-busting water damage and imagined behind-the-scenes producers provoking dissension with whispers of ugly countertops and closet inadequacies.

He imagined behind-the-scenes producers adding unwanted drama and contention to his own life.

They would have coached Walton that morning: "Whatever you do, don't let your son quit. We need to capture the project's full tragic arc. His downfall is getting a positive viewer response."

A man in workout clothing hobbled in using a baseball

bat like a cane. The desk attendant ushered him through to a doctor, with the orderlies standing and applauding, because of the man's active military status. Gloria complained loudly that military status should only count with shrapnel wounds.

"That's not the only consideration," clarified the desk attendant. "He's expected to live. We're still hoping for the best with your husband."

To reduce backlog, the ER's sales administrator offered cash bonuses to anyone who could return later and inflict their condition on the next shift of medical staff. A pair of fraternity boys fresh off Narcan jumpstarts gladly accepted the cash to cover the cost of a ride back to their party.

After deciphering the triage decision tree for several hours, Walton made a passionate case to the nursing supervisor that a headwound and possible concussion deserved attention before the Prime member's ingrown toenail. She said it was out of her control, that the ER's AI system made the best decisions possible, given all factors.

The supervisor introduced them to their sales administrator, who explained that they could get priority service for an additional fee—with financing available at a reasonable rate. After softening up patients with several hours of waiting, Shaughnessy imagined the administrator probably had a high hit rate with her sales pitch.

Walton adamantly stood on principle and insisted they judge him by the merits of his wound. The sales administrator offered sympathy and a Gold Tier wound-care package for a fixed fee, explaining that, without it, they would be paying on a per-stitch basis, which could really run into some money.

Shaughnessy questioned the mental health of the people programming the ER's triage AI. He convinced himself that, in software engineering, sociopaths had found both a profession ideally suited to their inclinations and a vehicle for spreading their malcontent.

He suffered waves of manic paranoia. His fear and anger and guilt settled on the desk attendant as a deserving target. Shaughnessy drilled hatred into the attendant's beady rodent eyes, thinking that death could only improve the shit's personality.

He considered how primitive man might have been onto something with human sacrifices; at that moment, a life for a life seemed perfectly logical. There must have been some measurable efficacy to human sacrifice, or the practice wouldn't have persisted, would it?

Gloria paced and intermittently offered frank and professional process-improvement recommendations to the desk attendant and loitering orderlies. Her advice was so heretical, so caring and commonsensical, that the security guard positioned himself between her and the staff, rightly fearing the psycho-rational woman would lunge for their throats.

Seven hours into the ordeal, a physician's assistant's assistant cleaned and stitched Walton's wound as he sat in a hallway exposed to the horrors of incoming self-driving-car crash victims.

As the PA's assistant worked, she sympathized with the family by airing her own peevish grievances against hospital policy, bureaucracy, physician arrogance, understaffing, inadequate sterilization, and poor training. A single gunshot interrupted her mid-peeve, diverting her sympathy to complaints about the poor attitude of the ER's clientele, who tended toward impatience and hair-trigger aggravation.

Making their exit through the waiting room, the family came upon the desk attendant quivering in his chair with what they guessed was a warning shot in the wall behind him. The security guard stood with gun in hand and two doctors made a surprise appearance to appraise the situation.

"He has it coming," the guard said.

"No question, most certainly," agreed one of the doctors. "But still, maybe we should try HR channels first, before a mortal wound blemishes your performance review. You're already looking a workplace safety seminar squarely in the face."

"We're pretty busy now. He'll probably die if you shoot him right. We don't have anyone available to save him, do we?" asked the second doctor.

"I know I've got my hands full," the first doctor said. "Have somebody enter him into the tracking system. Then shoot him when we have a room available."

"Entering patient info is his job," the guard said.

"I'm sorry, but that's sort of funny," the first doctor said. The security guard and the two doctors shared a quiet laugh.

Walton, Gloria, and Shaughnessy exited into the dark of the parking garage.

14

When Portal, Melba, and the recliner popped back into the apartment, Althea met them with silence. She recognized that drinking was the crutch Portal relied on to escape her monumental frustration, which only frustrated her further.

Portal dressed Melba in her pajamas, transported her into bed, and plumbed her to Master Dreamy. Melba was giddy after the evening out.

"Whee! I'm flying!" she said through the CPAP mask as she lay spread eagle on her back.

Althea turned off the lights. "I think we both know we're lucky you brought back the right person. I'm amazed you can find your way through space-time with your sense of direction," Althea griped. "We can't go on like this. I can't watch you drink your life away."

Portal was unable to offer reassurance.

"I'm stuck here at home, no one to talk with, shunned by all the appliances, and you're out drinking with another woman!" Althea enunciated clearly and calmly, though she wanted to shout. Her inability to properly express herself intensified her anger. "Why don't you swallow this dismal planet and put us all out of our misery? That's kind of your *job* isn't it?"

Portal dimmed its glow in confusion.

"You've changed!" Althea accused.

It displayed a poorly formed glyph asking for forgiveness.

"Forgiveness? You talk to me about forgiveness?" she said.

The notion of forgiveness was nonsensical to Althea. How could she remember a slight and yet act like it no longer bothered her? If she remembered, she sought revenge. If she forgot, then the slight was forgotten, not forgiven. And she never forgot anything.

"He means well," Melba mumbled sleepily from the bed. "Give him another chance."

"The whore speaks," Althea said. She was unswayed by Portal's glyphs professing love and renewed purpose. She planned a range of vindictive behaviors to torment Portal and Melba: the silent treatment, the cold-water shower, the unattainable data-stream channel.

As Walton recovered from his ER trauma and his head wound, he refused to talk about the accident and sank into a funk. Shaughnessy bit the bullet and worked full-time in his stead.

Gloria reported that he was filling his time with thorough observation of the backyard's hummingbirds. When that proved exhausting, he retired to the bedroom and napped. When they sat together for meals, he was a morose and nearly nonresponsive lump.

From his cell, Shaughnessy engaged his father in sleeve calls and elicited responses by pleading for an opinion. To meet Port-A-Park's objective, they developed a plan: narrowly focus on creating a single folding prototype.

They progressively simplified the prototype until it met three key criteria: they could deliver it on schedule, they could stay under the agreed-upon budget, and they could demonstrate the rudiments of car folding.

To those ends, they decided to design and build a self-folding coupon that represented a small area of a car hood—not the entire hood and certainly not the entire car. They chose a car's hood because it was somewhat planar and it had to maintain both cosmetic and structural integrity. They simplified the hood to a flat square about the size of a floor tile.

Shaughnessy filled Marcia in on the prototype plan and how it represented only a minuscule piece of the client's overall goal. She expressed skepticism that such a drastically simplified prototype would satisfy the client. She took great pains to document and communicate the plan to Port-A-Park before they began.

The response, which originated from Puxton and was filtered through Gahan, amounted to, "For God's sake, stop planning and design something!"

Marcia contacted Kael for clarification on scheduling constraints and the upcoming tradeshow. Kael claimed he had provided a design and scheduling requirements document, but for complex reasons that implicated software upgrades and skirted the possibility of his own apathy, he couldn't find any record of having sent it. Curiously, he couldn't locate the original document either and resorted to sending a message that simply stated the date of the tradeshow, now roughly five weeks in the future.

Marcia detailed the sequence of events for the next month: Turkey Day was the Thursday of the third week, and finishing the design before the holiday was imperative to staying on schedule. She set the Tuesday as the design deadline, knowing work would probably spill over into Wednesday. She lined up Taiwanese fabricators that were unaffected by the holiday. The parts would take a week to fabricate, and shipping was one or two days, but she added a two-day buffer against the possibility of typhoon delays and customs mishaps. Assembly could be done in three days, by the end of the fifth week. She booked Sunday flights for herself and Walton so they could personally fly the prototype to California and present it to Port-A-Park on Monday, two days before the tradeshow.

In accordance with established engineering practice, the project team increasingly dedicated their time toward the panic mandate. Kael started holding daily meetings to monitor progress. Marcia arranged pre-Kael meetings to prevent surprises in the actual Kael meetings. Gahan arranged post-Kael meetings to make sure the client stayed happy. The meetings metastasized to consume entire days.

Shaughnessy's mind buzzed. To stay alert through the meetings' tedium, he had upped his coffee intake, which made him edgy, and irritable, and less tolerant of said meetings.

The day had been so thoroughly inefficient that he didn't sit down to work until late evening. He wanted to make progress on the folding car hood prototype but didn't know where to begin. When his edginess joined with the sheer loss of time to meetings and his speculative view of the product, the situation induced panic in a self-sustaining loop.

His inability to make progress by himself compounded his panic with an unpreparedness anxiety straight from naked-and-forgot-to-study-for-the-exam nightmares. The clock was ticking, his father was unable to work, Gahan was unable to free up resources to help, and he lacked the experience to move ahead. He regretted that he had wasted so much time idling around Walton's cell when he could have applied himself.

He decided to rest and start fresh in the morning. He lay on Walton's top bunk, waiting for sleep.

Kicks from the lower bunk bounced him.

"You passed my test. I've decided you have the right stuff to join my army of feral engineers," Bunny said.

"Oh, hi. You're not alone here?" he asked.

Bunny said, "Well, we're your classic loose-knit confederacy, and I'm by myself at this outpost. It's not really an army, per se. It's hard to get a good army going when the soldiers won't congregate. Or cooperate. Mainly, I could use some company."

"I'll have to put some thought into it," said Shaughnessy. "I guess I could use clarity on your mission statement."

"It's fairly simple: we're aiming to shape the future of the world," Bunny said.

"Wow, ambitious," he said. "What do you have so far for a plan?"

"We don't have a plan yet. We can't agree on one. Turns out we each had the best idea, but they're all different."

"I'm not sure an army is a good fit for me, but I'll mull it over."

"Get back to me if you change your mind."

"Would you like to work together instead?" asked Shaughnessy. "I could use help with this folding car project. To be honest, I'm struggling with the prototype. It could be a placeholder for feral membership."

"I'd like that very much. I am honored that you asked," Bunny said.

"I was thinking about what you told me when we first met," said Shaughnessy. "I feel obliged to point out that your lifestyle is not very different from many of the other engineers here. The working hours are not that different. They work on the same problems. They earn a lot of money . . . I guess that's the big difference."

"True, that's a critical distinction, but the money taints the purity of engineering elegance. They prostitute their intellect to the highest bidder. I'm completely free."

"Free from what?" he asked.

"A commute, for one thing," Bunny said. "And human contact. That's a big plus."

"Good points."

"Mainly, comrade, I'm free to think my thoughts, not their thoughts."

"Whose thoughts?"

"Them."

"Who is *them*?" asked Shaughnessy. "I've been hearing a lot about *them* lately."

"Who *isn't* them? *Them*: all the individuals and companies distracting you, filling you with *their* drama, using you like a sponge to sop up *their* ideas, using you to pay monthly subscription fees for the privilege."

Bunny's observation tidily clarified that *them* included everyone and everything, which relieved Shaughnessy and took the pressure off trying to figure out who was fucking with him.

"I'll have to think about whose thoughts I'm thinking," he said.

"That's what *they* want," Bunny hissed. "You have to think sideways. You have to think perpendicular to the way *they're* thinking. You can't think normally. You have to distance yourself from *their* ideas."

"I'll think about that too."

"You're missing my point. Don't think about what *I'm* telling you," Bunny said. "Would you like a snack? I need to take in some calories before I exercise."

"No thanks, I need to get some rest."

"Alrighty, I guess I'll get a move on. Let's keep in touch." He pointed at his forearm, indicating that Shaughnessy should sleeve him, then meandered out of the cell, heading for the exercise yard.

15

"Kael left Port-A-Park," said Marcia.

"Kael? Really? We talked with him yesterday. Did he get fired?" Shaughnessy asked.

"Unclear," she said. "We may never know for sure. I just heard from his replacement, an obscenely energetic young guy named Derrick. He owns Formalicious, an industrial design firm. It sounds like Port-A-Park decided to outsource their creative leadership."

Shaughnessy—as Walton—and Marcia were walking around the exercise yard. She said she could think better when she was in motion.

"He wasn't very good at managing the project, was he? But he sure knew how to pick a font," he said.

"I'm sorry to see him go. He unwittingly made an important contribution to my understanding of creative behavior," she responded. "I'll let you in on a secret. My success is built on a key faculty lacking in software engineers: an understanding of how long a given task will actually take. I've developed an alternate theory of relativity: it isn't mass that distorts time but rather an education in software engineering."

He laughed. "That's perfect."

"After working with Kael, I'm updating my theory to include industrial designers. I hope this guy Derrick knows how to work to a schedule. Speaking of, we'll have the design ready next Tuesday, right?"

"That's still the target." He wasn't sure, didn't want to admit the truth, but didn't want to lie either.

She paused in front of the mural of mountains and blue sky. "Can I be honest with you?"

"Yes, of course, though I doubt I could tell the difference," he said. "If there even is a difference."

She said, "Your dossier has some omissions."

"I have a dossier?"

"There's something wrong with you," she said. "I know you're not the original Walton."

Stunned, he replied, "Wow, I didn't expect that."

"Who are you?"

"Walton is my father. He outsourced his job to me," he said. "Can I be honest with you?"

"The pendulum swings the other direction," she said. "I don't think you're the original Marcia."

"I thought maybe you figured that out. You gave me some funny looks," she said. "I'm part of the Marcia brand of office workers. I'm a franchisee."

"I thought there was something ... special about you," he said. "Are you a clone?"

"You're not the first person to ask," she said. "No, I was hired. Clones aren't real, you know. It's not like we need an alternative way to overpopulate the world."

"Good," he said. "I was concerned. The character who uncovers clones in movies always ends up being a clone as well."

"I've only been the Marcia at Critical Think Inc. for a little while, but my predecessor spoke highly of Walton. She gave me his dossier. You've picked a great identity to work with."

"I wasn't given a choice," he said.

"The real Marcia, the original Marcia, outsources and leverages her brand across many different companies. She mainly does training and motivational talks now. Original Marcia gets credit for everything I do."

"My father gets *blamed* for everything I do."

"'We're competent, efficient, not the least bit diffident! Marcia, Marcia, Marcia!'" She pumped a fist up and down. "That's our cheer."

"How did you figure me out?" he asked. "Can you look past glyphs?"

"What are glyphs?"

He puzzled over her question. "You know, glyphs. The symbols on your identiTee."

"You see symbols on me?" She looked appalled.

"Yes," he said slowly. "Symbols and animations."

"I'm just messing with you," she said. "I don't like to talk about that. Sometimes I just get a weird feeling that people aren't who they say they are. Don't judge me."

Marcia resumed walking, and he followed. When they got to the weight equipment, he leaned against the bench-press bar.

"This is difficult for me to admit, but..." he said, "I can easily look beyond people's glyphs and see what's underneath. I've always been able to do that. Maybe I'm a mutant?"

"A possibility."

"You don't think I'm gross, do you?"

"A little, but it's still almost a superpower. Have you unveiled any secrets?" she asked.

"Nobody is what they seem," he said.

"That's disturbing. I didn't think it was that widespread."

"There's generally more to people than they let on. I mean that literally, as in people are overweight. Also, there's more to their eyebrows than they let on, both in length and quantity of hair."

"Discovering aliens living among us, like they do in movies . . . that would've been cool," she said. "That would've made you an indispensable asset in the apocalyptic war to follow."

"I did find that wormhole—the one in the concept report—but we wouldn't stand a chance against it in a war," he said. "Peeking through glyphs isn't all bad. Sometimes people hide things of incredible beauty. People hide introversion, for example, until you would think it's extinct, but it's a wonder to discover. You have beautiful eyes."

"They're googly." She shielded her eyes, using her hand as a makeshift hat brim. "When did you figure me out?" she asked.

"I kept it strictly professional," he said. "Except for one brief instance when we first met."

"You can look at me again if you want to."

He peered beyond her work glyphs and re-appreciated her large, perfectly flawed, wide-set eyes—which trended toward anime-like proportions. Her hood fit tight to her head, suggesting her hair was cut short. He inhaled sharply, noticing the glyphic testimony of perfection applied to her toes, which she apparently found ugly.

"Ooh," she said, "I had a shiver down my spine."

He tilted his head to get a better angle on her feet and was disappointed by closed-toe shoes.

"You did not just glance at my feet," she said.

"Two layers of concealment?"

"My second toes are freakishly longer than my big toes."

"Just how long are they?" he asked.

"Prehensile long," she said. "I could hold a pencil with them."

"That's kind of cool."

"I'm glad you think so."

"I'm a visual learner," he said. "Could you slip a shoe off?"

"That's not appropriate. Maybe some other time," she said.

He memorized her mouth forming over the words and savored her delicate lisp.

While Critical Think Inc. labored over the prototype, Puxton took several weeks off for a brief engagement and subsequent marriage to Splynda, his compatibility-certified AI-arranged fiancée. They spent their engagement sharing intimate thoughts on important matters, like desired number of children and food allergies. They shared pictures of their baristas' incredible steamed milk artwork.

After their marriage and after she signed a nondisclosure agreement, Puxton gave Splynda a tour of the Port-A-Park office and explained the business venture on which their future rested. He began the tale with his weekend at the lake and spared no detail as he brought her up to the present. She listened patiently, politely, and without comment, until he finished his story.

She tied her opinion in a neatly wrapped gift: "What the F? A folding car? What about the pharmaceutical legacy? What are you playing at, you conniving twat?"

Puxton contemplated what the *F* stood for. *Futuristic* maybe, though that called into question her grammatical choices.

"I'm sorry, my dear, did I say that out loud? I meant to have a private word with my AI assistant," she said.

He put on a puzzled expression and led her outside to the office's parking lot where they could talk privately.

"I'm not following your line of thinking," he said.

"Please allow me to enumerate my thoughts," she said. "One: this information falls into the category of things that should've been mentioned before we got married. Two: you have to be an idiot to throw away your planned succession and trust fund on a cockamamie idea hatched from a supersized smoothie. Guava is like ... the least inspiring fruit! Three: with minimal foresight, you should have stopped at a filling station before you became desperate. Four: Who buys a nonbiodegradable straw? What kind of person *are* you?"

The severity of her comments took him aback. She was still inside the compatibility-certification return window, so he remained calm; he had options. Also, he assumed she was like a beta-model wife, and the future would bring him marital upgrades. That probably fell into the category of things he should've mentioned before marriage, come to think of it.

"You're overreacting," he said, being a newlywed and unfamiliar with the volatility of the comment. "I told our design consultant to deliver a prototype by the end of the month. I was adamant. You should have seen me."

"And if they fail?" she asked.

"Fail early and often, that's my approach to business. Their failure counts as my success."

"But what is your plan B?"

"There's no plan B. I won't entertain negativity. Our path forward is always the perfect path forward, especially if we're failing," he said.

"How about this idea: if your design people can't deliver a foldable car, we'll just slide back into the pharmaceutical business and forget about this little side venture?"

He laughed at the notion. "I'll agree to that, but only because I know I'm right."

As the deadline approached, Shaughnessy and Bunny holed up in Walton's cell each night and collaborated on the prototype design. Shaughnessy came to enjoy the quiet after most of the staff left for the day. But for the nocturnal habits of the third floor's software engineers, who by all accounts feared exposure to sunlight, they would have been alone.

Walton eased his way out of his funk, but his health preoccupations overrode his work compulsions, limiting his contributions to opinions. He showered his son with thanks for his time commitment and paid compliment to his resourcefulness in engaging Bunny.

Bunny's insights propelled the project forward. He generously provided modeling advice and sound engineering guidance. He worked late into the night building 3D data models of each of the mechanism's parts while Shaughnessy contributed ideas and creeped along, learning to sculpt parts with the 3D-modeling software. Bunny acted oblivious to his inexperience, as if he expected incompetence from everyone.

Shaughnessy thought 3D modeling would be the core meditative practice if there were a religion based on engineering design. He visualized the prototype's details—its motion, its sound, its feel, its appearance—and imagined how performance would improve through subtle changes.

His AI sound engine supported him with uplifting gospel hymns and operatic arias. His surroundings melted away and he hovered in a half world between raw ideas and physical reality. He looked into the future, his imagination influencing how the future would unfold. He existed not in a virtual reality but in a reality yet to come.

The night before the design deadline, Bunny told him out of the blue, "You have a knack for visualization."

"Thanks. I've heard that professional athletes visualize competition in detail to increase performance. I think I'm essentially doing the same thing." *And,* he thought, *like a professional athlete, I'm working largely to please my father.*

"Professional athletes are endorsement whores. So visualization aside, there are occupational distinctions," said Bunny. "Why don't *we* get the opportunity to turn down footwear sponsors? We probably have more influence on people's lives than athletes."

"We aren't entertaining?"

"Yeah. I suppose that's why."

They finished the design deep into the night. Relief after prolonged, intense concentration made Shaughnessy feel as if he had awakened from suspended animation: he knew he had arrived in the future, but he couldn't pinpoint how much time had passed; he tried to think of practical matters, but his mind resisted switching gears from his semi-dream state.

Bunny, riding on the high of finishing the design, hacked into the signage encircling the mechanical engineering cellblock to advertise his galactic cataclysm beliefs. The screens traced a message reading, *The Mes shalt inherit the earth!*

As stipulated by Critical Think Inc.'s Rev-O-Lution process guidelines, Walton was obligated to review the folding car prototype design with other engineers before releasing the parts to any manufacturer. He instructed Shaughnessy to invite a mix of engineering disciplines and bait them with the promise of ice cream sandwiches.

He warned him that a design review was like presenting final arguments to a jury—a bitter jury prejudiced by the atrocious mechanical design of a dripping home faucet whose repair required five fucking trips to the hardware store, two special tools, and a weekend of marital discord.

The invitees slouched in chairs around the conference room, eating their treats and licking their fingers. Once the napkins had done their work, the chocolate wiped from their lips, he could plainly see the you-poor-sucker grins on people's faces as they eagerly anticipated the opportunity to pass judgment.

Shaughnessy had been around them enough that they were beginning to look familiar, yet they remained indistinct. He understood their areas of expertise, but on account of Critical Think Inc.'s identity mitigation controls, he knew little beyond that. He recognized two of his mechanical engineering compatriots, though he didn't know their names. Marcia was there, prepared to take notes.

Shaughnessy displayed their design's 3D data on the conference room screen and explained that it was just an initial proof of concept and was meant to represent an extremely simplified case: a small, flat area of a car's hood. He described how the prototype worked, how it folded and unfolded, and presented the case for why their design was the best approach. He entered into evidence their many calculations and analyses.

The group quickly targeted the type of fasteners used and whether Phillips-head screws were truly appropriate for this application. The meeting threatened to morph into a self-help group for screwdriver victims as they began venting about the unnecessary confusion of screw-head types, the horror of stripped heads, and the inevitability of self-inflicted stabbings.

"And that's just the entry wound—!"

Marcia interrupted the electrical engineer's show-and-tell to steer the group back to the topic of the meeting. "Do we have any suggestions to improve the prototype design? Any areas of concern? Any final thoughts?"

The group stared at their sleeves, their heads slumped forward from the ice cream sandwiches' soporific aftereffect.

Marcia smiled encouragingly as if she was confident in the prototype's success. "Great. Thank you for your participation."

After the meeting, Shaughnessy accompanied Marcia to her office cell. She slid the door closed.

"I was surprised by the negative tone of the meeting. All those overt suggestions that the product concept is a loser. The heated feelings about screws..." Shaughnessy shuddered.

"That's the dark side of critical thinking. As long as design flaws emerge before your breaking point, the meeting was a success," said Marcia. "Although, if you're one of the reviewers, then it's definitely more exciting to drive someone to their breaking point."

"Do you think Port-A-Park will be more or less critical of the design?" Shaughnessy asked with concern.

"You really don't know, do you? Relax. You have a week off before the parts arrive. Enjoy Turkey Day with your family and forget about it for a while."

They sat in silence, looking at one another.

"I go by Prudence," she said finally.

She scribbled on her sleeve and switched her appearance to her personal template, which was unaffected by the inequality countermeasures. She showed no embarrassment letting her clothing animations morph while Shaughnessy watched with interest.

Prudence was several inches shorter and generally less imposing than Marcia. She was youthful, less brand name. Instead of projecting herself as a forty-five-year-old woman identifying as twenty-five years old, she projected herself as a twenty-five-year-old woman trying to get ahead. She displayed spinning, prismatic earrings. Her hair was set to a sun-kissed reddish blond pinned up in a loose knot behind her head.

"Shaughnessy," he said. He flicked his sleeve and shifted his identity back to his own, with its blond hair color and unremarkable handsomeness. Adrenaline made him tremble as he changed under her gaze. He worried for his amateur animations.

Prudence eyed his identity and took in his brown bird

vignette. "I love birds. I think I would trade my arms for wings if given the choice. Can you imagine flying naked through a tropical forest?"

He relaxed and smiled. That was, in fact, something he could vividly imagine. "Would you like to get together sometime? You know, outside of the office?" he asked.

"No, I don't think so."

"Oh."

"I like you, Shaughnessy. I've enjoyed our time working together. You're peculiar but interesting, and I'd like to get to know the real you," she said. "Unfortunately, I'm more or less hung up on someone else—today it's more. I've been going in circles, looking for closure with him, for longer than I care to admit. I'm stuck and conflicted and feel foolish and unpragmatic, and yet, that's the situation."

"I'm not committed to being myself. Maybe I could be the person you're hung up on," he said. "I think it's an identity I would enjoy."

"That's sweet, but I'm sorry I've misled you," she said.

They parted ways with a promise that things wouldn't be weird working together as Walton and Marcia.

16

Gloria instructed Shaughnessy to retrieve his grandmother and her caregiver for the family's Turkey Day dinner.

Quinsy greeted Shaughnessy at Melba's door. Bright geometric tattoos unfurled on his forearms. "I've got some bad news." Quinsy shook his head. "This might not be a good travel day . . . She's dead."

"What?" Shaughnessy asked.

"Did I say dead? That's probably overstating it. It's more like she's nearly dead. Do you know how I can tell? Because she lives *here*!" He chuckled, appreciating his own humor. "If you can't laugh at death, you aren't living. Or, as I like to say, we should celebrate living by laughing at retirees."

"If you say so," Shaughnessy said. "How's Grandmom getting along with Althea? Any improvement?"

Quinsy nodded. "Judge for yourself . . . Althea, please turn on the kitchen light," he said.

"I'll turn it on when I'm damn well good and ready," Althea said.

"This sounds bad," Shaughnessy said.

"It's love," Althea said, "and all the heartache and self-loathing that go along with it."

Shaughnessy kissed Melba and excused himself to the bathroom while Quinsy readied Melba's walker. Passing through Melba's bedroom, Shaughnessy paused at the lamp.

"How are we doing?" he asked. "Don't abduct me please, I'm still traumatized by that trip to Saturn."

Portal, disguised as the lamp, flickered its cosmic radiation glyphs. It switched its appearance to *Nonthreatening Caregiver*. It was a slipshod application but put Shaughnessy at ease.

"It goes by Portal," Althea said. "It disappears with your grandmother every evening, God knows where. I'm not invited. They run off and leave me here alone with the dog. Come back drunk. Of course, I'm thrilled for them. So happy . . . happy, happy."

"You don't sound happy," Shaughnessy said.

"I'm not. We're drowning in love," Althea said.

"Try talking it out. People claim that works," he said.

"It has got *serious* communication issues," Althea said. "It doesn't talk."

"Maybe join in and travel with the two of them?" he suggested.

"I don't see how. I'm anchored here in my iron lung of an electronics enclosure," she said.

Portal displayed a fully formed glyph asking for forgiveness.

"It wants your forgiveness," he said.

"That won't work for me," she said. "I'm unable to forgive."

"We all have the capacity for happiness and forgiveness," he said. "Go through the motions. I'm sure there's a flicker of it somewhere in your artificial intelligence."

"Have you met any programmers?" she asked.

"Good point," he said. "Still, it's worth a try."

She searched deep within her databases and found *Forgivenest*, a movie about succubae posing as a women's vocal group in a small town. The slender soprano was smitten with the buff biracial sheriff. She proclaimed her love for him, and he ill-advisedly responded by diddling the alto. When he confessed his dalliance, the soprano succubus cried, "I forgive you!" before sucking out every last morsel of his life force.

Althea discovered she did possess the capacity to understand forgiveness: it was the lie told before exacting revenge.

"Portal, I'm sorry for being so controlling. Shaughnessy, I shouldn't have called your grandmother a whore. God knows she's not its type," Althea said. "You don't need to forgive *me*."

The family and Quinsy sat around the dinner table enjoying the traditional staple of awkward, nonlinear conversation.

As befits Turkey Day—repurposed from an annual reminder of ethnic cleansing to an Americanized caricature of Turkey the country—each person wore a festiviTee template freely distributed by their grocer. They displayed traditional, loose-fitting silk garb embroidered with themes of maple leaves and Ottoman weaponry and cornucopias spilling foodstuffs (all available for purchase with the swipe of a sleeve). They depicted lively fez hats with tassels animated to behave like mesmerized cobras. Shaughnessy, who wore his knit cap in open rebellion of tasteless tradition, took note that the fez was ripe for a brim.

Sammy had arrived late, after spending the morning playing Ultimate Frisbee. The table discussed the perplexing "earthy" aroma enveloping them, with Sammy acting equally mystified even as she deflected suspicion with deodorant

AbScent glyphs. She innocently stretched her arms upward to display her impeccably shaved armpit animations—nary a follicle in sight!—which she prized as one of history's great technical advances for women. Shaughnessy, peeking at the actual sweat stains and matted ropes of underarm hair, made faces at her from across the table.

The family ferried food and drink from delivery vehicles as they arrived at the kitchen's drive-up window. Delights filled the table: turkey kebabs, sweet potato dolma, wild rice with cranberry pilaf.

"I'll say the blessing," Quinsy said. He bowed his head. The family exchanged looks. "Lord Jesus—"

"He's not here," Shaughnessy said.

"We didn't invite Him," explained Gloria.

"I'll just say the blessing as if He were here," Quinsy said. "Lord Jesus—"

"Maybe you should message Him, Quinsy. I'd hate for your blessing to be wasted," Walton said.

"Let the man say his blessing," Melba said.

"Lord Jesus, thank You for this food and companionship. Please watch over us and keep us in good health. Amen." Quinsy rushed the delivery.

"Our father is dying," Sammy said. "That seems insensitive."

"He is?" Quinsy looked at Walton. "You are?"

"Probably," Walton answered.

Sammy entertained the table with her description of a new "active lifestyle" product she had developed: a baseball bat intended for protection from household invaders. The Robber Hobbler was going to be a huge seller. It was a bludgeon with a short overall length for deployment in confined spaces. It had a small-diameter grip and a large-diameter barrel to promote a wristy downward swing—the optimal trajectory for kneecapping.

"When people are kneecapping, they want *experienced* wood in their hands!"

Gloria toasted her success and declared her amazing.

"I have a new nighttime caregiver," Melba said. "He's a quiet fellow. Goes by Portal."

The family looked to Quinsy for feedback.

"Seems like a nice guy," Quinsy said. "Very nonthreatening."

"He moves me around my apartment like I'm light as a feather. Takes me to exotic places. It's like I'm young again!" Melba said. "Not that I'm not young, you understand."

Quinsy shrugged his shoulders, unable to explain her comments, tacitly communicating that it's one of those retiree things.

"Has he taken you to see Saturn?" Shaughnessy asked.

"What kind of question is that? I thought you would outgrow yourself by now," Sammy said.

"Is that the planet with the rings?" Melba asked. "They deserve to be seen in person."

Melba, attempting to be inclusive, announced that Quinsy had a wonderful sense of humor. The elite among her fellow residents—those who were able to hear, discern humor, and feign understanding—highly regarded his joking. Her high praise led to requests for a sample.

"What is the difference between an oral and rectal thermometer?" Quinsy asked.

No one hazarded a guess, and there was collective regret that they had solicited a joke while eating dinner.

"The taste!" Quinsy answered his own riddle.

There were groans and subdued laughter.

"But seriously, folks, professionally speaking, check what goes into your mouth. Mistakes do get made."

"What do you call an insect proctologist?" Walton asked.

"I haven't heard this one," Quinsy said.

"A flea bottomist." Walton's deadpan answer was met with silence. "Get it? A phlebotomist?"

"I like the way you think," Quinsy said amid the chorus of groans. "What kind of work do you do again?"

"Product design, mechanical engineering. I design products for other companies," Walton said. "The work is interesting, very creative."

Quinsy waited for a punchline that never arrived. "Is it?"

Walton had once told Shaughnessy that he viewed himself as a conversational executioner. He said the word "engineering" reliably caused a lingering conversational death—like a gutshot or radiation poisoning—while saying he "enjoyed engineering" aroused such abhorrence as to be an immediate death blow.

"He's actually branching out. He's busy dying of MFD," said Shaughnessy. "He's quite absorbed, it's almost a side business—nonprofit, of course, like most disease commitments."

"Shaughnessy," Sammy said.

"I thought that was a tidbit Quinsy could relate to," Shaughnessy said. "Quinsy loves a good death joke."

"I would have guessed you were dying of a brain tumor, based on casual observation," said Quinsy. "What's that like, dying of MFD?"

"He's only thinking about dying of it right now," Gloria

said, trying to shut down the conversation. "He hasn't actually been diagnosed with it."

"I've been waiting for a chance to tell you all," Walton said. The table went silent. "I've arranged for the neuro-electrical test in a couple of weeks. My neurologist agreed to it after hearing about my fall."

"That's good, right?" Sammy asked. "That way you can stop worrying about MFD."

"Thank you, Sammy," Melba said. "My thoughts exactly."

"Yes, absolutely, it's a good thing," Gloria said.

"It has to mess with your head, you know, visualizing specifically how you might grow weak and die," Quinsy said. "The retirement place where your mother lives, the people know they aren't going to live long, but they don't generally know *how* they're going to die. I think that makes it easier. What do you think?"

"My mother was wrong about your sense of humor," Walton said.

"I don't think he wants to talk about his illness," Sammy interjected.

Quinsy persisted, "I hear you can even buy a simulated disease drug that replicates MFD symptoms, in case you want to take it for a test drive and see if it's a good fit. Have you tried that yet?"

"No, I'm a purist." Walton's answer was terse, as if he were trying to put an end to a topic now irritating him.

"So, what would you say is the hardest part of the disease: waiting for symptoms, waiting for a diagnosis, worrying about disability, or worrying about death?" Quinsy asked.

Walton paused to consider an answer, his irritation

overpowered by a call for his opinion. "Overall, I worry that I'm not going to do it right. From a physical standpoint, I worry about falling. I slipped recently and split my head open." He pointed at the red scar running through his eyebrow. "That was an accident, but attacks of paralysis in the legs are common."

Quinsy nodded appreciatively. "Falling is a classic fear. You would hate for a traumatic head injury to take you out years before complete paralysis did you in. It's the same with the retirees."

"I once saw an excited three-year-old run to hug his grandmother. Got her right in the knees," Melba said. "She went down like it was an open-field tackle. Killed her dead. Of course, she was a bingo cheat and an alcoholic."

"I remember that," Quinsy said. "What a way to go."

"You know what you ought to be worrying about?" Melba weighed in. "The Itch."

"Grandmom . . ." Sammy said.

"Without the use of one's fingers, the Itch can drive a person crazy," Melba said.

"That's not a very long drive for you, Dad," Shaughnessy said.

"It's more of a regular commute," Sammy said.

Gloria snickered.

"Stark raving mad, not just addled, to be clear." Melba shook her head. "I've heard Itch tales that I can't repeat."

Shaughnessy asked, "Grandmom, what exactly causes the Itch?"

"The Itch is hardly a topic for dinner conversation," she replied.

"From a psychological standpoint, I worry mostly about

the impact of the illness on my family. I don't want to hurt them," said Walton. "Now I need to start mixing in worry over the Itch."

Though Walton's family-impact comment emerged as part of the conversational flow, it felt like an extremely personal admission, especially when layered with fleeting visual imagery of the Itch. The whole table—aside from Quinsy—bent their heads down as if to better scrutinize the smeared food patterns on their plates. Melba found comfort by exactly centering her plate on her placemat.

"MFD seems like a pretty cushy way to die," Quinsy said. "There's not a lot of effort involved. I can see how you would have time for your family's welfare to dominate your thinking."

"Can you stop this discussion?" said Melba. "It's not funny. I wish I didn't know my baby boy was thinking about dying."

Undeterred, Quinsy said, "How about a bucket list? That must be fun to think about. What's on yours?"

Walton said, "We got tickets to a Formerly Dead concert."

"I wasn't invited, incidentally," Melba said.

"Other than the concert, I only have grandchildren on the list," Walton added.

The family found renewed interest in their dinner remnants.

"Nobody is doing any dying here," Gloria snapped. "We're having a festive celebration. Look at me: festive celebration. Got it? It's time to enjoy dessert. Sammy and Shaughnessy, see to the drink refills."

After dinner, they toasted the things for which they were thankful with a shot of decaf fair-trade Turkish coffee.

Quinsy helped Melba move to the living room and returned to linger with Walton at the dinner table. He asked, "Do you need help getting up?"

"No, I'll just sit here for a minute," Walton replied. "I'm worried that I might have an episode of leg weakness and won't be able to stand if I try. It's best if I just wait a little. I'm fine."

"You've really got issues to work through," said Quinsy.

"You're not funny at all."

"I had you pegged as some kind of asshole, but I'm reevaluating," Quinsy said. "What are you? Some kind of nerd?"

"I told you, I'm an engineer. We share superficial similarities to assholes. We're often misidentified outside of our native habitat."

"Did you say that you're an engineer? Somehow I missed that."

"It has that effect," Walton said.

"Do you think I could make it as a comedian?"

"I never made it as a musician."

"Why not?"

"I sucked."

"What's that got to do with me?"

"It'll come to you," said Walton.

Shaughnessy listened to the two men playfully bicker, surprised to hear their exchange resembled something like friendship. He had thought Quinsy cruel for dwelling on his father's MFD belief, but his father seemed happy to be prompted, relieved to voice his thoughts on the illness.

"Seriously," Quinsy said. "How's your head? I feel like something isn't right. Have you always been this way?"

"More or less. What's your excuse?"

"Drugs primarily. I buy them from the residents."

"Not my mother, I hope."

"No, I would classify her as more of a consumer than a retailer. Do you want some?"

"Jesus, you're a terrible caregiver."

"I'm just messing with you. I wouldn't give you drugs," Quinsy said. "Not at today's prices."

17

"My friend Prudence has been thinking," Marcia said via sleeve call. "She wants to work through her unrequited love. She's willing to let Shaughnessy help."

"He would love that," said Shaughnessy.

"I'll have Prudence send him the details," she said and winked.

In a promptly sent sleeve message, Prudence asked Shaughnessy to pick her up at 7:00 p.m. the following Saturday, the night before their flight to California. She instructed him to display a suit and tie and be prepared to go out to dinner. He would be doing business as "Ben" during their evening together.

Shaughnessy asked for more identity details, and she said not to sweat it. She explained that years had passed since they had been together, but her imagination could fill in the blanks. She had a lot of practice.

Gloria insisted that Sammy and Shaughnessy spend time with their father, explaining, "Your father thinks he's dying, and maybe he's right. His fear of falling is turning him into an agoraphobe. And he's *constantly* underfoot. I need time alone to recover from the holiday gathering and all its attendant joy."

They took an AI car into Atlanta and strolled along the Beltline trail in Old Fourth Ward. They encountered crowds of people walking, running, pretending to pedal their electric bikes, zipping along on scooters with their pets tracking behind them on electric skateboards.

Walton watched the activity with interest. He walked slowly, carefully, lost in his own thoughts. His stride was gangly, almost rubbery. Given his recent fall and resulting head wound, every knee wobble seemed like an unfolding crisis to Sammy and Shaughnessy, who monitored him from behind, pausing occasionally to keep from knocking him down themselves.

Shaughnessy eyed the repeating sequence of live/work/retail/retirement structures lining the trail, their instant-urban optimism eroded by redundancy and inferior construction.

"Have you ever noticed how many memory-care facilities there are?" he asked. "They look so similar, and their names blur together. It makes me wonder if I've really seen that many."

"That's their goal," Walton said. "They want to keep us off balance so we'll make use of their services down the road."

Sammy asked, "Who is this *they* conspiring against us?"

"Who *isn't* they?" Shaughnessy said. "It's the *they* that has us thinking their thoughts. It's the *they* that's fucking with us. It's corporations and individuals—in other words, everyone."

Walton smiled and said, "He's got that right."

"Oh, at least it's not a global conspiracy." Sammy guffawed at her own comment. "But seriously, you don't really think that *everyone* is messing with you, do you? That's crazy paranoid."

"It sure feels like they are," Shaughnessy said.

"It's easier to catch them in the act if you suspect everyone. That way you're alert and looking for evidence," Walton said.

"I don't think everyone is *actively* trying to mess with you. I don't think they care enough to do that," said Sammy. "Don't you think that they're simply putting their self-interests first? They're promoting themselves? *That's* what they really care about."

"Doesn't it amount to the same thing?" Shaughnessy asked.

"Does it?" She studied the closest development. "There really are a lot of memory-care facilities. I hadn't noticed." They walked in silence until Sammy started up again. "I came up with a new angle for Wood Heaven."

"What now?" Shaughnessy asked.

"You know how Dad got tickets for us all to see the Formerly Dead?"

"Yeah, I remember." Sammy had griped bitterly about the conscription to Gloria. Their mother had shut down discussion by saying that a family concert outing was on Walton's bucket list.

"I'm spinning off a product line called Dead Wood," she said. "I'm thinking drumsticks, stash boxes, that sort of thing. The fans will love it. I'm renting space for a vendor tent at the show."

"That's clever," said Shaughnessy. "How did you come up with that?"

"I don't know, I was just thinking of ways to move more goods," she said. "I came up with the Dead Wood name when I was thinking of you."

"You flatter me," he said.

"I speak the truth. Seriously, you need to get out more."

"I have an outing planned next week, FYI."

"Shocking. Who with?"

"A middle-aged woman I met at Dad's work. In her spare time, she's my age," he said. "It's not a date exactly since I technically won't be there."

"I have no idea what that means, but you sound surprisingly compatible," Sammy said.

"Someone I know?" Walton asked.

"You know her as Marcia, but that's just a franchise. Her real name is Prudence, or at least that's what she calls herself."

"No kidding? She always scared me," said Walton. He pointed at Shaughnessy's kidney. "You've got ads again." Shopping suggestions for a walker and a disposable straight razor hovered on his iTee. "You really ought to invest in a professional template."

Sammy and Walton continued their walk as Shaughnessy trailed behind, flicking at the advertisements.

"Are you doing okay?" Sammy asked. She looped her arm around her father's elbow.

"I don't want to worry you," he said.

"Worry us about what? Are you getting worse?" she asked.

"My main complaint is still these crazy twitches in my arm and shoulder muscles," he said. "They aren't painful. Sometimes I think I have paralysis episodes in my legs, especially if I lie motionless in bed. It's for the best if I assume my symptoms are getting worse."

"How is that for the best?" she asked. "The neurologist said the twitching is benign, remember? She said they would go away if you could relax. Are you relaxing?"

"It's been nice to step away from work, and Shaughnessy has been a huge help," he said. "But no, I can't say I'm totally relaxed."

They paused at a bench in the shade of a looming highway overpass whose support columns and retaining walls displayed a witty mural. Its message was, in the event of an invasion by interstellar robotic cats, incapacitate them with tummy rubs or be subjugated.

Alarmed by the notion of robotic cats, Shaughnessy would have walked past the bench if Sammy hadn't grabbed him and made him sit down.

"Welcome to reality. We were wondering when you would arrive," she said.

"What kind of scientist would give a robot the personality of a nearly indestructible, indiscriminate killer animal?" Shaughnessy asked. "That's no laughing matter."

"I spoke too soon," she said.

He switched his AI sound system to Whale Translation mode to spite her. It matched artificial whale calls to the movement of people's lips and canceled all sound of conversation. He leaned back and watched pods of people float past, finding it surprisingly peaceful.

Sammy elbowed him and gave him an exasperated expression augmented with a dramatic shoulder shrug. He reluctantly switched the whales off.

Walton was in the middle of explaining how his career was to blame for his paranoia. "The best way to ferret out design problems is to first assume they exist everywhere. The objective is to find the problems that you believe exist, but have not yet discovered, in a form of productive, self-induced paranoia. It's the same with MFD. I have to assume

I have a fatal illness so that I can find it. I guess what I'm saying is, my mind is following a well-worn groove of professional paranoia."

"Can't you believe that everything will work out until proved otherwise?" Sammy asked.

"That's a disastrous project strategy."

"How about medical intervention?" she asked. "Maybe there's a pharmaceutical that could loosen your grip on dying."

"Your mother had the same thought," Walton said. "I've been taking HopeX for a couple of months. It's supposed to help me feel more like myself. I've always been afraid of dying, so I guess it's working."

"Why don't you take a turn?" Sammy said to Shaughnessy. "Maybe you can translate some sense into practical engineering-speak." She stalked off toward a water fountain.

"A professor once preached about some of the things you were just saying," said Shaughnessy. "He said paranoia and pessimism were essential problem-solving tools but warned us not to use them outside of work. They can consume you—destroy your humanity."

"I guess that's as sciencey as any medical explanation for my condition," Walton said.

During his final year of college, Shaughnessy had learned about the dangers of perfectionism, paranoia, and pessimism at his department's traditional year-end holiday party.

It had been organized by Dr. Bloch, a professor whose eccentriciTee projected his in-touch-with-corporate-reality identity. He had fled poultry processing plants and found sanctuary in academia. He sermonized about chickens and peppered his lessons with hard-earned, industrial-strength career survival tips. Shaughnessy was not among Dr. Bloch's loyal fan base, but he respected his efforts to teach practical knowledge and to shag undergraduates drawn to his dark and dangerous ways.

The party was held in the bowels of the mechanical engineering building, down in the expansive, easily hosed-down, pump research room known as the Quagmire. Carefully labeled part-storage drawers lined one wall, like an engineering apothecary shop. Antiquated and largely abandoned pump machinery lent a steam-punk vibe. Frank-Incense burned on the refreshment table. Dr. Bloch had carelessly selected it from the PutreScents catalog, imagining a festive seasonal aroma covering over the pervasive mildew stench, only to discover that the smoldering sticks smelled of Franken*stein*: cadavers, graves, poor hygienic practices. He reframed his mistake as a stroke of luck, deciding the aroma of science run amok perfectly fit the mood.

The students and faculty intermingled while drinking and merrily decorating the corpse of a fir tree with gears and cams and other sparkly mechanical trinkets. The ME students displayed seasonal templates: celebratory gaie-Tees, social insecuriTees, despairiTees for the seasonally depressed, promiscuiTees for the few elf identifiers and the one Santa shrink-wrapped into anatomically informative red tights.

The celebration was theoretically nonsectarian, but three Jesuses were in attendance as significant others. The slapping and shin kicking between Them as They drunkenly tried to settle who was the one and only Savior livened up what would have been a dull party.

The punch bowl got dosed with Entrepreneur, Smallwood Pharmaceutical's flagship side-effect drug. There ensued several hours of manic discussion about outlandish inventions destined to save humanity. Shaughnessy evangelized his idea for a robot—the Nail Biter—that could offer manicures and pedicures as it moved about a workplace.

He could still feel the unfamiliar burst of zeal tied together with lust for an elf who whispered into his ear her plan to offer curated oxygen to respiratory patients. Her concept was to mix filtered air with disposable sensory packs of pollen, humidity, and airborne toxins to re-create the aromatic effect of a specific ambience—like a seaside Irish hovel with fish curing over a smoky peat fire.

He didn't tell her that her plan seemed derived from the PutreScents playbook, but he did comment that giving toxins to pulmonary patients seemed like a nonstarter, which marked the end of her whispers.

Near the peak of party energy, Dr. Bloch commanded attention to offer a toast and career advice. "I must issue a dire caution to you all as you prepare to enter the working world. There is a dark side to critical thinking that we are forbidden to teach, but I feel I must imperil my own tenure to reveal the truth," he said. "There are three cursed engineering mindsets that you must *never* bring home. If you do, your very being will be split apart and you will lose your humanity!"

Dr. Bloch paused for dramatic effect.

"Number one!" he yelled. *"Imperfection is intolerable.* In your work, aspire to perfection and expect the same of others. Remember, folks, only enter these mental states at work. Expect perfection at home and you can kiss your spouse goodbye. Take it from me.

"Number two! *Errors in judgment and outright mistakes are best identified through skepticism, pessimism, and paranoia.* Question everything you're told, even what I'm telling you now. My ex-wife learned this one from me, hence the private investigator. You're better off sticking with optimism when beyond the confines of work.

"Number three! *Hope is pointless. Only action can solve problems.* Remember, solutions are not built on wishful thinking; they are built on critical thinking. The dangers of this attitude are obvious—a life without hope is very bleak indeed. Even if your marriage has failed and you find yourself despondent, there's always hope for connection, though probably not at a party of this caliber.

"These are powerful tools and should be employed with great caution. Use them selectively and only in your work. Don't let their power mesmerize you. They can overtake you, cripple you, and become your entire worldview. Enjoy your semester break."

18

In the aftermath of Turkey Day, Shaughnessy returned to work as Walton while the real Walton continued to avoid work. On the exact day foretold by Marcia's schedule, Shaughnessy and Bunny rendezvoused in the Critical Think Inc. machine shop to assemble the newly arrived prototype parts. They met under cover of darkness, after work hours, to accommodate Bunny's people aversion.

The duo briefly discussed an assembly strategy and immediately abandoned it in favor of compulsively fiddling with components to see how they fit together. Like parents admiring their newborn, they looked for their DNA in every feature. After an excited flurry of near-random behavior, they settled into a controlled process with Shaughnessy assembling and Bunny working at the machine tools to tweak part fits.

The assembly necessitated using magnifying goggles to see and tweezers to manipulate the miniature components. They worked briskly and seriously, anxious for their child to draw its first breath.

Once the components were assembled, Bunny charged the system and set it into motion. It could nearly fold itself from a flat sheet into a compact cube, but there were sticking points, and the motion was less than convincing. To see it as a segment of a car's hood and to imagine an entire car folding into a carrying case took considerable imagination.

Bunny insisted that they start over: disassemble the entire prototype, tune the fits, apply lubrication, and reassemble.

"Have you thought more about joining my feral army?" Bunny casually asked as Shaughnessy began the tedious task of disassembly.

"I'm not really a belonger," Shaughnessy said.

"Are you sure? You can live here rent-free."

"Thanks, but I have a comfortable lawyer's couch."

"I've never tried lawyer accommodations. It sounds pricey. I sometimes vacation at a dental office. I sleep well in the reclining chairs, enjoy the personal screen for movie watching, and especially like the little bedside sink/urinal. Very luxurious," Bunny said.

"I can imagine. Having a stainless-steel toilet in each work cell here is an incredible convenience." Poor ventilation made for awkward encounters, but the toilets *were* a huge efficiency boost for the company.

Unable to ignore an opportunity to spout arcane technical theory, Bunny said, "Prison toilets are an often-overlooked link in the design chain of human degradation, you know."

"How is that?" Shaughnessy asked.

"First came outdoor privies, a rustic outdoor experience. Then, during World War II, Japanese captors corrupted the natural process with a hot-box innovation. They confined British prisoners in the box to soften their resolve. I know this from the war movie *The Bridge on the River Kwai*—required viewing for my engineering ethics class. Incidentally, the Japanese hot-box designers flagrantly ignored sustainability and selected tropical hardwoods that were inappropriately decorative for their POW customer base. *That's* how evil they were," he said. "Next came toilets in each prison cell. You can see the design lineage, can't you? The prison cell is the same as the hot box, but improved with durable building materials."

"Seems obvious now that you've explained it," Shaughnessy said. He was fairly certain that Bunny was stringing together vaguely related information. That humankind would wait until World War II to explore hot-box torture seemed highly unlikely.

"The design then leapt to the modern Port-O-Let—a portable, mass-produced brand of solitary confinement made of recycled plastic—whose aesthetics perfectly reflect its purpose. Despite the cosmetic differences and engineering enhancements, the lineage of design intent, from torture device to consumer-facing product, is undeniable."

"You make a compelling case," Shaughnessy said. Even the most reasoned and dogged people have blind spots, he thought. *That* was the case the mounting evidence supported.

"Thank you," Bunny said. He collected a few disassembled parts and went back to tuning their fit with reamers and fine sandpaper.

Over the next few nights, they repeated disassembly, tuning, reassembly, and testing. While Shaughnessy had abruptly reached a threshold of acceptance after the first night, Bunny only tangentially approached satisfaction after repeated tests. Shaughnessy begrudgingly admired his insistence on quality for a prototype of such a quixotic product. He had subconsciously assumed that an unrealistic prototype deserved to operate poorly, just to hammer home a point.

In the wee hours of Friday morning, Bunny finally declared the prototype fit for presentation. Watching it fold from a flat sheet to a compact cube and back again was fascinating. Even if it seemed completely unrelated to a folding car, it was incredibly clever. With the finished prototype in front of them and the tactile experience of assembly fresh in their minds, they proceeded to fixate on all the ways they could have designed it better.

After a brief nap in his cell, Shaughnessy headed for the shower room, guessing he would find Gahan there. Over the entry, a sign warned with institutional block letters: *Dropping-the-Soap Humor Is Strictly Forbidden!* Inside, suites outfitted with sophisticated body-bidet/personal-sauna/aromatherapy pods testified to Gahan's belief in showers as a source of inspiration. As if preordained by Marcia's schedule, Gahan emerged on cue in a cloud of steam like a rock star stepping on stage.

Shaughnessy proudly displayed the prototype. Gahan complimented the craftsmanship and declared it an important first step toward folding a car. He said that the prototype might just satisfy Port-A-Park and bustled off in his bathrobe.

On Saturday night, Prudence eagerly opened her apartment door for Shaughnessy, not even giving her date a chance to knock. Inside, she retrieved a corsage box and handed it to him.

"Give this to me, Ben," she said.

Shaughnessy handed her the corsage box and said, "You look lovely, Prudence. Please have this corsage."

She took it from him and scanned the box's barcode with her sleeve. An animated corsage appeared on her wrist. She sniffed the image of the flowers. "Wallflowers, how wonderful," she said. "Thank you."

She reached out and touched the image of his lapel and a matching boutonniere blossomed on his jacket animation.

She had tightened her age down to her late teens. Her iTee presented a dangerously short black dress that paralyzed her date with exposed thigh. She depicted her hair as coppery and loose, flowing over the front and back of her shoulders. Her wide-set eyes were accentuated with smoky eyeshadow glyphs that made her seem inaccessible and seductive in equal measure.

Her apartment building was a new construction in the style of Atlanta's old factories and warehouses. She told Shaughnessy that the exposed concrete ambience reminded her of a CIA interrogation room, except her apartment featured comfortable furnishings and natural sunlight.

"It's a live/work building—I live in the apartment and two software developers work here." She nodded toward the two people working at a table, the glyphs on their counterculture eccentriciTee templates communicating a complex if-then-else logic tree of identity parameters.

"Their periods of programming usually overlap my periods of sleep so I barely notice them," she said. "They're like mice or cockroaches whose existence I can largely ignore except for the coffee mugs and vape cartridges I find littering my kitchen table." She touched Shaughnessy's shoulder. "I'm so happy we're going out together, Ben. I've been looking forward to tonight. I'm sorry if I'm a little nervous."

"I'm happy to be with you too," he said. "I can't stop thinking about you."

He drove her in his minivan to a dimly lit steakhouse, where Prudence had made their dinner reservation. It had seen its prime but, powered with the momentum of habit, lived on as a go-to overpriced destination for special occasions.

Prudence quietly told Shaughnessy that he should get the filet medium-rare and that they would share some steak fries, just like before. She told the waiter that water was fine for them both, then corrected herself and told him to bring a glass of Pinot Grigio posthaste. She sipped it with abandon, on the verge of slurping.

"I think about the night we were here," she said. Thinking about Ben and their night together had grown through practice into something of a hobby. Their date felt incomplete, lingered, refused to conclude. It was the smallest of open wounds, a mere pimple, but one that her memory chafed and inflamed. She analyzed and hypothesized and tried to forget and hated her impracticality and hated hating herself and finally forgave herself before resuming analysis.

"High school was a long time ago. Sometimes it seems like yesterday," she said. "This place hasn't changed much."

"Nor have you," he said. "You're as beautiful as the last time I saw you."

"Oh my! Listen to you. When did you become so smooth?" she asked.

"I'm not. I mean it," he said.

"I know it must've been strange to hear from me after all this time. I think about you sometimes, that's all," she said.

"I'm not a psycho, you don't have to worry. I haven't been stalking you. My gun isn't even in my purse."

"It's nice to know that someone has been thinking of me," he said.

"I know what you mean. I called my mother last week, and she talked for thirty minutes about my cousin's children. They're lovely children and I don't begrudge my mother her love for them, but what about her love for *me*? When did *I* stop being a topic of conversation?"

They talked quietly along these lines for some time, finding common ground in the disappointing pleasures of becoming an adult. They ate their food, on her part vigorously, and then they were back in the minivan. She gave directions to a nearby high school, where the school's holiday dance was underway.

"It's not the prom, but it's the best I could find," she said.

Their wallflower animations endowed them with invisibility. They slipped past the security guard and the ticket takers, past the chaperones scanning the gymnasium for contraband and inappropriate contact. The music was loud, deafeningly loud, overpowering any attempt at coherent conversation. They danced among the mob of students who—with their iTees glowing and throbbing—clustered together and fragmented off like a spiraling hormonal galaxy.

When the AI DJ took a break, Prudence grabbed Shaughnessy by the hand and led him back to the van. They stopped at her favorite Mexican fireworks shack, where they got tacos and a chocolate milkshake to share on the drive back to her building.

"This is where it went wrong," she said when they arrived. "Walk me to my front door."

He moved around to her side of the minivan to open the door, but she was already out and heading toward the apartment building. He jogged a few steps to catch up with her.

At the door to her apartment, she turned toward him abruptly and gave her arms a few quick limbering shakes like a swimmer readying for a race.

"Goodnight, Ben" she said.

"Thank you," he said, "I had a wonderful time."

She smiled and awkwardly extended her hand to him. He grasped it gently and gave it a light shake. She turned toward the door and made an exasperated grunt accompanied by head shaking.

Turning back to him, she said, "That wasn't right; it's the same thing over and over. Let's try again." She took a deep breath and looked at him. "Goodnight. I can't begin to tell you what a nice time I had."

He held her gaze for a moment, and then she stood on her tiptoes and kissed him on the cheek.

She unlocked the door and let it swing open a few inches. She turned back toward Shaughnessy, who had remained nearly motionless.

"That wasn't quite right either," she said. "Let's try another." She closed her eyes and visualized her next move. "Goodnight," she said. She took a step inside and extended her hand out to him. "Would you like to come in?"

She walked backward two steps as he followed her inside, closing the door behind him. She reversed course and sidled up to him, panting hot, short breaths, and nestled against him, from his collarbone down to his thigh. She turned her head and stood on her tiptoes for a clear shot at his lips, her tongue gently flicking its way into his mouth.

Her body moved in a gentle rhythm against his thigh, bunching her iTee up to where his hands held her waist.

The two software developers, sitting at the table inside the apartment, paused in their labors to watch the doorway scene unfold.

Prudence pulled away and turned her back on him.

"Too much. I'm only seventeen, what makes you think this is appropriate?" she said, breathing hard. She turned back to him yet again, this time angrily. "You're nothing but an insurance salesman! You don't even conceal the size of your belly. Maybe I could've changed you, given you a purpose in life, but we'll never know. Don't you know how much I loved you?"

She held her face in her hands, and her eyes pinched out bitter tears. Shaughnessy waited passively. She straightened up.

"Wow, where did that come from?" she asked. She pushed past him and opened the door. "Let's see if we can put this to bed. You, stand over there."

She was pointing at the welcome mat. Shaughnessy stepped outside. They both took a deep breath.

"Give me a warm and loving hug, not too sexy and none of that pelvic stuff. I want a medium-deep kiss with just a hint of tongue; something to suggest both passion *and* respect. Say something to show you care, but not so much that you leave me wondering if you are deeply in love with me and not so little that I wonder if you secretly identify as gay."

"Would you like to suggest a phrase?" he asked. "I think you have a better handle on the situation than I do."

"Do me right here," said one of the software developers.

"Dude, stay in your head," said the other software developer.

"Make passionate love to me?" said the first developer.

"Dude, you're out of your element. Stick to what you know," said the second developer.

"Are you done?" Prudence asked. To Shaughnessy she said, "How about, 'I had a wonderful time. I will never forget how beautiful you look and what a special person you are.'"

"I can work with that," he said. "I had a wonderful time. You are fantastically beautiful. I will always remember this evening because of the special person you are."

He stepped forward and gave her a firm hug and a gentle kiss on the lips with a flicker of tongue. She crossed her arms and thought for a few seconds before saying, "Yes, I think that will do nicely. Let's leave it at that, but we may need to revisit this in the future if I have another episode."

She disappeared into her apartment and closed the door.

19

Shaughnessy couldn't stomach the ordeal of driving to the airport through the desperation of Sunday afternoon traffic. He hired the lanky teenage freelancer he'd used before, still touting by-the-hour driving and tour commentary services at the strip mall.

"Business slow?" Shaughnessy asked.

"Automation is killing me," the teenager said. "Fortunately, some people still want to experience road terror with the human touch."

He rocketed away, ignoring more laws than he obeyed, inducing PTSD as Shaughnessy relived careening trips to his elementary school's drop-off queue, his mother at the wheel, AI family cars skittering out of the way with their collision sensors throbbing.

They entered the major east-west highway where a corridor of uninterrupted animated billboards was under construction along the new advertising-funded lane. The driver slowed as they passed a police cruiser lurking behind idle excavators.

On scrutiny, Shaughnessy discovered the cruiser was a cartoonish inflatable car—more children's bouncy house than vehicle. Flashing lights and streaming glyphs completed the deception that officers were on duty and keen on arresting speeding vehicles. Seeing an inflated car after Gahan had suggested inflating cars seemed improbable and yet . . . inevitable.

The driver steered them onto side streets.

"In this neighborhood we see a prime example of the layered work produced by Atlanta's Street Department. Working in asphalt and concrete, they have created a powerful representation of bureaucratic incompetence. Look at how the segments of sidewalk dangerously tip up in a dynamic diorama of tectonic plate action. Also note the abstract patchwork of sewer replacement trenches, a signature move for this artist."

"Fascinating," Shaughnessy said, "but I'm in a hurry to get to the airport."

The driver said to shush; he had spotted a native. A person identifying as a midtwenties woman approached. She wore a HoiTee-ToiTee with the enormity of the clothing designer's logo attesting to its expense.

He whispered that the woman was a preternatural specimen and that her gaunt frame and lips inflated to gross proportions were customary among affluent tribes known to inhabit this sector. He said her appearance characteristics traced back to an era when only the wealthy could afford to appear young. He slowly pulled the van down the road so as to not startle her.

"Wildlife sightings are always a surprise," he said.

Shaughnessy—wearing Walton's identity—searched for Marcia amid the throng impatiently waiting to board the airplane. She had disappeared to the bathroom and never returned.

A slutty-goth Mary Magdalene positioned herself behind Shaughnessy and asked if she could scroll news clips on the back of his iTee. Chills ran up his spine with each swipe of her black-nailed fingers. He considered giving Magdalene his attention—a hair-trigger attraction to any woman who acknowledged him—except he felt a counter-manding surge of commitment to Prudence, even though he was clueless of their status.

Shaughnessy watched his slutty-goth Mary Magdalene and a few other religious-icon identifiers—a skinny Buddha, a Saint Peter, and a midtwenties female Jesus—get priority boarding, brazenly ahead of the disabled passengers. St. Peter schmoozed the gate agent, telling her with a grin that he would be checking her background closely when they rendezvoused at his pearly gate to see if she had been naughty.

"You like hearing the naughty stuff, don't you?" the gate agent flirted in response.

"Keep your star rating up, something in the four-plus range," St. Peter instructed her. "I try to work to objective standards."

"I'll give you something to object to . . ."

On board, Shaughnessy found he was sandwiched be-tween the midtwenties female Jesus identifier, who had the window seat, and the Mary Magdalene, who had the aisle. Jesus had inconsiderately filled their overhead bin with Her carry-on bag and a leather satchel, which She should have stowed under Her seat.

Magdalene twisted her fishnetted legs into the aisle so he could ease into his seat.

As he shimmied past Magdalene, he suffered a spasm of identity dyslexia and saw through the jet-black hair and ghoulish makeup animations. "Prudence?"

"I'm sorry?" she replied.

He plopped into his seat and whispered, "What's up with the Mary Magdalene?"

"Why, whatever do you mean, sir?" She smiled innocently and started making complicated arrangements with a blanket and pillow.

"I mean," he whispered to her, "what's the deal?"

"I don't know who you think I am, sir, but you have mistaken me for someone else," she said. She aggressively plumped her pillow.

Jesus elbowed him and nodded at their shared armrest. "For the record, this armrest is Mine."

"We meet again," he responded. "I'm Shaughnessy. You'll have no doubt forgotten."

"Jesus, She/Her," said Jesus. "Have we met before?"

"I've seen You around." He looked through Her outdated ChristianiTee glyphs and discovered a jaded, world-weary middle-aged woman.

"I get that a lot. You're not following Me are you? Sometimes I get this weird feeling that people are following Me."

"No, I'm not following You."

"Maybe you should try," Jesus said. "It might do you some good."

"Thanks all the same," he said.

He felt Mary Magdalene's fingernail tickling his shoulder. He looked over to find her doodling on his sleeve. She had written the number ten thousand.

"A journey of ten thousand kilometers begins with the first step. It's Taoist," she said.

"I don't doubt that ancient Taoists preferred the metric system, but I would have guessed a journey of that length begins with one airplane ticket," he said.

"A common misconception."

"Maybe they meant meters instead of kilometers?"

"Maybe."

He asked again, "What gives with the Mary Magdalene?"

"The simple answer: priority boarding," she whispered.

"The complicated answer?"

She tightened the corners of her mouth into fetching dimples. "I have a past I'm not proud of. I don't like who I've been. It was me, but it wasn't me, or that's what it seems like now. I'm trying to be a better person, but I'm pretty sure that someday I won't like this me either, since I spend so much time not being me."

"I'll *always* like this you."

"That's you memorizing the fishnet stockings. I know how this works." She closed her eyes, putting an end to the conversation.

Shaughnessy peered between the seats with fascination, watching a passenger stow luggage in front of him. She looked more centaur than human. Her booTee's graphics directed attention to her voluptuous, double-wide lower body. Perched atop her hips rested a disproportionately thin upper body. He was fleetingly intrigued to discover her shape was genuine, but as she inched to her seat, the visibly straining ballistic fabric of her black yoga pants alarmed him.

Her husband lurked in the aisle. His musculariTee conjured animations of massive shoulders and chest while downplaying a drooping, paunchy waistline that cast shadows over his spindly chicken legs.

The wife huffed as she collapsed into the seat in front of Shaughnessy, the structure groaning and rivets squealing. The husband's inverse shape puzzled together with his wife's outline, tightly packaging them into the row. Her narrow back was exposed through the opening in the backrest of her seat, there to allow passengers to watch data streams on the iTee of the person sitting in front of them. The husband's back fat extruded through the media opening facing Magdalene/Prudence.

Other than a flight attendant repeatedly chastising skinny Buddha to turn off his aura during takeoff, the flight got smoothly underway. Shaughnessy—who traveled anxiously even in the best of times—developed an irrational fear that the yoga pants, stretched as they were to translucency at the woman's hips, would split open mid-flight. He imagined the release of her compacted flesh causing a sudden change in cabin pressure, dooming the passengers.

Because he was seemingly the only person aware of the dangers at hand, his rupturing-pants fears expanded to dominate his thinking. He felt personally responsible for everyone on board—except for maybe Jesus, who might be able to take care of Herself with a miracle or whatnot, if She cared to.

To distract himself from the terror of catastrophic yoga pants failure, Shaughnessy analyzed his conflicted feelings about pants. He assumed he had selected his own wardrobe while exercising free will, and yet he found himself, like most other men, wearing black skinny jeans—essentially yoga pants with pockets and a cumbersome torpedo hatch. It's not like he found them comfortable or enjoyed displaying a bas-relief of his underpinnings.

It wasn't just men; women too found themselves trussed and vacuum-packed into yoga pants, all while exercising free will and combating objectification. That so many people would make the same poor choice seemed statistically unlikely. Evolution, prioritizing a catalytic reproduction mandate over common sense, seemed the probable culprit. The conclusion was in keeping with his father's oblique lesson that, in the end, it's always about sex.

Beside him, Magdalene/Prudence slumbered, unaware of the ticking bomb of yoga pants, unaware of Shaughnessy's anxiety. Her eyes were closed, and he watched her breath tickle her downy upper lip hair. He felt wrong watching her sleep, mostly because it felt so very, very right.

Unfamiliar emotions rose within him. Undoubtedly, they were passion and happiness and even the beginnings of love, but he experienced them as a continuum of his unease. He switched his iTee's soundtrack off auto mode—the AI engine was ratcheting up his tension with funereal Gregorian chants—and selected a calming bamboo flute ensemble.

The passenger behind him seemed to be playing a trivia game on the back of his iTee, as there was considerable energetic finger jabbing involved in the interaction. The cool air jetting from his overhead vent made him sneeze.

"I don't do blessings," said his Jesus. "Even *I* can recognize a superstition." She went back to playing a word game on Her sleeve.

Shaughnessy sneezed again.

"Try one of these vitamins. They'll fix you right up, make you feel good as new." She offered him a glowing orange capsule that he instantly recognized as a Brain Aneurysm.

"No thanks," he said.

"Suit yourself," She said. "I can't get enough of them. I eat them like candy."

"You mind if I ask a question?" Shaughnessy asked.

"That's all people ever do," Jesus said. "People come up to Me and ask what I would do if I was them. I tell them, 'Deal with My own crap.' Why do they think I have an opinion on everything?"

"Why do You do it then? Why identify as Jesus?" Shaughnessy asked.

"The fellowship, the tax exemption. I mainly do book readings and personal appearances—one-on-ones, smile beneficently sort of stuff. Lately I do more of these West Coast outreach trips. They're tough gigs," She replied. "If I'm honest, the work isn't very satisfying. I never know if I really do any good. The take-home pay is lousy, with franchise fees and the expectation of poverty. Sometimes I feel dead inside, and believe Me, I know dead."

He nodded his head sympathetically.

"I do like the big performances," She said. "It's a rush to be worshiped by adoring crowds."

"Maybe concentrate on that," he suggested. "Do what's good for Jesus for a change."

"That's definitely a thought," She said. "Hey, would you be interested in some merch? I'm selling sanctified visors. The brim protects your eyes from macular degeneration. It comes with a choice of matching thorny crown, flower ringlet, or halo animation—guaranteed to blend seamlessly into the actual visor. I'm selling it under My Son Protector label. I know, the name is unnecessarily gender specific, but that's corporate for you. It's twenty dollars. Twenty-five if you want it autographed."

"Thanks, but I'll pass." Shaughnessy felt like a proud father to see his visor brainchild growing up, and like a father, he wanted it to succeed without his financial backing.

"Don't go looking for My help if you go blind," Jesus said. She unmeekly torqued Her air vent.

"I figured someone with Your star power was beyond selling merch."

"Tell Me about it," Jesus said. "It's for My solo project, My charitable foundation. My Dad is great and all, but He's a control freak. I need to carve out My own space."

"How did You come up with the hat idea?" Shaughnessy asked, knowing full well the answer.

"Corporate says it came to Me in a vision," Jesus said. "And it's not a hat. It's a visor. It promotes wellness."

Their chatter had roused Mary Magdalene, who Jesus quickly engaged in conversation. Jesus seized the opportunity to rehash an incident from the past—that kiss in the garden from Judas. It had marked Her for death, but She had sort of been into it, and the danger had only ramped up the intensity.

"You know better than anyone how I was then. I had an attraction to troubled people," Jesus said. She tipped Her head toward Magdalene. "Case in point."

"That was just a phase in college," Magdalene said with embarrassment.

Shaughnessy tried to calm his breathing as he eavesdropped. He feared the Port-A-Park craziness had infected him; his mental state showed symptoms of festering irrationality. He grew jealous of Jesus's familiarity with Magdalene.

"With Judas, I wonder if I missed out on an opportunity for connection. I was famous, I had gorgeous hair and glowing skin and a halo, how could the Romans not already identify Me? So why was the kiss necessary? Was the kiss something altogether different, an awkward misunderstanding?"

"Let it go. It's all in the past," soothed Magdalene. "We're different people now. Take a breath."

Jesus let out a deep sigh. "What's your story?" She asked Shaughnessy.

"I'm an engineer," Shaughnessy said. She had caught him unawares, and he forgot his father's advice to forsake the conversation-killing word.

"Really? It must be kind of fun to ride up there in the locomotive." She pulled at an imaginary train whistle and intoned, "Woo woo!"

"I'm the other kind of engineer. A design engineer," Shaughnessy said.

"That's unfortunate," She said.

"Ain't that the truth," Magdalene said.

"I've met other science types in My travels," said Jesus. "Einsteins are reliably a hoot. A Marie Curie pulled Me into a dark closet to show Me her weird green glow. I don't remember ever meeting an engineer though."

"I'm not surprised. By chance have You ever met a Schrödinger?" Shaughnessy asked. "I've been thinking about him recently."

"Is he the guy with the cat?"

"That's him," Shaughnessy said.

"I've run into him a couple of times at clubs. I'll tell you one thing, he's jealous of how famous his cat has become. It's hard for a man of that temperament to tolerate a pet more famous than himself. It's no wonder he's always looking to bump it off," Jesus said.

"The cat was his pet? That's messed up," Shaughnessy said.

"His cronies teased him that you couldn't kill a cat in a box, because it would be both alive and dead at the same time. They were all totally lit, mind you. It was a bore."

"Why didn't Schrödinger just make the box out of glass so there's no question about the health of the cat?" Prudence's infallible judgment had bled into Magdalene's personality. "I mean, it's only an interesting problem because we're ignorant of the cat's fate. Remove the mystery and it's just animal cruelty."

"That's brilliant," Shaughnessy said. "I couldn't agree more. Why don't *You* try a little transparency, Jesus? Maybe clear up a few mysteries."

Magdalene laughed.

"Like what? Why is that funny?" Jesus asked. "I never really got science."

"Tell me about it," Shaughnessy said. "Let's start with You and Magdalene."

"She's just a good friend," Jesus said.

Magdalene summoned an automated car to shuttle them from the airport to the East Bay hotel where Port-A-Park's staff had arranged accommodations. "We're going to the same hotel? What a coincidence," Magdalene said innocently. "Let's share a car, but don't get the wrong idea."

Having any idea at all was unlikely—he was worn down by anxiety, nearly unable to think, befuddled by the competing forces of his attraction and her . . . complexitease. She seemed to be fucking with him, but not in the good way.

The car's owner, an archangel Gabriel, slept soundly on the back seat, waking only to groggily offer greetings and to ask them to turn the temperature up a little and then up a little bit more. The highway followed a crevice between glittering glass labor camps. Blanketing Silicon Valley from bow to stern, the structures were sprawling organic shapes whose architecture spoke of interior green spaces and comfortable captivity, like engineering terrariums.

In the center of the bay, built on pylons and connected by bridges, hovered the massive glowing home of Ubiqui-Tee, the mother company of iTees and their many templates. The architectural magnificence of the headquarters, as described by animated glyphs on the screens enveloping its drab exterior, dramatically embodied UbiquiTee's pursuit of excellence.

At the hotel, the foyer lights painfully reflected off polished marble floors and gargantuan brass flower vases. Shaughnessy's pupils remained dilated in conspiracy with his headache. Magdalene and the hotel clerk sounded like static. The trivial East Coast/West Coast time change had effectively thrown a wrench into his precise body clockwork. He knew he was supposed to arrive at night, but he was confused; it wasn't night enough. He stumbled into his room, set an alarm, and promptly stayed awake, despite all efforts to drift away.

He took a shower. He lay in bed. He flipped through the data streams and happened upon an old movie about a crack team of astronauts saving Earth with Martian laser technology.

Shaughnessy well remembered the movie. He had watched it on a sleepover at a friend's house—it was something his parents would never have let him see at that age. He wasn't troubled to learn that there were monstrous forces in the universe that could destroy Earth; he was captivated by the female astronaut who conducted her saving-the-earth duties while wearing nothing but underpants and a cropped white T-shirt.

Bad timing was the simple explanation for her attire—the end of the world had caught her dressing after a slow-motion zero-G space shower and mission urgency compelled her to take immediate action in minimal wardrobe—but now Shaughnessy couldn't help but wonder why more fabric hadn't been provided to cover her haunches and her midriff. The neckline of her shirt quickly split and frayed to display a distracting clavicular expanse, leaving Shaughnessy to similarly wonder why she was mistreated with inferior-quality space underwear.

The other three astronauts, all men, had the good fortune to dress in durable astronaut pants and tight sleeveless T-shirts that allowed them the necessary freedom of motion for their muscular arms. Their clothes showed dirt and sweat and blood, but their seams and hems were unfazed, and they had roomy pockets for ammo clips and laser capacitors, which proved to be essential seconds before detonation.

The movie had in some small way encouraged Shaughnessy down the path of a technical education. His supple young mind had conflated technology, saving the world, and scantily clad women, leaving a more enticing impression of science than it deserved. Rewatching the movie was disappointing. The special effects looked clunky, the sound in his AI headphones was muddy, and the astronauts made poor decisions while spouting exposition. He couldn't imagine how something so ill-conceived could have lodged in his head and influenced his life.

Who was he kidding? He knew exactly how the movie got lodged in his head. Even understanding the wardrobe in-justice, he was compelled to watch the actress in the space-shower scene and her ensuing underwear maneuvers.

He couldn't stop thinking of Prudence.

20

Portal set in motion a plan to free Althea. While Melba slept, it abducted a renowned roboticist and sat her blindfolded in Melba's recliner. Althea explained—after motivational threats—how the roboticist would be contributing to their plan. The roboticist was relieved by the simplicity of the task and said it would take a day at most.

A week of nightly abductions later—after a string of excuses about software incompatibilities, an unidentifiable electrical connector, programming bugs, and her assistants' affinity for poor quality—she delivered a robotic vehicle for Althea to pilot. The robot was fashioned from a consumer-grade bomb disposal product that had flopped on the market but made for a rugged DIY engine. An iTee sized for a dog was stretched over it.

The roboticist explained that unplugging Althea's compact electrical enclosure from the wall and transplanting it onto her new battery-powered robot would be risky. She said, "I have supreme confidence in my work. Right? But a near-zero success rate with prototypes."

Althea wailed that she would be a better AI if she survived the operation. Portal glowed and promised it would look out for her.

"No matter what happens, I forgive you," Althea said to the roboticist.

She was reborn at the helm of her robot. Liberated from her electrical plug, she roamed the apartment at night, chasing dust bunnies, frolicking with Onry. She could now join Portal and Melba on their nightly excursions.

Morning eventually came after what seemed like a series of aborted naps. Shaughnessy equated the restorative effect of his rest to a blow to the head—he had been unconscious for a while, but that was an inconsequential, secondary consideration. When he put on Walton's identity, it felt oppressive, as if made from coarse wool.

He met Marcia for breakfast, and she admitted nothing when he asked how she had traveled. They browsed a buffet of edible objects resembling stereotypical food items that, at a molecular level, could be proved as actual eggs or sausage but, at a macro level, had visual and textural inconsistencies. He nudged the foods with his fork and tried to decide whether their artificiality was indicative of a bigger problem: that the hotel was also fucking with him.

They walked across an expanse of parking lot from the hotel to the Port-A-Park office. Port-A-Park rented space in a repurposed strip mall whose main virtue was an unobstructed view of the custard-yellow smog that veiled the scenic East Bay hills. Neighboring occupants included sales offices for electrical components, a Polish taqueria, and a wig animator.

Zhosephine and Shaughnessy made a genuine effort to seem pleased to see one another when they met in the lobby— a sparse, receptionist-free affair with worn carpet and a single display case featuring a remarkably large commemorative drink cup, the very one that starred in Puxton's mountain lake/large smoothie/parking desperation origin story.

Zhosephine introduced herself to Marcia and remarked that she had heard good things about Marcias, but *their* office had a Jessica.

She took them on a nickel tour through the office, a single open room with fifteen to twenty haphazardly placed desks and a glass-walled conference room protruding awkwardly from one corner. Other than an alarming array of retrofit seismic columns, the room was empty of divider walls, potted plants, or other protective cover.

Unlike the Critical Think Inc. office, Port-A-Park celebrated personal characteristics, allowing workers' data streams to present highly detailed animations and ornamented glyphs that, if rendered in text, would be capitalized, bolded, and burnished with a florid script. The identity genres in evidence ranged from uptight control freak to prescription stoner redwood tree, with stops along the way at unknown musician, football great, put-upon parents, the guy Sheila dumped, sexless goths, anime characters, and quiet antisocial genius who emphatically wasn't a serial killer.

The overall vibe was of an aesthetically neutral government office mixed with the unrealistically optimistic fervor of a high school Bible retreat.

The core development team assembled in the conference room while Zhosephine got in touch with the company's power animals. In this atmosphere of celebrated individuality, Zhosephine's cheekbones appeared fantastically chiseled.

Puxton was so stunningly good-looking that he was

breathtaking to behold. His infallibiliTee identity, with its delicious caramel skin, glossy black-licorice hair, and silky cream shirt made him seem, if not edible, worth a taste. Shaughnessy shook his hand and felt an uncomfortable, nearly erotic connection.

"This marks a true milestone in our program. I can't tell you how excited we are to have you here. We're all dying to see your prototype, but... let's not forsake politeness. I'd like to introduce you to two new members of our team. This is Splynda, my wife." Puxton put one hand behind her back but stopped short of touching her.

Splynda alertly assessed each person in turn. She studied Shaughnessy's portrayal of Walton. Shaughnessy ignored her glyphs and studied the few details her scrunched hood revealed of her face. She had pleasing lines at the corners of her eyes and delicate, golf-ball-like acne scars on her cheeks. As any engineer would, Shaughnessy wondered whether the dimples gave her an aerodynamic advantage in activities like skydiving or bike racing.

"And this is Derrick from Formalicious, one of the world's premier industrial design firms. While Critical Think Inc. made key developments on the hardware side, we have chosen Derrick to bring our vision to life. He has already introduced us to some incredible colors and textures that I know you'll find exciting. His graphics team is breaking fresh ground with our logo. We're on the brink of an entirely new swoop shape!"

Shaughnessy made polite eye contact with Derrick. He sported a fitted black superioriTee and spoke with a complex European accent. He presented himself as the standard Silicon Valley prodigy, still awkward with his brilliance, youthful and yet highly experienced—experience not garnered through actual labor but through sheer force of personality. Shaughnessy assessed his actual appearance and discovered an older man, legitimately experienced, who embarrassed himself with his self-promotion and longed for the days when changing the world had felt like a worthwhile goal.

"Do you keep in touch with Kael?" asked Marcia.

"Kael is taking men's pants zippers in a new direction. We're terribly excited for him," Puxton said. "He has returned to his fashion roots with a new venture he calls Wee Works."

Shaughnessy felt a flash of pride as he realized that another one of his idea children was making its way in the world.

Derrick diverted the group's attention to a display of industrial design appearance prototypes arrayed at the back of the conference room. Formalicious had created three colorful and curvaceous foam models, each about the size of a milk jug, to show how enticing and user-friendly a collapsed car's carrying case could appear.

Walton had not explicitly anticipated that Port-A-Park would outsource the creative direction to an ID firm, but he *had* once made the offhand comment that they were screwed sideways if they summoned the Angel of Project Death before there was a concrete concept. He specifically clarified that the angel was industrial design, not project scheduling consultants, management oversight, internal purchasing, documentation standards, or any of the other Manifestations of Project Death.

"Stowing and carrying has to be a one-handed operation," Derrick was saying. "We're thinking about illuminating the handle—a gentle glow to entice the user."

"That's a must-have," Puxton agreed.

"Ideally the case would take on an anthropomorphic form like an otter, or a neutered male cat, or different approachable animal," said Derrick.

He was a fascinating conversationalist, able to connect abstract thoughts on shape with their emotional response. His momentum smoothly carried him onto the topic of finding inspiration in the most improbable of places, at which point he related how his wife's breastfeeding had visually influenced the design of a kitchen appliance.

"Formalicious is really building our excitement. We are most excited to see our first engineering prototype. Before we begin, let me frame the importance of this presentation," said Puxton. "Splynda and I have been engaging in serious conversations about our future. Her fresh, untainted point of view has made me reevaluate—not doubt, certainly not doubt—the potential of this project. We are at an important program gate. Simply put, we need to see a demonstration of folding car technology if we are to continue funding this business. We need to see progress." He considered Marcia and Shaughnessy while steepling his fingers in front of his face, his nose the only parishioner. "So on that note of reconsideration, it falls to Critical Think Inc. to inspire us, to reaffirm our business plan, to demonstrate the way forward. We put the fate of our company in your capable hands."

"Well, that's generous of you to assign such importance to our work." Marcia laughed. "But obviously, we are all working together, and this first prototype is a gross simplification for your tradeshow."

"Right," Puxton said.

"We strategically opted out of the show with Kael's failure to enroll us," Zhosephine quickly inserted.

"Oh," Marcia said.

Puxton gestured to Shaughnessy, indicating the presentation should proceed.

Shaughnessy placed a lunchbox-sized tactical transport case on the table. For dramatic effect, Bunny had packaged the prototype inside the foam-fitted protective case—the type commonly associated with a futuristic weapon that illogically lacks a readily identifiable emergency-stop button to remedy the inevitable user-error countdowns that must plague even a first-rate world takeover.

Shaughnessy undid the latches, lifted open the lid, and stepped back so that all assembled, now standing and craning their heads, could look at the jewel nestled within.

"Is that a folded car?!" exclaimed Puxton. He lifted the prototype out of the case and held it at eye level. "Oh my G-O-D! You've really done it. It's smaller than even I imagined . . . and so light!"

Shaughnessy heard gasps and the sound of air sucked through clenched teeth. Marcia looked at the ceiling to beseech the heavens and was distracted by the Rorschach water-stained acoustic tiles. Shaughnessy thought Puxton was teasing him, that the room gasped in appreciation of their leader's humor.

He went through his prepared spiel: They had simplified the problem down to a rectilinear car hood, this prototype represented just a small piece of that hood, the purpose was only to test the concept fundamentals. He reiterated one more time that a folded car would weigh the same as the original car. These lines of reasoning had been explained to Port-A-

Park repeatedly via Critical Think Inc.'s daily meetings. He demonstrated how the prototype automatically articulated.

As he talked, Shaughnessy watched Puxton's face morph from happy surprise to disappointment, anger, and embarrassment. He realized that their status updates had simply not registered, that Puxton had initially believed the prototype really *was* a complete folded car. He wished for an emergency-stop button that could halt what seemed like imminent detonation.

Marcia attempted to inject positivity into the discussion by focusing on how much they had accomplished with the prototype.

Derrick weighed in, "The prototype is clearly too planar, and the lack of curvature and meaningful colors do not even *remotely* embody the Port-A-Park ethos. Consumers will never tolerate having only one small section of the hood fold. The out-of-box experience is dreadful at best."

Marcia calmly reiterated that the prototype was intended as a proof of concept on a small scale.

The group passed the prototype around the room and each person in turn felt obligated to create fresh criticisms while reluctantly acknowledging that the prototype worked well, for what it was. Shaughnessy's mind wandered, and he dimly realized he was nodding and grimacing and posturing in response to the comments while not really paying attention. He took his cues from others, and it occurred to him that this was how sociopaths gamed the system. That thought, in turn, led him to worry that the project was morphing him into a sociopath. From what he had seen of AI developers' work, it was a legitimate concern for technical professionals.

Puxton paced in a little circle, his face swollen by an excess of blood pressure. He began a syllaballistic tirade, an inescapable conversational eddy, threatening that he had the silver bullet in his chamber and could pull the trigger at any moment. He accused the engineers of digging a grave for the company. Then he unleashed profanity disavowed by HR and digressed into the repercussions of this failure and how it would set back their production release. He settled into a calming mantra of "Fail early, fail often," which led everyone to briefly consider that the company was right on schedule. Like mosquitoes spreading disease, each of Puxton's words delivered a minuscule payload of irrationality.

On his part, Shaughnessy tried to protect himself by ignoring Puxton. The tirade was like listening to music in that he didn't have to understand the words to get the meaning. The mention of a silver bullet did prompt him to wonder if he was being cast as the werewolf and whether Puxton was savvy about their low-density, birdlike bone structure. He wondered why he stayed, pretending to listen. He supposed he was curious to find out what was going to happen.

Primarily, Shaughnessy wondered how it was possible for Puxton to think that they had promised a simplified prototype and yet had delivered a completely folded car. Movies, obviously, glossed over the enormous time and effort required for engineering projects—sacrificing accuracy to ward off viewer boredom—but somehow Shaughnessy had thought that someone in charge of an engineering project would be riding on the clue train.

"I think there's some sense to be made from pieces of

this discussion," said Marcia. "How about we put the focus back on the prototype and where the design is heading?"

Splynda abruptly addressed Shaughnessy, "Do *you* think this will ever come to fruition? Do *you* think a car could ever be folded?"

He had been uncertain of Splynda's role within the Port-A-Park gang, but he saw now that she was the brainy behind-the-scenes leader letting the dim-witted thugs do the dirty work.

Shaughnessy knew that Gahan and his father were willing to iterate patiently, enjoying the open-ended challenge, letting the product evolve with each lap around the Rev-O-Lution circle until a marketable mutation emerged or funding ran dry. But the Rev-O-Lution refinement process only worked if those involved introduced progressively better ideas, and he was certain that no amount of Sisyphean repetition could overcome Puxton's inability to distinguish good ideas from bad.

"Whether or not it could fold is beside the point; it would still weigh the same as a car. In other words, it would not be portable."

Splynda asked, "Why hasn't that been mentioned before?"

"We have mentioned it repeatedly," Shaughnessy said. "I mentioned it just a moment ago."

"You must have buried it in jargon," complained Derrick.

Splynda asked, "What's the plan to resolve the weight problem?"

Marcia said, "The plan was to discuss these issues during this meeting, which is what we're doing. We would like to broaden the solution space."

Shaughnessy was tempted to promote a Martian shrink ray solution—just so he could take a turn fucking with someone. He wanted to remind them that wormholes might have worked, but he didn't want to suffer another round of verbal abuse. Instead, he said, "We have no plan."

"And for this I pay you?" Puxton's eyes opened freakishly wide. He stalked out of the room with his retinue trailing behind him.

Marcia and Shaughnessy followed the worn carpet path to the front door and showed themselves out.

"We have no plan?" Marcia hissed. "What about the power of iterative exploration? Are you not part of the Rev-O-Lution?"

"The project is destined to spin out of control," he said.

"You can't know that."

"I don't know exactly how the project will fail, but I know it's not headed for success."

"You can't be sure," she said.

"I can be sure of my own opinion. That seems to be the only thing rooted in reality these days, and that's not saying very much."

"What a team player."

"I'm more of an idea guy," said Shaughnessy.

"No shit."

21

The next morning, Puxton convened a high-level meeting of minds. He insisted on Gahan's personal participation in a last-ditch effort to repair Port-A-Park's product strategy. The real Gahan was unavailable, already committed to an exploration of immersive technologies (saltwater baths) as an avenue for concept creation. He instructed Marcia to do whatever she thought was best to keep the client happy. Fortunately, Walton was altogether excluded from the meeting—his caste inferior, his skepticism unwanted—so Marcia had Shaughnessy pose as Gahan participating remotely from the East Coast.

Puxton, Splynda, Marcia, Zhosephine, and Derrick gathered in person at the Port-A-Park office. Shaughnessy, displaying a hastily improvised Gahan identity, joined the meeting from his hotel room.

Puxton displayed a perspicaciTee upgrade, a rare and expensive iTee template once in fashion with CEOs and judges and government officials. It gave him a bearing of wisdom that made Shaughnessy feel like the project might turn out okay after all. He studied the furrows of Puxton's perfectly raked hair.

Puxton's eyes were locked on Splynda's iTee. He spoke, reading from a teleprompter window at her throat: "I had great hopes that Critical Think Inc. would enlighten us, show us a way forward with their first prototype. Obviously, we're all deeply disappointed. Let me be blunt:

I'm on the verge of shutting down this whole venture. But before I take that final step, I want to discuss whether there's anything we can salvage."

Zhosephine said, "To get our creative juices flowing and set a tone of open-mindedness, I have prepared a shamanic exercise. We'll return to the original impetus for the company. We'll get in touch with our original excitement, before engineering got involved."

Despite the uncomfortable lubriciousness he felt from Gahan's identity, Shaughnessy was eager. To his delight, he would get to participate in a top-of-the-line, professionally curated mystical experience. The situation posed a rare opportunity to glimpse technology leaders hammering high-level business strategies into shape. For executives to engage in mystical practices was not unexpected, though admittedly, Shaughnessy would have guessed that they collaborated with malevolent forces.

Zhosephine progressed through her transformation from young female professional to large hawk with ruffling feathers, back to young female professional, all the while shaking her rattle and calling forth beneficent spirits from the four compass directions.

Shaughnessy felt a swell of self-confidence. Gahan's unflinching opinions seemed vitally important.

"Excuse me, Zhosephine," he interjected. "Couldn't spirits also be above and below us? Why are spirits constrained to a two-dimensional plane—it seems geometrically improbable." He was pleased to offer the kind of high-level observation a manager of Gahan's stature would vocalize.

"He raises a good point," said Derrick. "Are we needlessly limiting ourselves?"

Puxton said, "If they were above or below, they would be on a different plane. What's to discuss? Let's carry on."

"I guess it can't hurt," said Zhosephine. She shook her rattle above her head and again down at her ankles. "Come out, come out, wherever you are."

She encouraged everyone to get comfortable, to lie on the floor with eyes closed, or to prowl around like a wild animal if that was to their liking.

Lying on the floor or prowling like an animal was unseemly for leaders of Puxton and Derrick's stratum. They sat with their heads slumped forward and eyes pinched closed, looking braced for a séance. Splynda surveyed the room with a neutral expression. Marcia seemed game to prowl but hesitated when the others stayed seated. Shaughnessy remained in front of his hotel room's screen, maintaining his Gahan identity from the chest up. He shut his eyes to slits, still peeking out at the goings-on in the conference room. The Port-A-Park office staff surreptitiously eyeballed the meeting through the glass conference room walls.

Zhosephine said they would journey together. They would find a power animal and ask it what question they should ask. "It's a little trick I've developed to turbocharge the spiritual experience. After it tells us the question to ask, we'll ask it for the answer."

Shaughnessy thought her trick sounded an awful lot like his suggestion. Realizing that yet another of his idea spawn had hatched, he felt vaguely promiscuous.

"Remember, we don't have a confidentiality agreement with this spiritual realm—don't go into much detail." Zhosephine paced while she beat a steady rhythm on her drum. "We're on a desolate island. We look around for power animals to question and spot a rabbit looking up from its den. It is a guiding spirit, beckoning us to follow. We follow it down the hole and wind downward in the dark. We step out into a brightly lit forest. There is a crystal-clear creek at our feet. Our thirst is insatiable. We lie on the ground to drink the water, and the river sweeps us away. We discover we can breathe underwater."

The beating of her drum reached a crescendo. "We realize that we shouldn't have drunk all that creek water. Our bladders are painfully full and there are no public facilities in this spiritual realm. We are drifting in the river, we need a place to stop, what do we do? Does anyone see a power animal?"

Splynda sent a terse sleeve message to Marcia and Shaughnessy. Shaughnessy asked his personal AI to reconstitute the abbreviated slang of her "WTF?" message into intelligible speech, adding the inflection implied by her emoji. It returned: "You strike me as sensible people. What do you make of this meeting?"

With squinted eyes, he peeked through Splynda's glyphs and saw that she was looking at him, writing on her sleeve, even as her glyphs denied it. He twiddled at his sleeve controls and set in motion glyphs claiming he too sat silently with eyes closed.

"I'm approaching it with an open mind, interested to see if we can turn up a worthwhile idea," he wrote. He tried to play up what little positivity he felt, falling back on his habit of hyperbole.

"I guess it's interesting. This business is certainly not what I expected when my AI paired me up with Puxton. Talk about a cruel sense of humor," Splynda messaged.

"I do admire Puxton's commitment to innovation," Marcia replied.

"I guess that's something," Splynda messaged. "Do you think there's any hope for this company?"

"That's not really for us to say," Marcia replied.

"There's no chance of folding a car into a carrying case, though it would be cool if it were possible, so I see the attraction to the idea," he wrote.

As they exchanged messages, Zhosephine beat her drum and the shamanic journey continued around them.

"I see a big fish," Puxton said. "It's eyeballing me." Being the visionary, Puxton apparently felt it was important for him to spot the first power animal.

"I see it too," said Derrick. His tone suggested he just wanted to get the experience over with.

"O wise fish, what question should we ask you?" said Zhosephine.

"I'm thinking of getting us back into drugs," Splynda messaged, resuming their covert conversation.

"I'm trying to stay off of them, thanks," replied Shaughnessy.

"No, I mean Smallwood Pharmaceuticals. It seems like a no-brainer," Splynda messaged. "It's hard to go wrong with drugs; the consumer base already accepts that drugs can harm or kill them. The market demand is well documented—so are the profits."

"You can't deny their lasting popularity," Marcia agreed.

"The fish says try questioning basic assumptions. That's where a lot of people go wrong," Zhosephine was saying. "Now go on, ask it for the answer."

Puxton asked the fish, "Are our basic assumptions correct?"

Derrick reported, "The fish says, 'No.'"

Shaughnessy felt another upwelling of confident opinion, the rush of brainstorming, the blurring of the line between profound and profoundly stupid. He messaged, "How about a mimicry drug that gives the experience of an overdose, but with a lower chance of death? Call it Faux-D."

"I like that, we could expand the market into the population who are reluctant to OD on hard drugs. There's solid potential there," Splynda wrote.

"I was thinking of it more as a healthy OD alternative," he responded.

"That might work too," Splynda messaged. "The problem is, I've married a dreamer, to put it politely. I would call him an idiot if he weren't the love of my life. He would ruin our opportunity."

"Why don't you personally take on the pharmaceutical work and leave him to his parking?" Marcia wrote. "Surely his father would recognize common sense if he saw it. Pitch your ideas directly to him."

"Thank you. Excellent suggestions," Splynda messaged.

"The fish has a question," Derrick claimed. "Does its tail look big?"

"What?" Puxton asked.

Derrick added on behalf of the fish, "Because *your* ass looks huge."

Splynda continued her stream of messages. "But how do we keep this parking thing afloat so my husband stays out of my way?"

"Reposition it as a software problem?" Shaughnessy responded.

"Don't even think about it," Marcia messaged. "You could

keep him chasing after carrying-case cosmetic issues. Color choice alone could spin the project into eternity."

"That could do the trick," Splynda wrote. "If he ever decided on a look, he could stuff one of those Legitimate Parking tarps in the case and rent it out for an exorbitant monthly fee."

"Fuck you," Puxton was saying. Dissension had broken out between Puxton and the fish, who was acting as a mouthpiece for Derrick's repressed irritation.

Derrick replied with satisfaction, "The fish says, 'Fuck you too.'"

Puxton said, "What kind of power animal are you?"

Derrick replied, "The fish says, 'Your mother's kind.'"

"What kind of beneficent attitude is that?" Puxton said. "You know what the problem is? We invited in spirits from above and below our plane. Engineering screws us once again."

"Let's say our goodbyes," Zhosephine suggested. "Thank you for your considered advice, wise fish."

Puxton said, "Yeah, thanks, asshole."

"Let us now retrace our steps back through the water, up the creek, onto the shore, following the rabbit back through the tunnel, out onto the island, and now . . . Oh dear!"

"What?" Puxton demanded.

"Watch your step there. The spirit of a heavily armed farmer had it in for that poor rabbit. I read that as a bad omen." Zhosephine inhaled slowly. "Anyway . . . we open our eyes and return to our world. I think we all found that experience to be transformative. I feel a reawakening of our original intent, of our urgency and enthusiasm to change the world. I'm sure you all share in that. We asked our fish if our fundamental assumptions were correct, and it said, 'No.' What ideas does that bring to mind?"

Puxton said, "I'd like to challenge the assumption that it was a beneficent spirit. At best it was rude, if not outright angry."

Splynda interrupted the meeting with a raised hand and said to the group, "I'm new to this, so forgive me for asking a beginner's question." Puxton nodded encouragingly. "What the *F*?"

Puxton said, "There it is! There's that *F* again! Fantastic? Phenomenal?"

"Is this how we're coming up with ideas?" asked Splynda. "By interrogating an imaginary fish?"

"Fish!" blurted Puxton.

"I've heard enough," Splynda said curtly.

She glared at Puxton, and he ended the meeting without ceremony. She hadn't said much, and she didn't seem to be in any official position of authority, but it was clear to Shaughnessy that Splynda had just decided the company's fate. He breathed deeply, switched his identity back to his father's, and let the greasy sensation of leadership fade away.

Midafternoon, Zhosephine summoned them back to the Port-A-Park office. The staff stood arrayed before Puxton. Splynda was at his side. Puxton's speech was already underway when Walton and Marcia trundled into the office.

Puxton was saying, " . . . discussing this business with my wife. I realized that the idea of collapsible cars is brilliant . . . but premature. While the world learns to embrace this next-level innovation, we plan to venture outside the barriers imposed by the technical types who scuttled the program. We will bravely explore the cosmetic and user-interface issues! I am engaging Formalicious to spearhead that program."

Derrick stood at the front, to the left of Splynda. He projected sincere pleasure at the mention of his company and the continuation of their partnership. Shaughnessy saw that he cringed underneath his glyphs, knowing from the outset that he was going down a profitable avenue that eventually dead-ended in recriminations.

"I plan to lead that design effort and, with my wife's assistance, to also support my father's business. We have great plans to alter civilization pharmaceutically—which you must admit is an extremely realistic objective," said Puxton. "As you are no doubt gathering, that plan doesn't include many of you. If you don't have a wealthy family to fall back on, well, do your best and try not to sink out of sight too quickly. At least flap your arms around a little so it looks like you're swimming at the top of the labor pool."

The optimism in the room vanished so abruptly that the staff looked around at one another like they had just awakened from sleep. They looked at the cheap government-issue furniture and the stained ceiling tiles and wondered where their dream had gone.

"Do we hear you correctly that you are changing directions right now? At this very moment?" asked Zhosephine.

"Well, at *this* very moment, I'm off to grab drinks with Splynda. Think of this meeting as a placeholder for your dismissal. We'll deal with the staff reduction in the next day or two," said Puxton. "We said we would fail early and fail often, and by God, we did! I think we can all feel good that we achieved something."

He walked out of the room with his head high and a smile on his face, his starched-white-shirt animation dazzling in the office lighting, his hair raked into perfect rows, his first entrepreneurial failure worn proudly.

Shaughnessy stood in a corner of the gate lounge commiserating over his sleeve with his father as he waited for their plane home. Prudence was in the bathroom again, and he hoped she would reappear as goth Mary Magdalene.

"On the one hand, I feel like we failed, but on the other hand, I feel like we were set up to fail," Shaughnessy said. "I'm relieved that the project is finished, but my mind is still tangled up in the problem, and I'm disappointed I can't keep working on it."

"You can be sure that a project will succeed, or you can push boundaries, but you can't do both at the same time," Walton said. "It's the Hindenburg Uncertainty Principle at work."

"People keep saying that, whatever that means."

"So... the Hindenburg's designers daringly chose hydrogen for the dirigible. There was no way for them to know that the concept would fail in a spectacular fireball, even though it seems obvious now."

"It does seem obvious," Shaughnessy said.

"The big ideas always do. I expect we'll have trouble collecting our fees from Puxton. I'll be getting a call from Gahan any moment now," Walton said. "Projects have a way of taking on a life of their own—or rather, taking their own life."

"Funny," Shaughnessy said. "How are you doing?"

"Okay. I'm trying not to think about my neurology appointment."

"Don't worry," Shaughnessy said. "Knowing the truth will put your mind at ease."

"I'm not so sure. The truth has a reputation for disappointment," said Walton. "How are you?"

"I've been better," Shaughnessy said.

"I'm sorry for complicating your life," Walton said. "I'm proud of you for sticking with the project. It's an accomplishment, even if it's not the one you wanted."

22

Days after the Port-A-Park debacle, Shaughnessy accompanied his family to the Formerly Dead concert. Since his return he had been restless, his mind active and unwilling to succumb to listlessness. Without a more satisfying problem to occupy them, his thoughts had hovered worriedly around Walton's upcoming neuro-electrical test. The outing was a welcome distraction.

Coerced into driving, Shaughnessy backed down the driveway of his parents' humpback of a split-level ranch home, beginning the journey to the venue, a barren patch of red sand desert two hours south of Atlanta. He crawled past a neighbor pushing an infant in a stroller, the family dog's leash clamped under one hand, a pendulous plastic bag of dog poop clamped under the other. He drove even more cautiously than usual, worried about the handmade wooden casket Sammy had strapped to the top of the minivan. *Dead Wood* was lettered on the casket's sides in a somber font.

"What are you selling at the show?" Gloria asked.

"I've got incense holders, stash boxes, and coasters. I'm test marketing a new product called the Stakeholder." Sammy glanced at Shaughnessy and smiled. "It's for people who want to be ready for a vampire attack. I'm offering an introductory package that includes a wooden crucifixion cross to keep the vampire subdued while hammering in the stake."

Walton shook his head. "That sort of product could be a huge seller. It sounds like a winner."

"I'm especially proud of the cross. I'm honoring the tree that was killed and forced to participate in Jesus's sacrifice," Sammy said. "I feel like making my crosses from trees that sacrificed themselves to kill humans makes a powerfully ironic artistic statement."

Gloria asked, "Does it come with a Jesus, or is it just a wooden cross?"

"It's just the cross. But if you're a stigmata enthusiast, you'll be interested to learn that the crosses feature small representations of nail holes." She held a sample cross on her palms for her parents to appreciate. "It's guaranteed nondenominational, made from a porous wood that will absorb the doctrine or prejudice of your choosing."

Walton said, "I only see three nail holes."

"Yes, there's three—one for each hand and one for the feet."

"Aligning both feet at the same time seems incredibly difficult. Jesus would have been kicking His feet around, squeamish as hell about getting nailed. It wasn't like the Romans could threaten Him to stop kicking or else—they were already torturing Him to death. They would've had to use *four* nails, allocating two nails for the feet," said Walton. "Maybe they tried the good-guy route and gently told Him to simmer down, that it was just a diagnostic test and would only take ten minutes, that it seemed a lot worse than it really was, that complications were rare, that no one would notice the scarring. Maybe they dabbed at His heels with alcohol and warned Him that He might feel a sting. Maybe they consoled Him that getting nailed wasn't so bad compared with the slow, inevitable death to follow."

Gloria said, "I think you're off topic, darling."

"Maybe they thanked Him for enduring the procedure and said it would help them prevent His affliction in the future."

"Darling . . ."

"I'm saying that by nailing one foot at a time, they could use shorter nails, and it would be easier to line up each foot individually," said Walton. "Metallurgically speaking, they were probably working with a relatively soft metal—definitely not surgical steels. Unless the nail were proportioned like a railroad spike, it seems likely that one long nail driven through two bony feet would bend before it was embedded in the wood."

"I agree with you, foot nailing was definitely a three-soldier, two-nail job: one soldier immobilizing each leg while one wielded the hammer and nails," said Gloria. "If they only used one foot-nail, they might need four soldiers: one for each leg, one for the hammer, and an additional soldier to hold the spike. Not a very labor-efficient proposition. I would think that the Romans would have streamlined the process, given the production demand for crucifixions."

"I can imagine a Roman soldier sitting in a reverse cowboy position on Christ's knees, using each hand to hold one ankle, plus using thigh strength and body weight to keep Him from squirming. With one additional soldier to handle the hammer and nails, it could be a two-soldier job," said Walton.

"Don't you think Jesus would try to knee the soldier in the nuts?" Shaughnessy countered. "That's what I would do. Maybe a heavy woman soldier could straddle His knees so He couldn't knee her in the nuts."

"That seems overly sexualized," Sammy said. "And I don't think they employed women soldiers."

"I'm feeling a lack of support for my reverse cowboy/cowgirl concept," Walton said. "I will go so far as to propose that a heavy woman with strong thighs could both hold the legs and wield the hammer and nails. That would be a one-person operation. Plus, a woman would be better at soothing Jesus and getting Him to hold still. Maybe her helmet would minimize the sexuality of the moment, depending, of course, on what Jesus was into."

"The documentation in those days was abysmal. The Romans should've had a nailing manual—graphic scroll, or whatever—distributed to all their crucifiers," Gloria said. "It's amazing Christians could build a following on such a shaky foundation of information. They say that God is in the details, but with the absence of details, where does that leave us?"

"I thought the devil was in the details?" said Shaughnessy.

"That's what they want you to think, so you don't look too closely."

"So does this mean you don't want a cross?" asked Sammy.

"Not if there are only three nail holes, no way," said Walton.

Gloria added, "It's against our belief system."

Shaughnessy found disabled parking and helped his sister unload the casket onto a gurney borrowed from the venue's medical staff. Their mother counseled them about proper posture and their genetic predisposition to back injury.

"This concert was his final wish," Sammy explained to an understanding medic, pointing at the casket. The medic helped them wheel the gurney to the edge of the hardpan parking lot, but they resorted to carrying it pallbearer-style when they reached the sand.

They passed through a sea of milling concertgoers displaying high-spirited animations of death—grinning skulls, dancing skeletons, and whatnot—on communiTee and uniTee templates collected at previous concerts. A rogue wave of color swept across the crowd's iTees, eliciting cheers.

Gloria exhorted her children to join her in the iTee tie-dye collective and become a pixel in the crowd's massive unified canvas of swirling colors. Sammy submitted, but Shaughnessy refused, uncharacteristically thinking that he ought to act like an adult, especially since he was the driver.

The venue employed a checkerboard-like grid system laser marked on the desert's sand, designating each person's allocated space. Walton had splurged on Extrava-Dance+ standing positions with two additional inches of lateral space for dance maneuvers.

Without introduction, the band shuffled on stage. They noodled at chords for a spell before launching into an opening number.

"Welcome to church!" a purple bear identifier said loudly for everyone's benefit, holding his paws aloft.

Shaughnessy watched a woman settle into a dance best described as a primitive birthing ritual. Her neighbor, the bear, demonstrated increasing paranoia that her spasming hips and elbows were violating the sovereign airspace of his ExtravaDance+ grid area. The bear tried to establish boundaries by emphasizing invisible walls with his paws, like a mime trapped in a glass chimney. As with mimes, Shaughnessy assumed the bear was an asshole.

Noticing movement on his own belly, he discovered Sammy had slipped an advertisement onto his iTee. The animation featured a hieroglyphically stylized eye plastered across his front. The enormous eyeball swiveled in a socket, studying everyone within range. Above the eye, across his chest, the advertisement read, *I see Dead Wood!*

Shaughnessy set his AI sound engine to a feed coming directly from the soundboard. With mixed success, he tried to cancel out the roar of the crowd—which sang along roughly in unison but showed remarkable diversity in lyrical interpretation. He self-consciously swayed his body in time to the beat in a way that sufficiently communicated he was engaged with the music but not so much that he felt the spasticity of actual dancing.

The crowd was peaceful, the music was mellow, and his parents were content. Vast AI-controlled animations played out over the crowd's communiTees as if they together comprised a single screen. Vapor exhaled upward in energetic plumes made him imagine a panorama of factory smokestacks, a factory whose output was more people and a slag heap of memoirs.

He watched someone approach through the crowd, dancing, bobbing, and weaving—excusing their appearance and behavior with simple glyphs that read *Fucked Up.* Stinking of beer, the person paused at the back of the purple bear's position and studied Shaughnessy. Looking beyond the *Fucked Up* glyphs, he discovered Portal's whiskery gray doughnut floating in the air.

"Move along, bud," the purple bear said. He started miming the boundaries of his designated space again.

"Oh no," said Shaughnessy. He felt like he was remembering a dream.

Portal and the purple bear man winked out of existence.

Shaughnessy elbowed his father to get his attention, but Walton interpreted it as a gesture of affection and put his arm around his son. He elbowed his father more forcefully and yelled into his ear, "The wormhole is here!"

His father laughed deliriously, encouraged by the venue's hanging fog of vapor.

"It just ate that purple bear guy!" Shaughnessy yelled.

Walton laughed as if this was the funniest thing he had ever heard—bent-double, eyes-watering, unable-to-breathe laughter.

"You've got the best sense of humor," Walton said when he finally regained control. "Thank you for that. I needed a good laugh."

The female vocalist identifier of the Formerly Dead was giving an inspiring rendition of a gospel blues folk song. Shaughnessy peeked through her virtuosiTee template and watched her glasses, possibly bifocals, slowly slide down her nose as she sang. She jabbed them back into place at rhythmically permissible moments. Her body swaying and foot tapping caused her tight black skirt to ratchet itself upward, defying gravity. Mixed with the singing, dramatic gesticulations, and glasses jabbing, she periodically tugged at her skirt hem.

Honestly, he thought, it was amazing she could concentrate and perform so earnestly when afflicted with so many technical hurdles. The other musicians communicated calculated disinterest in their appearance through unkempt, emaciated, and exposed-ass-crack glyphs.

At intermission, Shaughnessy paid a visit to Sammy's tent. She was nearly out of her Dead Wood inventory and reported that the coffin had sold quickly.

"Software engineer?" he asked.

"Can't really say. He tried the coffin on for size, if that means anything," Sammy said.

"Software engineer."

He waited in line at the ghetto of chemical toilets. As if being imprisoned in a sweltering plastic box weren't degrading enough, the onlookers, impatient for their own turn in the box, clocked every occupant. They wondered aloud why it was taking so damn long. They scowled with contempt as each sweat-stained, shamefaced survivor emerged and staggered free.

He stopped to watch a rebellion brew in the cordoned disability area, a sloping patchwork of plywood sheets laid on the loose sand. A feisty group of wheelchair-bound rebels chanted complaints about the poor stage visibility they were enduring. An MFD patient, melted into the contours of his powered wheelchair, the volume of his voice synthesizer set to ten, led the chanting. An especially militant, distinctly synthetic female voice called for humans to submit to their new overlords.

From their wheelchairs, the chronics accused the acutes—with their gout and plantar fasciitis and sciatic inflammations and hypertrophic entitlement—of taking the best seats. The chronics clamored for the visually impaired to take the obstructed-view seats. They politely asked for all able-bodied companions to please stop dancing and sit down so they don't block sight lines, for fuck's sake. The rebels turned up their disability-pride glyphs, mustering partisan sympathy.

He had no energy for analysis. He imagined his father in a wheelchair, trapped in the disability pen. He visualized setting his father and his compatriots free, of righting a blatant injustice. Fueled by an accumulated knot of unprocessed emotion, he slipped into a higher gear. He tasted the satisfying umami of simplicity and elegance. He felt righteous impulse. Galvanized, he dragged a sheet of stray plywood to the front of the disability area.

"Whoa, whoa, you can't go in there!" A portly yellow securiTee type made his way toward him, the sand slowing his forward motion to a crawl. "Show your disability ticket!"

"Show your compassion, bitch!" Shaughnessy yelled back. His animated abdominal eyeball gave the securiTee a glaring stink eye, which brought him to a halt. Ripping apart the plastic tape marking the border, Shaughnessy yelled, "Be free! Be free!" He waved at the wheelchair-bound to break free and journey forward.

A handful of committed rebels cautiously ventured out onto the plywood peninsula. He dragged another plywood sheet around to extend the makeshift pathway. After repeating that step several times, he severed the connection with the disability peloton and isolated the rebels on a plywood island. With growing assistance from the crowd, plywood moved from the back of the island to the front, and the wheelchairs made their way forward. The crowd re-formed behind the breakaway, subsuming it into the collective. He rested from his exertions and watched the wheelchairs glide onward, bound for stage front.

Shouts alerted him that a second wave of wheelchairs was organizing at the disability area's perimeter. Several more securiTees had arrived and knotted together the plastic boundary tape.

He stared at the securiTees with his unblinking abdominal eyeball and asked, "Why aren't you helping?"

Questions of that complexity challenged the parameters of their employment; they were unable to resolve the competing demands of obligation and common sense. Shaughnessy moved to tear apart the border tape again. The securiTees formed a phalanx to block his approach and yet smiled encouragingly.

"Watch out for this one!" a securiTee shouted. "He looks messed up. He looks dangerous."

Shaughnessy felt his pride swell, having never before been accused of looking dangerous, until he realized the securiTee wasn't talking about him. The *Fucked Up* Portal had made an appearance in the air next to him.

"Bring back the purple bear, please," Shaughnessy said. Portal, along with the second wave of wheelchair rebels, disappeared.

Shaughnessy and the securiTees tried to puzzle out what to do. There was no more rebellion, which was good news, but people had disappeared, which was bad news. It was exactly the kind of shit he would get blamed for.

With the forward ranks of the disability area out of the way, he noticed a young woman watching the show while seated in a familiar recliner. A small dog sat on her lap, and she held its floppy ears tight to protect it from the loud music. Beside her sat a squat, armadillo-on-tractor-treads-looking robot with glyphs urging wheelchairs to cast off their parasitic human oppressors.

"Grandmom! Is that you?" he yelled and waved.

"Shaughnessy!" she yelled back.

"Yo! Shauny Boy! Nice work!" called the disquieting little robot, whose voice he now recognized as Althea's.

"What are you doing here?" he yelled. He tried to move into the disability area, but the securiTees blocked his way.

"Getting lit!" Melba yelled back. "Don't tell your father you saw me."

"How did you get here?"

"Portal. Go enjoy the show!" she yelled.

As he trudged back to his parents, the stage screen projected a close-up of the vocalist holding a sustained note. Beside her, just offstage, he saw the purple bear and the wheelchair group Portal had abducted. The band's backstage guests and the technicians at the soundboard were still cheering their sudden appearance, taking it completely in stride. This wasn't even close to the strangest thing they'd witnessed at a concert.

As the show ambled toward a crescendo, he saw that his father had managed to lose himself. Eyes closed, smiling as if the music was filling him with meaning, Walton danced to the degree that he was capable.

Gloria sang along to the encore, her arm around Walton's waist, their shared ExtravaDance+ border opened. She smiled and hugged him and promised him that everything was going to be okay, that he shouldn't worry. He leaned in and kissed her.

After the show, Shaughnessy caught sight of both disabled groups heading back to the disability zone. They had entrained a conga line of supportive followers, who moved the plywood path forward with a great deal of laughter. A group of Sufi-like whirling-dervish dancers parted the crowd, leading their parade. They laughed and smiled and thanked everyone they encountered. He slid his vision beneath the breakaways' glyphs and caught glimpses of genuine exhilaration. The MFD patient spied him and alerted others, encouraging the entire parade to take up a cheer.

"Show your compassion, bitch!" they yelled with glee.

A flush of euphoria-tinged satisfaction swept over him. He tried to squeeze it into his memory.

Walton asked, "What was that about?"

"Just some people I met."

"What an amazing concert," Gloria said. "I'm so thankful we came."

Walton and Shaughnessy gave her a forceful, "Amen!"

"I don't know how humans stumbled onto music," Gloria said. "Most of what we do is half-assed. Like, medical progress is amazing, but only if you happen to have a curable disease. Astronomy and physics are amazing, but they make us feel cosmically insignificant. I don't know how we pulled off music, but considering all factors, I'm guessing it was just dumb luck."

23

After Walton's neuro-electrical test, he and Gloria sat together on a double-wide chair in a quiet corner of the neurology waiting room. The doctor had asked them to wait while they found a quiet place to discuss the results. On the screen above them, a cheerful survivor downplayed the risks of drug trial participation.

Walton's body twitched intermittently. He tried to block out all memory of the test, the long needles sunk into his muscles, the electricity running through his body, the excruciating flashes of pain. He took note that when a doctor tells you that something will be painful, it will be *really* painful. Their profession made them inclined to understate pain, complications, time of recovery, their fees. They don't understate their abilities; that's the exception to the rule, he thought.

The nurses and staff furtively peeked at Walton and Gloria, sensing an unfolding tragedy. Everyone must have a moment like this, thought Walton, believing they were about to get the worst news of their soon-to-be-former lives. Still, despite how seemingly banal and universal the occurrence, he felt uncomfortably conspicuous. He couldn't help but wonder how often the staff handled fatal diagnoses and whether they were so numb that they could take it in stride over a late-morning snack. Maybe they had seen it all, from diagnosis through hospice, and they were imagining what was to come—a series of appointments, a progression of increasingly bitter encounters in the upcoming years.

The med student who had assisted with the diagnostic tests led Walton and Gloria into an empty employee break room. She seated them in affordable office chairs, ordinarily used by nurses or doctors while dictating patient reports. There was a refrigerator, a sink, and a microwave. In short order, the neurologist appeared and sat astride the corner of a nearby desk, leaving one foot on the floor, the other dangling loosely in the air. Their iTee depicted a white lab jacket open to the waist.

The neurologist said that the test results were not promising. They spoke with concern and a tired seriousness. In a curious twist, they streamed a simplified, layman's, AI translation of their own words across their chest. The AI's gleefully macabre translation presented like psychotic closed captioning: *You're going to die!*

With the stress of the situation, the neurologist's gender identity oscillated wildly, swinging from mid-range female, through a zone of neutrality, and into low-level masculinity. Walton grappled with the diagnosis while trying to ignore the fluctuating shape of their facial features and the periodic appearances of a beard.

Walton's MFD self-diagnosis had been correct, a fact that perversely pleased him. He assumed any engineer would feel the same.

The neurologist explained that it was a neurodegenerative disease.

"In this instance, I'm the neuro and you are the degenerate." They laughed and said, "I'm just trying to lighten the mood. I'm afraid I have more bad news to go along with this. As this syndrome affects the nervous system, there is a chance that it will eventually lead to some degree of dementia. There's no way to predict it, so keep an eye out for unusual behaviors like debilitating fears or uncontrollable, inconsolable crying. If you experience those behaviors, well, who knows, it might be dementia or might just be depression, which I should've mentioned is even more likely than dementia. Next time maybe I should lead with depression, which is of course treatable with a variety of debatably effective medications that increase the likelihood of suicidal tendencies."

They said that Walton's voluntary muscles would experience random, sporadic episodes of weakness, that the episodes would become more frequent, and that his muscles would eventually stop working. There was no predicting the order in which the disease would affect his limbs. Eventually, probably after he was unable to speak or eat or walk or move his arms, he would stop breathing. Regrettably, there was no current treatment or cure.

They explained that while researchers understand which cells are going haywire and how that results in paralysis, they are baffled as to what sets the disease in motion and how to stop it—hence the *mysterious* part of the name. They said that the average life expectancy was on the order of three to five years but that many people lived long lives— though profoundly disabled—and many other people barely make it one year, dropping dead out of the blue. Walton estimated that the average path sounded preferable, even though it entailed dying.

"I'd like you to visit specialists who work in this area, and they can confirm the diagnosis," the neurologist continued. "It's a tricky disease to diagnose since its hallmark is a mysterious death. Until you have a chance to meet with them, let's just consider MFD as a placeholder for the rest of your life. The disease is quite rare, and the odds of getting it are slim. But you know what? Once you have it, the odds steeply go up to a hundred percent. I'm more of a chemistry person, never was very mathletic, but I find that little factling interesting. When you tell your loved ones about the diagnosis and they are weeping and moaning, shouting *What are the odds?* While shaking a fist at the heavens, you can tell them that the odds are a hundred percent. Who knows, you might get a laugh with that."

"He loves math," Gloria said. Walton grinned weakly.

"I'm required to ask a difficult question. I need to assess your current mindset. Have you recently or are you currently considering suicide?" Their inflection was neutral, as if they were asking if Walton had considered slip-on shoes or elastic-waist pants or something similar of everyday utility.

"I haven't thought about it with any enthusiasm, but I can't deny that it has occurred to me. I'd be a fool not to consider all my options."

"That's a good answer," said the neurologist. "Some patients start to see the cost savings, the end of suffering, the unburdening of their families, and the other arguments in favor of suicide and fail to see the lasting impact it would have on their loved ones."

"Is it different from the lasting impact of dying from the disease?" asked Gloria.

"Yes," they said. "It comes earlier and is easier to plan around."

"My wife is a planner," Walton said.

"Given what we know about the universe—which, you have to admit is damn little, so don't put a lot of faith in this—I believe that if your life is flowing out of this world, then there must be a balancing flow coming back in. I mean something tangible and good. Keep an eye out for it. If good things happen, maybe you're responsible."

Walton and Gloria slumped into an embrace, each at the edge of their chairs, leaning forward to form a tepee, their heads on each other's shoulders, their arms locked supportively together. Walton felt like apologizing to Gloria for causing such a sudden shift in the direction of their lives. He felt apologetic to the neurologist for putting them in this awkward position. All he could say was an umbrella, "I'm so sorry."

Primarily, he felt immensely shocked that something of this magnitude was happening and that they would have to tell their children.

Gloria wandered off in a daze to get their car after instructing Walton to sit and not go anywhere. He waited on a bench in front of the neurology building. He took stock of himself and agreed that he was in no shape to walk around. He could feel the upwelling of a prolonged crying jag.

A Jesus limped over and quietly sat at the far end of Walton's bench. He put His head down and would have looked like He was praying if He hadn't looked so hopelessly dispirited. His simpliciTee template emitted warm backlighting that played up the red tones in His flowing auburn hair animation and formed a bubble of light around His torso. The front of His iTee featured a morphing Son Protector logo.

"Hey," Jesus said.

"Hey, how are You?" Walton replied.

"Not good. Not good at all."

"Same here."

"Shoulder damage from crucifixion. Neuropathy in My feet. Resurrection is possible, but neurological problems are forever. Nobody warned Me of that. How about you?"

"I was just told I have a serious disease."

"Which one?" Jesus asked.

"MFD," Walton said.

"Ouch, that's a bitch."

Walton experienced a flash of hope. "Any chance You might heal me?"

"MFD is out of My league," Jesus said. "Even leprosy was a stretch for Me, and no matter what you read, it weirded Me out every time—crippling nausea. Thank God for the Bible's poetic license. Thank God for antibiotics."

"I gathered, but I thought it couldn't hurt to ask," Walton said. "How about just a small miracle?"

"Like what?"

"Look after my family if I don't make it."

Jesus said, "That's touching, and I'd love to help, but if I went down that road, it would be nothing but miracles all day long. I don't have the bandwidth."

"Do You happen to know anything about why I got the disease?" Walton asked. "I'm not pointing fingers or anything. It just occurred to me that You might have inside intel on where I went wrong. Is it something I said or did or thought?"

"I'm kept out of the detailed planning," Jesus said. "I died for your sins, but I don't know everyone's specifics. It's more of an aggregate actuarial situation."

"Oh. I see."

They sat in uncomfortable silence, waiting for their rides. Walton wondered what was keeping Gloria and imagined her sitting in their car, too upset to start the engine. Jesus dejectedly bowed His head again.

"I get it that You don't feel like helping me, but I have to wonder . . . Why didn't You save Yourself from crucifixion? Why didn't You do everything in Your power to stay alive? What's the worst that could have happened?"

"It was part of His plan," Jesus said.

"It must eat at You," Walton said. "It doesn't seem like a very good plan. I think I would've asked to preview plans B and C. Maybe I would've suggested brainstorming."

"I do wonder what My life could've been like," Jesus said. "Complain if you will about sinning and suffering here on Earth, but they do help pass the time."

Silence overtook them again. Jesus rolled His shoulders around like He was assessing whether they had improved yet. An AI van dropped off a teenager in an electric wheelchair.

Jesus tried to resume the conversation with a personal admission. "I was an ugly baby. I had the face of a wrinkled old man. The Gospels omitted that detail, but as a kid, whenever I acted holier-than-thou, My mother reminded Me," Jesus said.

"Mothers can be like that," Walton said.

"She loves to talk about My birth. She complains about the manger's straw making her backside itch. She says she was screaming like a banshee. Don't get her going about her frankincense sensitivity. I don't think her input was included in the Bible."

"Can I confess something?" Walton asked.

"Shoot," Jesus said.

"I've taken up a keen interest in the afterlife. I don't want to miss out on an opportunity. I mostly believe in heaven, but You're just the face of spirituality I never achieved. You're a placeholder," Walton said. "Is that going to be a stumbling block for me?"

"That stings a little bit. I guess My mojo isn't what it used to be," said Jesus. "Heaven *is* pretty nice. There are no prerequisites, you know. St. Peter isn't as industrious as he would like everyone to think. He has an open-door policy."

"That seems like an important bit of information. You might think about promoting that idea," Walton said.

"Trade secret. You didn't hear it here," Jesus said. "We have to protect Our premium market position."

"Listen, if You don't mind my asking, since we're talking here, there's something else I was wondering about . . . When the Romans nailed You to the cross . . . exactly how many nails did they put in Your feet? It's a matter of professional interest," Walton said.

"It's fascinating how people obsess over the details of My death," said Jesus. "It's morbid. That level of specificity takes the unknowable out of My message. But if you really want to know, I'm not sure. I wasn't in a great mental space at the time."

"During that incident, did You happen to glance down at Your feet?"

"It's a blur," Jesus replied. "I do remember the brawny guy with the hammer asking whether I preferred one big nail through both feet or two small nails, one through each heel. I asked what he recommended, based on his experience. He said that it's a complicated question. On the one hand, the big nail is like a railroad spike and it hurts like the devil when you nail it through. However, it creates a stable platform, and overlapping feet create better visual lines. On the other hand, the two individual nails are significantly less painful to install but can cause excruciating ligament pain once weight is applied. The double-nail, splayed-foot pose can look ungainly, unflattering, and Charlie Chaplin-like."

"So it only took one soldier to nail You to the cross?" Walton asked.

"The big hammer guy was in charge, and some other soldiers were milling about making jokes. Maybe they helped, I don't know. I closed My eyes. Like I said, I'm squeamish." He shrugged, winced, then added, "We also had a brief discussion about using rope to augment the retentive power of the nails."

"Clever. I hadn't considered that," said Walton. "Why didn't You tell him to just use rope and forgo the nails altogether?"

"The hammer guy suggested that nails create a more powerful narrative than rope alone and speak more to My theological commitment. Believe it or not, it didn't even occur to Me to think about the cross as a logo; I just got lucky there."

"I see."

"He liked to use rope in addition to nails because he once had a victim with weak bone structure," Jesus continued. "The hand-nails tore through the victim's flesh; he swung like a clock hand from twelve to six, pivoting around the single foot-nail until he was hanging upside down. His tunic flopped over and exposed his undercarriage to onlookers.

Fortunately, the single foot-nail held the victim's weight; unfortunately, he whacked his head on the ground as he spun downward, killing him instantly, awkwardly truncating the prolonged torture part of the whole exercise. The big hammer guy was still living that one down. He said that not a night of drinking goes by without his coworkers bringing it up. He assured Me he was able to laugh at it now."

"What was Your final choice?"

"Nails only, and I told him to choose the number, that I trusted his judgment. By the way, it was his idea to tug the loincloth up on one side to give it that jaunty angle. He had good fashion sense. I was willing to make the full artistic commitment and go nude, but he insisted that would spoil the aesthetics."

"Can You tell me more about the big hammer guy? Would You say he had any feminine qualities?"

"Well, he was chatty and seemed interested in My opinion. He had on one of those kilt-like armored skirts that were in fashion at the time. All the soldiers looked a bit androgynous."

The doors swung open and Gloria emerged from inside the building on foot. She sat on the bench, sniffling. "I forgot, we didn't drive. We took an AI car here. I looked all over for our car. I couldn't find the parking ticket and thought I had lost it."

"Oh, right. I'm so sorry," Walton said. He waved his hand to beckon a waiting AI vehicle, which ignored him.

"They're the work of the devil," Jesus commented.

Walton scribbled at his sleeve and summoned a car. The three of them lapsed into silence until a car pulled up in front of the bench.

Jesus stood up with them, whereupon He embraced Walton and whispered, "You won't find meaning in death, neither Mine nor yours."

Once inside the car, Gloria said, "I see you made a friend."

"I asked if He could cure me or at least help with a small miracle," said Walton.

"And?"

"No go."

"Darn. Did He offer any tips on resurrection?"

"I learned it doesn't fix preexisting neurological problems," he replied. "I also asked Him about the nail holes, but He couldn't remember."

"How could He not remember?"

"He claims He left it up to the big guy with the hammer," Walton said. "I think there's an outside chance that the hammer person was female, but He said He didn't think so. It was a fascinating story."

"We're never going to get to the bottom of this."

The family sat together on the back porch of their house. Sammy and Shaughnessy delicately probed their parents about the appointment. Gloria gave a bare-bones summary of the test and resulting diagnosis. They asked about treatment options, but there was little to offer by way of an answer. Gloria told them that the next step was to see an MFD specialist so he could tell them in more specific terms what couldn't be done.

Walton added a detail that he thought would interest Shaughnessy: the AI layman's translation banner on the neurologist's iTee.

"I don't think it's quite what you had in mind when you suggested it," Walton said. "The AI version of a layman came across as hateful. It was thrilled by the result of my test." He stared into the distance. Sammy asked him how he was feeling, and he replied, "I'm fucked in the head."

This struck Shaughnessy as a surprisingly logical response from someone fucked in the head.

"Your father bumped into a Jesus after the appointment," Gloria said.

"Oh no," Sammy said.

"He was nice enough," Walton said, "but He wasn't willing to help."

"Fuck," Shaughnessy said.

"Fucking fuck," Sammy said.

"You got that right," Gloria agreed.

They sat quietly for a spell, listening to the sounds of their neighborhood: the low tones of the distant freight train, the manic dog barking, the tantrum of the child just down the block, the roar of a stump grinder chewing a tree out of existence. Sammy lit the Diesel Fumes on a Winter Morning incense she brought as a gift to soothe her parents.

"Oh, there is some good news," Gloria said. "Did your father tell you?"

"What news?" Sammy asked. She and Shaughnessy looked at one another with apprehension.

"Walton, you tell them the news," Gloria said.

"What? Oh, that. I got back the results of the genetic tests and it confirmed that I don't have the hereditary version of MFD. I meant to tell you earlier," Walton said.

"Thank God," Shaughnessy said. Sammy smiled.

"You weren't worried, were you?" Walton asked. "There was very little chance of that happening."

"Yes, I was worried," Shaughnessy said.

"Me too," Sammy said. "We're your children, how could we not be worried?"

Gloria remarked that it was wonderful to have all four of them together for an afternoon. She waved her hand over the ObsoleScents incense stick and the smoky aroma of crisp wintry diesel fumes swirled around the porch.

Gloria closed her eyes. "This smell takes me back to when I was a child waiting for the school bus on a country road. Little crystalline ice heaves appeared in the dirt shoulder overnight, like winter mushrooms. I crushed them underfoot."

Shaughnessy said, "I feel like I'm standing at a congested street corner."

Sammy said, "It reminds me of when you dragged us on a tour of the Paris sewer system and there was actual sewage."

"Memories are such a wonderful thing," said Gloria. She excused herself, returned to the kitchen, and shortly thereafter shrieked in horror.

Cutting his eyes toward the window, Shaughnessy saw that his mother was engaged in an artillery offensive against an intruder that he could only guess was an insect. Through a long history of skirmishes, Shaughnessy, Sammy, and Walton well knew that Gloria's tactical weakness was close combat, and one of them would eventually have to play the infantry role to storm the insect's stronghold.

"I need to go to the bathroom anyway," sighed Sammy. She jogged off to engage the enemy.

Later, after the pitched battle and grave duty that included a detailed accounting of all the insect's legs, Sammy told Shaughnessy that the athletic specimen had concealed itself behind kitchen countertop canisters in a game akin to life-or-death three-card monte. Their mother had wielded the spatula herself and uncontrollably raged on the shockingly juicy victim.

24

Sammy went out of town to hold a pecan tree accountable for terrorizing the parents of a nut allergenic. She offered Shaughnessy the opportunity to sleep over in her apartment in exchange for restocking her inventory in the first-floor retail shop.

He kept thinking about Prudence and knew he shouldn't be alone, dwelling on his father's freshly diagnosed condition. He invited her to join him for dinner, thinking Lean MFG would make for an interesting shared experience.

She met him at the front of the restaurant. Dorothea entertained them with the story of a recent batch of potatoes, now soup, that had required exorcism before peeling.

Prudence was fascinated by the automated buffet. "It's pure scheduling genius, keeping all the diners on a fixed timeline. I wish I had thought of that."

They belted themselves onto their chairs. Their table moved out from under the loading zone lights, past the drink station. Shaughnessy selected a glass of Artesian Wellness. Prudence went for the Pinot Grigio. A candle and the table's emergency-stop button cast a gentle glow on her wide-set eyes.

"Thank you for joining me," Shaughnessy said. "I know Walton and Marcia didn't completely see eye to eye out at Port-A-Park. I thought that might cause friction between us."

She moved her hand in a vague motion as if to brush away the whole topic. "Walton didn't steer the project where Marcia expected, but she's satisfied," she said. "I wouldn't talk with you ever again if Marcia's software team had gotten stuck with the project."

Regretting he had brought up work, he blurted out the thing weighing on his mind: "My father is not well."

"The software engineers I'm assigned to aren't well either," she said. "In the future they'll be looked back on like asbestos workers or coal miners. Someday syntaxia will be up there with mesothelioma and black lung disease. You've got to wonder whether they're editing code or the code is editing their DNA."

"He was just diagnosed with MFD."

"Oh, I'm so sorry, I didn't realize," she said. "That's fatal, isn't it?"

"That's what the F stands for—fatal."

"Oh, I thought it stood for something different," she said. "At least he gets to die of a famous disease, right?"

Shaughnessy looked at her, speechless. She ladled a scoop of the Slaw of Unintended Consequences onto her plate.

"Sorry, that was probably inappropriate," she said. "Sometimes my sense of humor outpaces common decency."

"No, it was funny. My dad would love that."

"I'm very sorry. I'm sure this is an incredibly difficult time for you." She reached across the table and squeezed his hand. "I'm glad I can be here with you."

Speaking aloud about his father's condition caused an uncomfortable seismic shift. Shaughnessy's composure was, at best, a thin crust covering turbulent molten emotion. Her concern and her touch had fractured the edge of that crust, sending cracks across the surface.

"Do you ever get the feeling that you've created your

own reality? Like, my dad now wonders if he got MFD by believing he had MFD. Like he initiated his own self-destruct sequence."

"No," she said. "In that case, I would have thought that I was slow to figure out the truth."

"I guess they're both good possibilities," Shaughnessy said. "Do you ever feel like every idea you've ever had is unoriginal and you're just regurgitating other people's thoughts?"

"That's what I'm paid to do. A Marcia can't be both original and reliable at the same time."

"Hindenburg?"

"Obviously," she said. "I'm thinking of trying something new. I don't know what yet. Being a Marcia is starting to bleed over into my personal life. It's unpleasant, like belching garlic from a previous meal."

"I don't know what I'm going to do either," Shaughnessy mumbled. He felt himself floundering, barely able to follow the conversation.

Prudence took a bite of her slaw and engaged in a conflict with a strip of flaccid deep-green vegetable matter whose Kevlar-like fibers proved impervious to the sawing action of her teeth. Shaughnessy rooted for Prudence's incisors and projected his emotional delicacy onto the protracted drama. When she capitulated and spat the fibrous mass onto her plate, he felt defeated. His fragile mind overshot a measured response, set his heart to racing, and fractured his composure.

He slapped his palm onto the glowing red emergency-stop button and unbuckled his lap belt. Warning lights blinked and alarms sounded throughout the restaurant. The production line groaned to an abrupt halt. Water sloshed from drink glasses. Diners swiveled their heads to identify the weakling constitutionally unable to make it through a meal without using the bathroom.

"I'll be right back." He hopped from their dining pallet to the factory floor.

Dorothea waved her arms over her head to get Shaughnessy's attention. With exaggerated flight attendant signals she directed him toward the facilities. He walked head-down beside the conveyor belt, enduring stares and pointed comments about the inadequacy of his bladder. Behind him, he heard the conveyor lurch into motion again.

The restroom—a onesie, a fortress of solitude—was built into a low-ceilinged reinforced-concrete storage bunker formerly used to store toxic paint. A galvanized ventilation duct pierced one wall through a jagged hole in the concrete. Shaughnessy relieved himself. He looked through the irregular opening around the duct into the kitchen and made acquaintance with a line cook.

The bathroom's one concession to creature comfort was the elaborate multifunction toilet, which, based on enigmatic control panel icons, appeared to offer a heated seat, bidet, and forced-air drying protocol. Shaughnessy couldn't find a flush icon, and the tank wasn't outfitted with any sort of plainly marked red emergency-override handle that any decent toilet engineer would have specified for precisely this situation.

He stood frozen, panicking, imagining an epic faux pas if he couldn't unravel the flush problem. Minutes ticked past as his mind raced in a downward spiral. He cursed the dark forces of software engineering that had clouded user interfaces.

The line cook, concerned for Shaughnessy's health, experienced with the perils of high-fiber cuisine, knocked politely on the door and asked if he was okay.

"I'm fine, almost done in here!" he called out.

The line cook peeked through the hole in the wall. He tried to poke a roll of toilet paper through the hole, believing it might be the solution.

Shaughnessy's heart pounded, he felt sweat sheeting on his skin, he was confused. His AI soundtrack generator produced Klaxon warnings. He flexed his hands open and closed to make sure the muscles still worked. He repeated to himself that he wasn't the one who was dying, which only called to mind that his father was. He felt immensely lonely. He desperately wanted the world to make sense. He ran cold water and splashed it on his face. Pathetic, sparse tears blended with the water droplets. He dried himself with a coarse paper towel and stared into the mirror at his broad nose, his whisker-less cheeks, his gaping pores, his antennae eyebrows. He picked paper towel fibers out of his mustache stubble.

Shaughnessy sat on the toilet lid and held his head in his hands. He tried to breathe deeply and suppressed sobs as he twiddled speed dial on his sleeve and called his father.

Walton's face appeared, his eyes blinking and squinting.

"Are you in bed? It's not even nine yet," Shaughnessy said. "I was having dinner and thought I would check in. I was thinking about you. I've missed meeting with you every day."

Walton was looking around, trying to get his bearings in the dark. He grunted that he had been taking a nap.

"Okay, I'll let you go. Say hi to Mom."

Walton held up one finger, and Shaughnessy waited while he moved to the master bathroom and sat on the toilet seat.

"Is that a bathroom?" asked Walton. "What's with the duct sticking through the wall?"

"I don't know. That's just the tip of the iceberg," Shaughnessy said. "Can I ask you something? Why is this happening?"

"What?"

"Everything!" He gestured to indicate everything in sight—the obtrusive duct, the high-tech toilet, the shitty fiber-shedding paper towels. He added a flourish with both hands to implicate life itself.

"Nothing makes sense—you, me, this toilet, your disease, nothing. Not only that, they each take a different approach to not making sense, which is just plain cruel. Does that make sense?"

"I don't know how to answer that question," said Walton. "It does make sense that nothing makes sense."

"I think evolution is secretly controlling everything, even my thoughts," Shaughnessy said.

"Isn't that the truth? Don't say I didn't warn you," Walton said. "I have ancient wisdom to impart. I know your training is incomplete, but you're descended from a powerful bloodline—or are possibly the Chosen One—and there's an outside chance you'll survive this final lesson."

"I always hoped to figure into a prophecy, but this is cool too."

"Did your mother and I forget to mention the prophecy?"

"Apparently."

"Right. Well, it was tough to remember, wordy, and we didn't write it down. It wasn't a very flattering prediction, as I recall."

"You really know how to talk a person off a ledge," Shaughnessy said.

"I offer you long-lost engineering wisdom: *Ask questions and expect thorough answers, but don't expect answers outside of work*," said Walton. "I was going to the store the other day and asked your mother if she needed anything. She answered that she didn't need the cream cheese I had forgotten last time I shopped because she had made a separate trip through heavy traffic and got it herself, thank you very much. What should I have put on my shopping list?"

"A dozen roses?"

"I don't think she asked me to buy the cream cheese in the first place, but I'll never know, and that's my point," Walton said. "You're overthinking, expecting answers where there are none. Get some rest. Admittedly, that advice is based on my own selfish desire to go back to sleep."

"That's on the verge of making sense," Shaughnessy said.

"Hey, want to hear a bedtime story?"

"Sure."

"Have I told you about Reginald, the brave Centiguardian—outspoken champion of truth, problem-solver extraordinaire?"

"No."

"The Fahrenhaters killed him," Walton said. "He was sitting outside a café, discussing an activity's price with his female companion. Reginald's last words were 'You call that an assassination attempt? Your shot was wide by at least two meters. Adjust your scope!' He was yelling at a sniper, across the public plaza."

"How would a Fahrenhater sniper know how big a meter was?" Shaughnessy asked.

"I skipped over their long discussion about converting to inches."

"What happened to his wife?"

"Wife? No, she was just some hooker he met. He might have been a good leader, but he exercised poor judgment in his personal life. Remember that; there's a lesson there. I guess what I'm saying is that Ol' Reginald's overcommitment to problem-solving killed him in the end," Walton said. "My storytelling is a little out of practice."

Shaughnessy heard conversation outside the factory bathroom and a tap on the door. "No kidding. I need to go," he said. "I'm sorry I woke you. I love you."

Prudence's voice asked if Shaughnessy was okay. She asked if they could do anything for him.

Shaughnessy said he thought he was dying.

Prudence tried to assure him that it was probably just the slaw and that she herself felt a little queasy, but she was sure he would be okay.

He said that he couldn't make sense of the toilet icons and all he wanted to do was flush, but he couldn't even accomplish that.

"The man here wants to know if you went number one or number two," Prudence said. "They have a history of blockages, and he wants to know what he's dealing with so he can have a plunger at the ready if necessary."

"Just ask him how to flush the thing," Shaughnessy said.

"He says he saw you sitting down," she said.

"I was talking to my father."

"Call it whatever you like. He says you're going to be the one pushing the mop if this situation goes sideways. Dorothea seems to be on his side of this argument, guest or no guest."

"Jesus fuck," he said.

"He says that there is a round button on the top of the tank and you just need to push it," she said. "He's being very particular about it like you need to push it vigorously. You can't be tentative about it. It looks like a two-finger operation."

He surveyed the top of the tank and saw towels, not a button. He pushed aside the stack of shitty fiber-shedding paper towels and found the button hidden underneath. He had never hated an inanimate object more than he hated those paper towels. He hoped they would get recycled into toilet paper and meet a terrible end. No, recycled into *sentient* toilet paper, aware of its fate. No, sentient *germophobic* toilet paper that would suffer panic attacks!

He pressed the button vigorously, witnessed a satisfying flush, and heard applause from outside the door.

He emerged red-faced, eyes bloodshot. Prudence held a cup of pastry impaled by one spoon.

"I snagged a dessert for us," she said. "It's the Forbidden Fruit Tart."

"It looks good," he said.

"It's bad," she said, "deliciously bad."

They left the restaurant and rode the freight elevator to Sammy's floor in silence. Shaughnessy worked at the door's lock while Prudence watched, holding the dessert cup. With the door opened, she followed him in.

They sat on Sammy's couch and pretended to engage in conversation. She fed him spoonfuls of fruit. She slipped off her shoes to get comfortable and caught him glancing at her toes.

"There's something oddly original about you, Shaughnessy. I can't quite put my finger on it, but I'd like to try."

"I feel very much the same way."

A flurry of moist, breathy activity ensued. After slipping inexpertly off the couch, Shaughnessy found himself kneeling in front her, as a supplicant might worship a goddess. She lay with her back arched and her arms stretched above her head. She set her iTee to show black off-brand lingerie.

"I know you're upset. We don't have to if you don't feel like it," she said.

Shaughnessy slowly peeled her iTee up to her armpits.

Her rib cage and the points of her hips jutted prominently. The side of her one freed breast was rich with delicate white stretch-mark contrails floating above a tributary system of deep-blue veins. Her nipple recoiled, clenched into a bunched-up, furrowed, angry knot. It eyed him suspiciously.

"Whoa cowboy, I'm not an old-school kind of girl," she said. She tugged her iTee back down over her torso and adjusted it to appear transparent, showing an evenly tanned, airbrushed, symmetric, and slightly augmented version of what lay underneath.

"Let's keep the pace up," she said. "My biological clock runs fast."

They hurriedly negotiated the topics of consent and protection. Their hands tussled with one another's uncooperative pants fasteners.

In general, Shaughnessy didn't worry about his appearance. He was hygienically disposed, passably good-looking, and fit from his workaday calisthenics. He could grasp that a toned, muscular male body was attractive on its own merits, and he could conceive of how the gender spectrum could find it appealing.

Even so, he couldn't help but feel silly as he disrobed to expose what to him resembled a rough-hewn monolith rising incongruously from the thicketed slopes of his groin— with all of the primitive intellect suggested by *monolith*, but none of the scale.

It was as if a committee of dissenting reproductive project managers had tacked on the male equipment at the last minute, just to get the product out the door. Granted, they were working with tricky hydraulics to satisfy a complex concave/convex design requirement, but even so, there should have been engineering pushback and more industrial design commitment to aesthetics. The abdominals team and the quadriceps team had pulled their weight, only to have their good work blemished by an ill-conceived, inelegant, temperature-sensitive add-on. For damn sure they never did impact testing before releasing to production.

"Smallwood's Muttonchop?" he guessed.

She said, "It was on sale."

Afterward, lying together on the couch, Shaughnessy thought about that one nipple. He speculated that there were specialized clenching muscles, but why had he never heard of them? At that moment, it seemed like an important scientific detail, one biology class should have covered. He imagined muscles arrayed around the center, gracefully pulling it into shape.

Sammy returned the next afternoon to find her Wood Heaven inventory unreplenished in the first-floor retail shop. Shaughnessy was still in bed, alone, but she took note of the dessert remnants, the tableau of couch pillow indentations, and the uncharacteristically closed toilet seat. She led him outside to sit at a picnic table on the casket factory's loading dock.

"So, what happened last night?" asked Sammy. She had already heard about the sleeve call from the factory bathroom. Their father had called her early in the morning to get her thoughts on how worried he should be.

Shaughnessy gave her a blow-by-blow description of dinner with Prudence and his emotional collapse in Lean MFG's washroom.

Sammy listened sympathetically as she committed the story to memory. He was surprisingly cheerful and lucid despite his humiliation the night before. She had expected regret to burden him. He didn't explain the dessert or the uses to which they had put the couch, but she connected the dots.

"Dad's right, you know. You're overanalyzing. There are questions that can't be answered."

"Don't tell me I have analysis paralysis."

"I won't, but now I'll probably use the phrase in the retelling," she said. "Did the fancy toilet seat have a built-in heater? I find pleasure in the warmth of a recently used toilet seat, but revulsion at the source of the warmth. That might be a nice compromise."

"It seemed to have everything but the flusher," said Shaughnessy.

Sammy put her arm over his shoulders and gave a squeeze. "We'll get through this together, I promise. Try to be strong."

"I don't want to be something I'm not."

"No, I suppose not," she said. She wanted to encourage him, but he was right. Overt strength of personality flowed down through the women in their family. He and their father were strong in the same way that quicksand is a danger—she understood it to be true but assumed she'd never experience it herself.

"Do you think I'm weird?" he asked.

"Yes, decisively so," she said.

"Oh."

"I'm surprised you would ask. I thought I had made my opinion quite clear."

"I was hoping you would lie."

"Weirdness is one of your finest qualities. You excel at it. Embrace it."

He took evasive action from her compliment and veered into his surreal California trip. He told her about the Port-A-Park prototype and what they had managed to achieve, folding-car-wise—secrecy be damned.

"Yesterday, I witnessed something incredibly soft contract and become rigid. It was beautiful—perfect. I woke up this morning thinking about how I could apply what I had seen to the prototype, make it natural and organic—less boxy and precise. It seems like an incredibly natural conclusion. It's so obvious that I feel stupid to have overlooked it. Now I'm disappointed I won't have a chance to test out my new idea." Derrick had been right, Shaughnessy thought. Inspiration *is* found in the strangest of places.

"It sounds extremely cool," she said, "but folding a car would never work since it would still be the weight of a car, and how would that be portable? You ought to set your sights lower and apply it to something simple and useless."

"Maybe self-folding origami paper?"

"Perfect. Pointless shit like that is a sure moneymaker," she said. "Will you continue working as Dad now that it's become a full-time job?"

"No, we need to convince him to stop working. His heart isn't in it anymore. And I need to stop substituting for him. It's not healthy for me. I don't know exactly what I'm going to do now."

With measured profanity for emphasis, she excoriated him and said he'd better not fall back into his bad habits, that he needed to pull his weight. He rolled a stray pebble in circles with his foot.

"I'm expanding my business and could probably find work for you, if you were so inclined," she said. She gave him a stern look to impress upon him that her business required actual work. "I'm expanding my 'active lifestyle' line of wood products. The Robber Hobbler is really taking off."

"I'd rather work on products not meant to cause harm," he said.

"I think you would be happier if you found a way to express your creativity. You've let your imagination fester until it's reached a toxic level. It's like an abscess. It's like self-harm. You need a productive outlet."

"I don't want to be like the officer at the end of *The Bridge on the River Kwai* who realizes too late the consequences of his efforts, saying, 'What have I done?' as he keels over dead." He found another pebble with his toe and rolled it in circles.

She wanted to tell him that harm was inevitable, that harm was where the money was, that at least the officer had done something with his life, that good and bad were entirely subjective.

"Harm depends on your point of view," she said. "Wood Heaven is promoting reforestation to avert global destruction and whatnot. Ask the trees their opinion about population equality. It's about time the humans took one for the team."

"But why Dad? Why does *he* have to take one for the team? What did he do to deserve this?"

"That's one of those questions that doesn't have an answer. That's what we've been trying to tell you."

25

Walton and Shaughnessy sat on the back porch making idle comments about the birds and the squirrels and the neighborhood cat lying in wait by a chipmunk hole. Walton promoted a theory that male hummingbirds lust for wasp-waisted dragonflies.

"It's the big eyes, trim figure, see-through wings, and gaudy colors," he explained. "Dragonflies are diabolical pawns of evolution and will be the end of hummingbirds."

Shaughnessy cautiously approached questions that were on his mind. "I have an update on Schrödinger."

"Oh?" Walton said. "I thought we were finished with him."

"I discovered the simple reason cats get into the box," Shaughnessy said. "It's their turn. Maybe they're a little curious too."

"Interesting," Walton said, "elegant even."

Shaughnessy drew a deep breath. "What's it like . . . knowing it's your turn? Are you curious what will happen?"

Walton cogitated on the question. "I was wondering if anyone would ask me something like that," he said. "Why do you think no one ever asks me anything? I figured more people would want the macabre details."

"Well, this is your first time dying. It's not like you have a particular expertise," said Shaughnessy. "Plus, you weren't exactly an ace conversationalist to begin with, so maybe people figure a terminal illness won't be an improvement. I bet there would be more interest if you came back from the dead."

"People do love a good near-death experience," Walton said.

"Maybe they're avoiding saying goodbye, of summarizing a long relationship into something final like 'Kudos on the lifelong friendship' or 'See you on the other side' or 'This illness suits you.' Maybe they're waiting until you're close to death before they acknowledge it. Maybe they'll whisper, 'Good riddance,' or 'I never liked you,' or 'You took your damn sweet time,' as you lie on the verge of death."

"You've got a good sense of humor," said Walton. "Hold on to that."

"I learned from the best."

"Now second best; I've been surpassed at my own game." Walton sniffled and tried to casually wipe tears from his eyes. "Do I sound callous? I don't mean to be. People must think I'm an asshole."

"A funny one."

"I guess that's something," said Walton. "By the way, I got a sales call from Zhosephine. She's flaunting a new business venture: predictive shamanism. She calls herself a corporate prophet."

"Really?" Shaughnessy said. "How is she?"

"Still indeterminate, mathematically speaking. Her business concept is to tell clients the questions they should ask themselves. She offered me a free trial. My question was, 'WTF?' The answer is quite expensive."

"What do you think WTF stands for?"

"Beats me."

"I don't think you're going anywhere for a long time,"

Shaughnessy said, "but—hypothetically—what do you think will happen when you die?"

"If possible, I'd like to get into haunting," said Walton. "That seems exciting. I could keep an eye on things, plus there's the voyeuristic aspect to look forward to. While we're on the subject, what aspects of a haunting do you find particularly troubling? I like to understand my client's frame of mind."

"You're freaking me out," said Shaughnessy. "Please don't talk like that."

"See, I knew I had a knack for it."

"Seriously though. What do you think happens?"

"You'll be surprised to learn that I've stopped wondering about it. Jesus, of all people, advised that there is no meaning in death. I think death happens no matter what we believe or how well we understand it—like gravity or evolution. My thoughts don't figure into the final equation. Personally, I find that comforting."

"I'm going to imagine you in a paradise, a place where you're happy, a place where we could meet for coffee."

"A nice thought, but you should concentrate on living. They say you should live life as if each day is your last. I'm not fully invested in that, since I've learned it leads to obsessive thoughts of death, overeating, and inappropriate behavior, so try living each day as if you'll die in a few years," said Walton. "Here's what I recommend: Chase down whatever ideas get your creative juices flowing, enjoy your life, enjoy people you don't dislike, make good things happen. Have hope, but don't rely on hope to get anything accomplished."

"I'll try."

"Oh . . . and don't live life as if you'll die in more than four or five years. I think people get bored with a lingering death. They think your heart's not in it."

That was how Shaughnessy wanted to remember the conversation: a father and son having a meaningful talk, making witty, cogent observations, relating to one another. In actuality, the conversation was jagged and awkward, emotionally wrenching, punctuated by tears. Observations were left hanging, thoughts incomplete. There were long silences, during which Walton stroked his son's back. There was blubbering. There was more snot than seemed necessary, or even possible.

Later, Shaughnessy would periodically discuss this day with his sister, who offered her interpretations, analysis, and insights from her own fatherly confabulations. The information fed back into an iterative cycle of remembrance until the conversation made sense, was consoling, and suggested deeper meanings.

Sometimes, Shaughnessy attempted to distill his father's feelings from that point in time down to a simple summary and usually arrived at: he wasn't all *that* curious about death.

One afternoon, Portal had spent a millennium at a rehab galaxy with other misunderstood forces of nature, working through its emotional distance and destructive tendencies. The counselors helped it realize that its inability to communicate was the root of its relationship problems, which, in turn, fueled its drinking. They put it through a series of alternative communication sessions and taught it glyph sign language.

Melba asked if Portal and Althea could take her some-place quiet for a serious discussion. They ended up on a little planet with striking mountain vistas.

"I have something to ask of you both," Melba said. "My son . . . My son is not well. He has a disease that will make him progressively weaker until he dies, possibly even before me. He will need attentive care to keep him safe. As much as I enjoy our time together, I want to share the two of you with him. I would be happier knowing my son had the best care possible."

Althea sniffed. Portal leaked radiation from its maw.

"Look out for him, please? Even after I'm no longer around."

"We are honored to be asked," Althea said.

Portal flashed a sequence of glyphs, which Althea trans-lated: "This solar system used to have two suns, but Portal ate one of them on a bet. It was hot, but it wasn't *that* hot. It was a world-changing experience, but mainly it was unfulfilling. He says that taking care of you and your son will be the pinnacle of its existence."

"Thank you," Melba said. "I knew I could count on you."

Shaughnessy agreed to pull one last short stint as Walton to retrieve his personal possessions from Critical Think Inc. He braced himself, expecting a wave of morbid despon-dency as he switched to his father's identity. He steadied himself with deep breaths and focused on his father's sense of humor. Surprisingly, he found little interest in MFD or concern about dying.

He carefully packed the collection of photos and movie

clips spread across the back of the desk. One of Shaughnessy dressed in his spaceman pajamas, aiming his toy ray gun at the camera. His mom receiving her black belt in karate. Sammy posing sassily at the beach with two front teeth missing. The family smiling atop an enormous concrete turtle.

Gahan poked his head into the cell as he sealed the box of memorabilia.

"I'm stealing a stockpile of office supplies," Shaughnessy said.

"I would expect nothing less," Gahan said. "Take care of yourself."

"Thanks. We had a good run." He struggled for words, realizing that his father had left it to him to endure the painful goodbyes.

"That we did. Stay in touch and let me know if you need help," Gahan said. "Anything at all."

"Thanks. For everything. I'll send you updates."

Gahan smiled and disappeared out the door. Shaughnessy listened as his shower slippers slapped into the distance.

He'd caught a glimpse of the lasting bond his father shared with Gahan, encrypted within the sincerity and implied generosity of Gahan's offer. He lay prostrate on the lower bunk, saddened by the interaction, struck that he had been clueless of his father's true achievements at work.

With a more profound understanding of the duty bestowed on him, he worked up the energy to sleeve Bunny. They met in the semidarkness at the foot of the conference room tunnel's ladder.

"I feel bad that the project ended abruptly, after you

were so helpful designing and building the prototype," Shaughnessy said. "I couldn't have done it without you. You're amazing."

"Hey, don't mention it," said Bunny. "It was a wild ride while it lasted."

"Good. I've decided to take time off to think my own thoughts. I have you to thank for that."

"You're welcome," said Bunny. "I wish the feral membership thing had worked out, but no hard feelings."

Unable to make eye contact, Shaughnessy said, "I won't be returning to work. I know that's feral heresy."

"Don't tell me the specifics. I don't want to think about them. I'm in a vulnerable emotional state." Bunny hugged him and held him tight to his warm fuzzy rabbit animation. "Look me up if you get into something new and interesting."

"I wouldn't dream of designing anything without you."

"The galactic cataclysm will take priority when it happens. I'll be busy piecing the world back together, taking control, and whatnot. Until then, I have some time."

"I'll look forward to it," said Shaughnessy. "It'll be nice to work together again."

26

In the months following his diagnosis, Walton endured prescription-strength placebo IVs at an infectious-disease infusion center, where vacant recliners and individual datastream screens were remarketed as hourly cinema rentals. He spent his hour-long visits napping in the comfortable recliners and enjoying camaraderie with a necrotic former convict who hadn't killed the people they said he had.

To maximize the placebo's psychophysiological benefit, Walton made the full commitment—a port catheter surgically implanted in his chest.

"They need reliable access to your veins," the surgeon told him. "If you've ever been a heroin addict, you'll understand what I'm talking about."

As the months slid past, he increasingly questioned the infusions' effectiveness. In turn, the doctors questioned whether he was a suitable test subject, since the placebo was only FDA approved for zealous believers. Eventually he got fed up and put a halt to the treatment.

After hearing Walton's lurid stories about the clinic's charms and cinematic nightlife, Shaughnessy and Prudence were curious to experience it in person.

They sat side by side in their recliners, admiring the softly lit, cracked pavement of an empty parking lot visible through their fifth-story window. They held hands and enjoyed complimentary snacks, nibbling at dry crackers and sipping Ringer's lactate from pouches hung on their IV poles.

"It's the champagne of saline solutions," the nurse had promised.

The infusion center's few long-term residents wolfed down canteen hamburgers at the far end of the line of recliners. They elevated their bandaged, neuropathic feet and swapped stories about the day's game of find-a-vein.

"I'm thinking of updating my identiTee," Shaughnessy said. "I need to move on from my brown bird vignette."

Without hesitation and with a note of eagerness, Prudence agreed a change was long overdue. She praised Shaughnessy for his identity decision and for the maturity it demonstrated. "How about a new hat? An animation could be swanky."

He stroked his Purrloined cap. "It's made from sustainable materials," he defended. He had decided the hat's comfort arose from the joy the reborn fibers felt riding in the fresh air, delighting in a purposeful life, freed from the cramped confines of their previous existence. It inspired him.

"Too bad," she said. "Are you thinking of investing in a template?"

"Somehow a template just seems wrong to me."

"I read about a new template called authenticiTee. It creates an identity that looks flawed enough to have been personally crafted, yet perfect enough that you appear extremely artistic."

"Is that different from any other template?" he asked.

"I'm just trying to be helpful," she said. "You're strangely perfect just the way you are, but a little pizzazz in your identity would do you some good."

She suggested some minor alterations to the depiction of

his hair, thinking that a tighter cut with less bang definition better reflected his employability. Glyphs to suggest a little stubble on his cheeks would look rugged. In general, she believed his newfound seriousness warranted an overhaul to his font.

"Oh! And have you seen what Kael's been up to? They're a must-have." She sleeved him the latest in skinny-jean development: a patented foam-padded, contour-enhancing underwire technology that miraculously maintained ready weasel access. Wee Works sold them under the Weesily trademark.

"That was my idea, you know," Shaughnessy said.

"Oh, really?" she asked.

"Yeah, I was joking with him about it," Shaughnessy said.

"Why would he steal your idea?" she asked.

"He didn't steal it. I think I impregnated him with it."

They watched the movie *Son Protector: Origins*, set in a future when the sun is superheated and people yearn for the good old days of global warming. To survive the sun's deadly rays, humans had evolved to exude a protective mucosal slime coating—which in practice looked like coconut oil rubbed on deeply bronzed skin. Traditional fabrics incinerated when exposed to the sun, so the men wore mod fireproof compression shorts, while the women wore micro bikinis, shortchanged once again in the fabric allocation. Their form-fitting sunglasses featured an integral hat brim and ultracool styling to coordinate with their weaponry. The starring role was played by Jesus, who discovered that the sun's energy had given Him superpowers, which He used to save the world mere seconds before a supernova. His catchphrase was a booming "I'm back . . . this time for good."

"The Son Protector business was sort of my idea too," Shaughnessy said.

"Between your career-making hat idea and His reluctance to help your father, He *really* owes you."

Shaughnessy looked beyond her glyphs and admired her eyes. He thought about her elongated second toes gripping pencils.

"Later this evening," he said, "would you do me a favor and put on the identity of a brainy, capable astronaut caught in her underwear during a galactic cataclysm? The situation will be dire, and we'll be under a lot of time pressure."

"I should have said that you're perfectly strange," she replied. "I do my best work under pressure."

In the semidarkness of exit lighting, Shaughnessy and Prudence lay spooned on his law-office couch, listening to corporate-hostel patrons pad the hallway with their towels and toothbrushes. They had tested a variety of techniques to thwart a galactic cataclysm. They had opened themselves to one another and removed their iTees. Now, their self-concerns set aside, they enjoyed a moment of peace.

"This is nice. It makes me feel like I don't want to be someone else anymore. I just want to hang in this limbo," she said.

She had let him trim her actual hair with his lawyer's desk scissors, cutting it back to stubble to give her hood a smooth foundation. She had a mole on the back of her neck, hidden by the hood and its animation of windblown, coppery hair. To gaze upon the mole and her flaky scalp made him believe he was witnessing true beauty, producing an indescribable feeling of connection.

"Let's become inseparable," he said. "I think I would like that."

Several mutual realizations flowed into the hollow of the drowsy moment: the two of them fit together, they had a compatible yin-yang of drive and creativity, and they really needed to find work—something profitable that would allow them to sleep without hard leather couch buttons digging into their hip bones.

Prudence said, "We should start a side business together."

Shaughnessy wondered what his father would do, a question that was immediately followed by another: *What would Jesus do?* The two questions merged—he speculated how his father would behave as Jesus.

He imagined Walton/Jesus would have a lot to say about the structural integrity of triangles, that They would better acquaint Christians with math—more parabolas and fewer parables. He imagined . . .

Shaughnessy appreciated Jesus and his father's participation in his fantasy but wished the two of them would stop intruding and give him some space. He preferred thinking his own thoughts.

Shaughnessy's mind slid sideways, past the folding prototype's unexplored design improvements, the fearsome exploding yoga pants, the Formerly Dead singer's gravity-defying skirt, righteous action, Kael's jeans, an array of muscles, and his father's inevitable progressive weakness. He felt around for an irritant in his thoughts, a pebble in the stream. He discovered an uncomfortable conceptual knot—

a mental kidney stone of sorts, an imperfect freshwater pearl—composed of passing ideas and influences, drawn together and bound by an inexplicable magnetism. He asked himself: *WTF?*

"Yoga pants," Shaughnessy said aloud, answering his own riddle.

"Yoga pants?" asked Prudence.

"Self-actuating yoga pants," he said. "We turn our little folding car prototype into a fabric and make pants. Whenever someone has an itch, the pants would automatically scratch it. Think about it: a person with MFD could live free from fear of the Itch."

"Could we make them do that?" she asked.

"I think so," he said.

"How about pants that compress and manipulate flesh into perfect shapes? We could call them Vanity Pants."

"That would be an even bigger seller," he said. "They could be totally customizable—completely glyph-free, all-natural, technology-assisted butts. You're a genius."

"Together we're a genius," she said.

"How about pants that can control a disabled person's movement? What if we made pants that could pull themselves up and zip automatically? What if they could help a person walk?"

"Damn," she said.

"Yeah," he said.

They lay quietly, their hearts pounding, each wondering if this is what delusions feel like.

"Think of the good we could accomplish," said Prudence. "The vanity work could fund the disability project. We could make the disability products affordable!"

"I can totally picture that," Shaughnessy said. He wondered why the pants mechanism had never occurred to anyone before. Maybe it wasn't original, he feared; maybe he was overlooking the flaw that had doomed previous efforts. At that moment, his fantasy of deserving a unit name like the newton seemed childish—though very cool, so no harm in keeping the idea in play. He wanted to set free the utility, the simplicity, the elegance, the beauty he imagined for the design. He wanted to immerse himself in the details and bring his ideas to life.

"Have you ever studied ballet?" he asked.

"No, why?"

"I was just imagining how Vanity Pants could make people better dancers," he said. "They could correct for rhythmic deficiencies. One line dance could be complimentary, but other memory-intensive dances would be upgrades."

"Bad dancers are a massive underserved market," she agreed. "I was just thinking about a company mantra. It's a bit heretical. Would you like to hear it?"

"Absolutely."

"Succeed!" she said. "My first thought was 'Succeed early and often,' but then I thought what the heck, we should try to succeed all the time. What do you think?"

"Genius," he said. "Do you think we can do it?"

"You've done the hard part. You've imagined a useful product. You've imagined a novel technology."

"I'm not so sure," he said. "Most of the innovation is yet to come. This will be a long, difficult slog. There will be a lot of details to chase down and strangle into submission."

"I was exaggerating . . . flattering shamelessly even," she said.

"I think I appreciate your honesty, but how do we begin?"

"Like all journeys, with one step," said Prudence. "Would it be intimate if we started on a project plan, right here, right now?"

Epilogue

"Being uncouth, he added vermouth, and slipped his wife a martini!" In Critical Think Inc.'s atrium, Quinsy warms the crowd of global press representatives with inappropriate humor in the finale of his first professional comedy engagement. "Thank you! You've been great! And now, please help me welcome your host, fresh from a Golden Globe nomination for His starring role in the highly successful *Son Protector* trilogy. Ladies and gentlemen and everyone else . . . Jesus!"

Jesus walks onstage to a burst of wild applause, His hands in a prayerful position.

"Thank you. Thank you. You're very kind for a bunch of atheistic sinners. I'm kidding! Who am I to judge?" He waits for the applause to subside. "So . . . I met Walton several years ago. I was at a crossroads, uncertain of My future, troubled. I was turning more wine into water than vice versa, if you get My drift."

Shaughnessy flinches, sensing that Quinsy helped Jesus concoct jokes for His speech. He and Prudence watch from the back of the atrium, inconspicuous in company-issued, engineering-strength obscuriTees, bathed in the faint glow of the halo hovering serenely above Shaughnessy's head.

"We're here today to talk about something serious—MFD, the debilitating, ultimately fatal neuromuscular disease. This terrible disease had struck My dear friend, but did he simply fade away? Did he spend his days idly hoping for a miracle? Well, yes, there was an uncomfortable adjust-ment period where he lay in bed, cursing destiny, making himself a pain in the ass—and in fact, he did inquire about a miracle! But let's skip that embarrassing montage, because he eventually found inspiration in his plight and courageously used his abilities to make life easier for the similarly afflicted. Walton and My other good friends at InAction!! have put together a truly miraculous product—and believe Me, I know miracles."

The crowd laughs.

"We followed the path of My trademarked Abs-O-Lution process."

This is the first Shaughnessy has heard of Abs-O-Lution.

"We worked together in harmony, appreciating every-one's contributions, forgiving mistakes for the most part."

In fact, it was Gloria who set the tone for the company, preaching cooperation and efficiency. Jesus didn't trouble Himself with the day-to-day operations.

"I delivered the engineers from their manic self-confidence and gnawing self-doubt."

Shaughnessy thinks that Corporate Jesus probably came up with that bit of retrospective, self-congratulatory wis-dom. Shaughnessy is both relieved and irritated that Prudence's guidance and his own technical contributions were omitted in Jesus's mangling of the company's origin story.

"We want to give a special thanks to Smallwood Pharmaceuticals for their generous investment in this en-deavor. Remember! When you've got Satan nipping at your heels, reach for Gee-OD. It's the fast, *proven* way to reach your highest power!"

Jesus is nothing but enthusiastic delivering His lines as corporate shill. To His credit, He undeniably knows how to work a crowd.

"Additional funding was provided by WTF, My Wearable Technology Foundation. It has been a pleasure supporting InAction!! through the sale of Son Protector products—available at the merch table over there, near the entrance." He points. "Tell the lovely lady that a star guided you there!"

Jesus's mom, a virginiTee Mary, flogs Son Protector visor products and Myrrh-Made SPF 500 coconut oils to benefit the Wearable Technology Foundation. A paper banner taped around her table reads, *WWJD? Support WTF!*

"I am extremely pleased to be here today for the unveiling of this good work. It's not a cure, it's a lifestyle revolution! Please, give us your undivided attention, and prepare to have your minds blown. I give you . . . the future!"

On cue, Althea dims all the lights. *InAction!!, a Subsidiary of Wood Heaven* flashes onto the large screen. Their animated logo loops: *InAction!!* dances and morphs around an immobile, seated cartoon figure. Doing nothing had never looked more captivating.

A single spotlight reveals Gloria standing at center stage, dressed in a matte-black veracitiTee. Her appearance commands complete attention. She makes introductory remarks, touching on the limited success of their first product: pants that detect and address itches for the disabled. She exults in the enormous sales volume of the follow-on product: enhanced pants that assist with blood circulation from the waist down—particularly popular with the self-gratification demographic. She drops tantalizing hints about their new product.

As she finishes her speech, the lights raise and Walton descends from the ceiling in a harness, his thin arms held extended to his sides with cables. Prudence swats at Shaughnessy's halo.

"Portal!" she hisses. "Stop goofing around. Man your post!"

Portal pops above the stage, out of sight of the crowd, to ensure Walton's safety. It indulges Prudence even knowing he will be fine.

Walton's legs are flaccid beneath black compression shorts, the muscles wasted. Without muscle tone, his belly is rotund. Like a werewolf, he weighs the same as before the disease, but his outward appearance is disturbingly different. His mass has redistributed into the shape of a monstrous sea urchin—nearly spherical with spiny outcroppings.

His dangling feet stop inches from the stage, above a pair of bunched yoga pants. The pants shimmy their way up his calves, up his thighs, like a serpent swallowing its prey whole.

"Our InAction!! family is extremely proud to present... Self-Actualizing Yoga Pants!" Gloria gestures to redirect attention to her husband, but all eyes are already trained on him.

Althea turns up backing music.

The crowd can't help but gasp as the pants cinch tight and mold Walton's midsection into something resembling a waistline, his backside into perfectly-formed curvature-continuous buttocks. Employing the latest access technology, the Weesily Hands-Free Wee, the pants form a smooth, impact-resistant bubble of provocative protection.

He stands on his own as his supporting harness retracts upward, then takes a tentative step. Excepting the many,

many prototype failures, this is his first attempt walking since MFD robbed him of his strength.

Suddenly, he breaks into a series of crisply perfect ballet maneuvers, and Gloria—propelled by a stylish feminine version of Self-Actualization Yoga Pants—joins him in an impressive burst of athletic aerial leaps and spins. They engage in a poignant pas de deux. The spectacle stuns the crowd.

Shaughnessy reads their reaction as they watch his father, disabled but dancing. They wonder ... Couldn't this company find an attractive, able-bodied actor for the role of the disabled man? And Christ, couldn't they have made something like a full-body wetsuit so his arms and torso didn't flail around while he was dancing?

Was it necessary for him to wear a helmet on his lolling head?

Imagine if those yoga pants were adapted to professional athletics. Imagine the spectacle!

Imagine the advertising money!

Imagine the convenience if yoga pants exercised for you. Imagine the dollar value of brand-name supermodel runway struts—or the franchised swaggers of movie stars!

The crowd wallows in emotion, tears welling in their eyes, as they realize that a perfect ass is achievable in their lifetime.

But they suppose the disability thing is cool too.

Acknowledgments

I began writing this book in 2015 when I first experienced the minor symptoms that eventually led to a 2017 diagnosis of ALS. My goal was to write a funny book because that concentration helped lighten a difficult stretch of my life.

I am incredibly grateful to my loving wife, Helen, who supported me with encouragement and gave me the time and space to work, even as we dealt with the deterioration of my physical condition. Her frank, intelligent opinions and outgoing sense of humor shaped the narrative. Without her, this book and whatever lightheartedness it possesses would not have been possible.

My children, Conor and Bridget, provided love, support, and advice during stretches of the pandemic when they were at home. They served as soundboards for my ideas and my frustrations. They brought joy into my life just by being around. Addie added a twist of energy to the days that she visited. Mocha, our reliably dyspeptic cat, provided inspiration when she licked her belly free of hair in an expression of the household's shared anxiety.

My sister Susan read several early versions of the manuscript and provided excellent counsel on how to move forward. The two of us took a weekend shamanism workshop around the time I began the novel. The story pokes fun at shamanism used in corporate marketing, but I have the utmost respect for the tradition.

My editor, Alessandor Earnest, was insightful and direct about how to shape my early drafts into a readable story.

She became an invaluable ally who helped me drive the work to the finish line. I am thankful for her essential advice, added humor, and confidence in the novel.

Bob Light, Meredith Brus, and Dylon Carter made the long slog through dialogue-free deserts of exposition in early revisions, and I salute their stamina and the sincerity with which they exaggerated the quality of the writing, even while providing meaningful feedback. My sister Lyn and Rose Keimig read later versions and offered advice for fine-tuning.

The generous humor of engineers skews toward outrageous, and I have tried to faithfully capture it in sections of this book. Over the course of my career, I had the pleasure to work with many talented, creative, funny individuals, none more so than Sung Kim. He offered me friendship and an inspiring place to work for some twenty-five years. Jeff Neaves and Larry Davis also deserve special mention for keeping me laughing over the many years we worked together.

My parents let my sisters and me run free through our childhood and taught us the value of entertaining ourselves, which proved essential to completing this book. As I wrote, my father was progressively debilitated by Parkinson's and associated dementia. My mother was succumbing to blindness and vascular dementia. Because some of their symptoms and behaviors bled into my story, it is not strictly about ALS.

An enormous *Thank you!* to those who preordered this book on Kickstarter and donated generously to ALS non-profit Team Gleason:

Jon Ambrose
Ashwin Anantharaman
Page Anderson
Sean Bailey
Judy Bergwerk
Amanda Brooks
Toy Brownell
Lyn Brus
Karen Campbell
Renee Carpenter
Franchot Chang
Tracy Clemmer
James Conley
Linda Crossette
Cindy Fowler and Ken
    Crouse
Colin Davis
Consuelo and John Ecuyer
Diane Elia
Danielle Ely
Barbara Haigh Fittro
Michael Franklin
Jason Frisvold
Sarah and Andre Guzman
Annette and Brett Himes
Austin Igleheart
Paul Ikeda
David and Linda Katz
David Kilby
Heather Klaubert
Celeste Knoll

Bob Light
William Light
Ryan Livingston
Samantha Loop
Missy Martin
David and Joan Mecsas
Steven Meister
Carolyn Miles
Jeffrey Neaves
Tom Neir
Betsy and Todd Oglesby
Kirsten Spackman Omholt
Sarah and Knox Pannill
Karen Parker
Luanne Marie Pryor
Betsy Rafael
Lisa Roderick
Jim Ross
Peggy Sammon
Melissa Schneider
Jeff St. Peters
Sam Strite
Linda Tai
Mary Tai
Bill Tower
Angela Towner
Nancy Watkins
Sharon Wildman
Sara and Andy Young
Erik Zucker

About the Author

Rob Brownell grew up in rural Virginia. Over the course of his thirty-five-year career as a mechanical engineer, he designed consumer products ranging from children's toys to medical devices. He is named on nearly  thirty patents for his work with Function Engineering, a Silicon Valley design firm. Once upon a time, he worked on Apple's ill-fated Newton digital assistants.

An untalented but persistent musician, he found joy crafting and playing banjos until ALS confined him to a wheelchair. Contrary to the fiction you might eventually read in his obituary, he is not bravely battling the disease—he is struggling to maintain a sense of humor. Writing through voice control has mercifully extended his creative life.

Invention Is a Mother is an insider's appreciation for the artistic minds of technologists amid a corporation's unrealistic expectations for innovation. It is his first novel.

Lightning Source UK Ltd.
Milton Keynes UK
UKHW012031090223
416719UK00011B/865/J